SPECULATIVE LOS ANGELES

EDITED BY DENISE HAMILTON

BROOKLYN, NEW YORK

This collection consists of works of fiction. All names, characters, places, and incidents are the product of the authors' imaginations. Any resemblance to real events or persons, living or dead, is entirely coincidental.

Published by Akashic Books

Hardcover ISBN: 978-1-61775-864-5
Paperback ISBN: 978-1-61775-856-0
Library of Congress Control Number: 2020936297

Los Angeles map by Sohrab Habibion

First printing

Akashic Books
Brooklyn, New York
Twitter: @AkashicBooks
Facebook: AkashicBooks
E-mail: info@akashicbooks.com
Website: www.akashicbooks.com

For Octavia Butler

. . . everybody who really lived in L.A. was linked into the trance.

—Eve Babitz, *L.A. Woman*

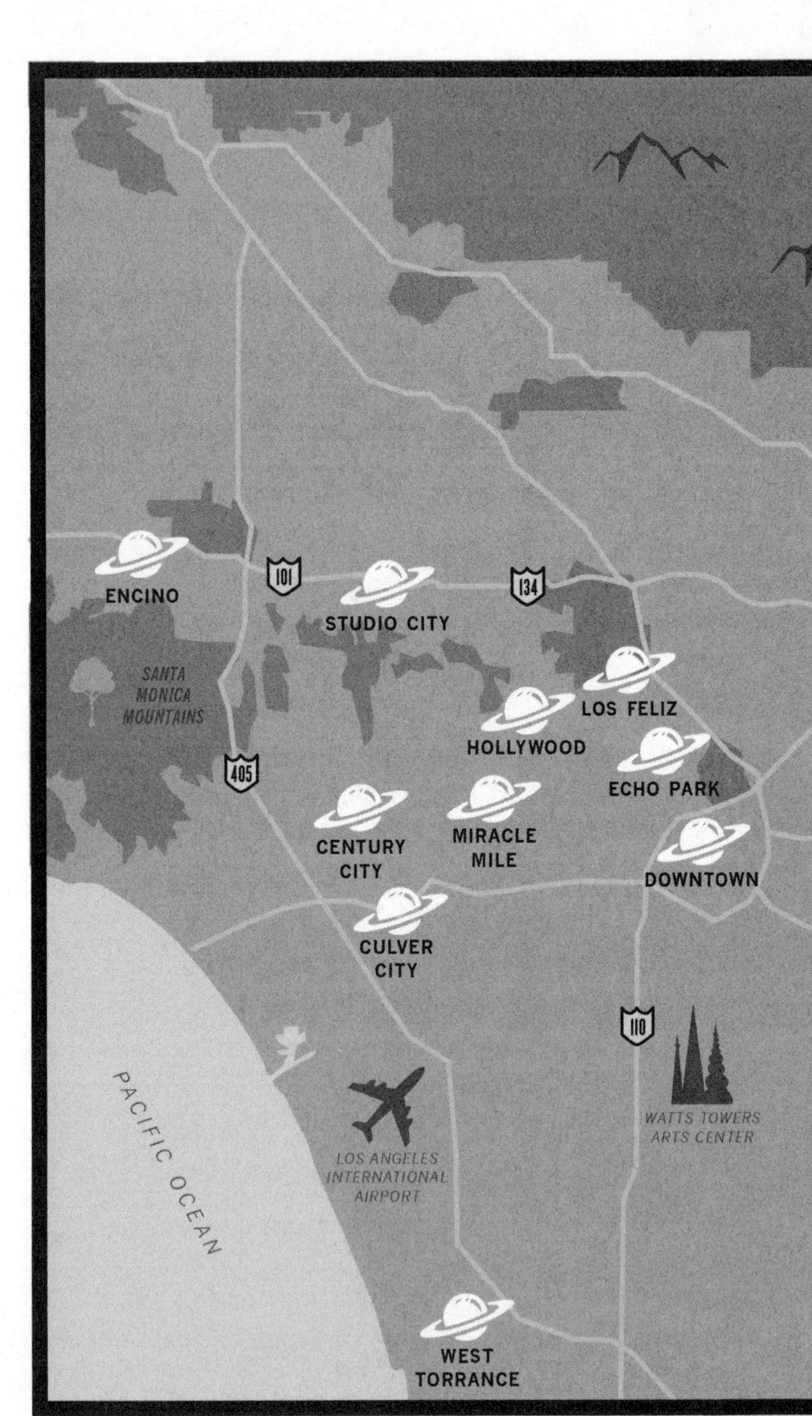
ENCINO
101
STUDIO CITY
134
SANTA MONICA MOUNTAINS
LOS FELIZ
HOLLYWOOD
405
ECHO PARK
CENTURY CITY
MIRACLE MILE
DOWNTOWN
CULVER CITY
110
PACIFIC OCEAN
LOS ANGELES INTERNATIONAL AIRPORT
WATTS TOWERS ARTS CENTER
WEST TORRANCE

LOS ANGELES

210

LA PUENTE

TABLE OF CONTENTS

PART III: A TEAR IN THE FABRIC OF REALITY

PART IV: COPS AND ROBOTS IN THE FUTURE RUINS OF LA

INTRODUCTION
CITY OF ILLUSIONS

Los Angeles is named after heavenly beings, but here at the continent's edge, it's always been the demons that inflame our imaginations and apocalypse that haunts our dreams.

As I write this, the world grapples with a deadly pandemic that has killed hundreds of thousands and upended civilization. Los Angeles is only one more data point in this tragedy, but residing in an incubator of the future, Angelenos have long lived with the tropes of dystopian fiction. In addition to plagues, reality for us also means giant forest fires that poison our air and block the sun; powerful earthquakes; extreme droughts; rising seas; Orwellian surveillance; exploding tent cities of the dispossessed; and Hollywood's dream factory, where the blight of celebrity worship began.

Indeed, one can argue that Los Angeles is already so weird, surreal, irrational, and mythic that *any* fiction emerging from this place should be considered speculative.

From the moment our ancestors founded El Pueblo de Nuestra Señora la Reina de los Ángeles del Río Porciúncula, we began to conjure up a fictional utopian past that suited us better than the blood-and-genocide-soaked reality of our Western frontier.

This land was built on ghosts. And over the centuries, each newcomer from Duluth, New Haven, Yerevan, and Tegucigalpa added her own wraiths, devils, and shape-shifters, contributing to an urban fantasy that only ever seems fully realized in our imaginations.

Los Angeles is like the hologram girlfriend in *Blade Runner 2049*, flickering in and out of reality. And like a thirsty starlet, LA can be anything you want it to be, plus what your worst nightmares can't imagine.

But don't take my word for it—read these stories. We've asked fourteen of the city's most prophetic voices to reimagine Los Angeles in any way they choose. In these pages, you'll encounter twenty-first-century changelings; a postapocalyptic landfill where humans piloting giant robots fight for survival; black holes and jacaranda men lurking in deepest suburbia; beachfront property in Century City; walled-off canyons and coastlines reserved for the wealthy; psychic death cults and robot nursemaids; guerrillas resisting fascism from deep in the San Gabriel Mountains; an alternate LA where Spanish land grants never gave way to urbanization; and lastly, you will visit a world where global pandemics have wreaked the ultimate havoc.

LA's speculative possibilities have long mesmerized writers. Nathanael West, Harlan Ellison, Octavia Butler, Philip K. Dick, and Aldous Huxley all lived and set stories in fragmented, tribal, destroyed, or creepily utopian Los Angeles. Moviemakers too. The visual genius of *Blade Runner* was transplanting Dick's novel from Northern California to LA, where a slickly decayed techno world mixed the Pacific Rim glam of Little Tokyo, the fortress architecture of Downtown, and the eerie art deco decayed elegance of the Bradbury Building.

In *Speculative Los Angeles*, you too can scramble through the ruins of Hollywood and NASA JPL, the fortified police sectors downtown, the squatter hills of Echo Park, the sacred springs of Los Encinos, the resistance tunnels below the Angeles National Forest, the once golden, now flooded coastline.

More than just disaster porn, these stories explore the bonds that make us human (or more than). If this genre has exploded in recent years, it's because it captures the free-floating anxiety in our souls as we grasp for ways to understand the profound, terrifying, and fundamental changes rocking society.

Writers have always been divining rods, dowsing for the future. So it's not surprising that some of these authors, writing before the coronavirus descended and Black Lives Matter protests surged following the police murder of George Floyd, were eerily prescient in capturing elements of what lay ahead. They also provide cautionary tales of what awaits if we're not careful.

Speculative Los Angeles is a new project for us at Akashic, an acknowledgment that in these real-life dystopian times, we crave the fortifying truth of stories that ask *What if?* then take us there in visions designed to warn, scare, tempt, laugh, and predict. Speculative fiction provides a wormhole into other LA worlds, but it also resonates with universal themes of good vs. evil and with how we live (and die) in this one.

Consider Lisa Morton's alternate history pastoral. As her story opens, an agricultural realm called Rancho Los Feliz thrives and prospers, thanks to the oversight of its managers, a Latina and a Native American woman. But their Garden of Eden changes forever when a horribly burned man carrying a high-tech weapon staggers out of an oak grove.

In "Detainment," Alex Espinoza creates a twenty-first-century changeling myth ripped from the headlines but rooted in ancient folklore when an immigrant toddler detained for months in ICE custody is returned to his grief-stricken mother in El Sereno. The mute, withdrawn child looks exactly like her son, but the mother swears he's a replicant.

S. Qiouyi Lu creates a dystopian love story bristling with junkyard steel in which a young engineer driven underground by the resurrection of the Chinese Exclusion Act spends her days scavenging tech scrap at the sprawling Puente Hills landfill. At night she becomes a warrior, battling to the death in her robot "chomper" before cheering, gambling crowds. This propulsive, incandescent tale might be the first San Gabriel Valley steampunk story ever written, but it won't be the last.

Stephen Blackmoore dives into demonology as real-life aerospace engineer, Jet Propulsion Labs cofounder, and Aleister Crowley occultist Jack Parsons summons a supernatural being in a 1940s Pasadena ritual. Aimee Bender examines a child's obsession with the La Brea Tar Pits, that bubbling prehistoric lake of fenced-off black ooze that we drive past each day but barely register because it no longer fits into our worldview.

Luis J. Rodriguez imagines guerrilla fighters hiding out in San Gabriel Mountain caves making a last stand for freedom against a totalitarian America First government. In Duane Swierczynski's pulpy horror and pop culture mash-up "Walk of Fame," a father and daughter infiltrate the ruins of Hollywood, where psychic anarchists have declared war on celebrity, leaving the famous scrambling for that most precious of new commodities—anonymity. The showrunner of a runaway hit about teen suicide gets his otherworldly comeuppance in Ben H. Winters's "Peak TV," set on a Culver City studio lot.

In his futuristic noir story, "Garbo on the Skids," A.G. Lombardo plunges us into a desolate police state featuring a tech-savvy cop and a desperate femme fatale. In Lynell George's "If Memory Serves," dystopia erodes the fabric of life in slow, incremental, and devastating ways for a young woman quixotically saving fragments of the past as she navigates a harrowing future in Echo Park.

Speculative fiction thrives in suburbia too, where Francesca Lia Block weaves a dark fairy tale about high school friends from Studio City who reunite as adults and realize the past was stranger than they ever knew. Charles Yu topples us into alternate universes lurking in a suburban backyard in his poignant family tale "West Torrance 2BR 2BA w/Pool and Black Hole." In both these stories, normality is stealthily overtaken by a creeping sense that our safe homes and families are only fronts for something more strange.

And what about the robo-apocalypse, the artificial intelligence that we fear could soon decide that humanity is redundant? Kathleen Kaufman's story, which closes the book, turns this premise on its head as she imagines a very different coda to the human race.

As with our city-based Akashic Noir Series, each story in *Speculative Los Angeles* is set in a distinct neighborhood filled with local color, landmarks, and flavor. But their boundaries are limited only by their authors' imaginations. We hope these stories will inspire, terrify, thrill, and inhabit these familiar locales in entirely new, um, dimensions. What you hold in your hand is a portal, just waiting to be activated. Now it's time to pass through the doors of perception and enter a strange new world, a city caught between shadow and light, past, future, and the uncanny present. You've just crossed over. Prepare to disembark into *Speculative Los Angeles*. We hope you enjoy your journey.

Denise Hamilton
Los Angeles, CA
October 2020

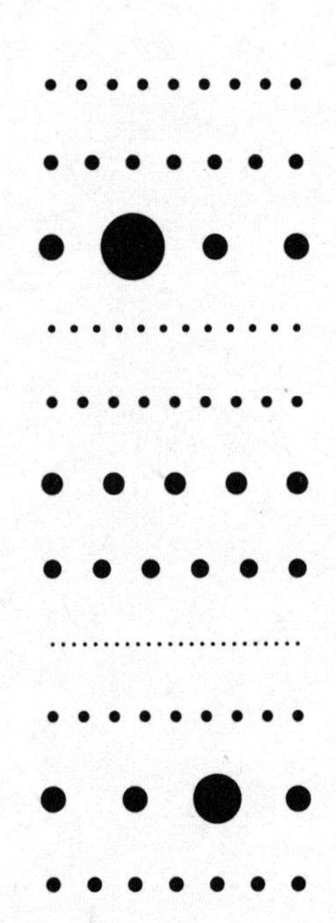

PART I

CHANGELINGS, GHOSTS,
AND PARALLEL WORLDS

ANTONIA AND THE STRANGER WHO CAME TO RANCHO LOS FELIZ

BY **LISA MORTON**

Los Feliz

At 9:31 a.m. on April 30, 1955, Antonia Feliz discovered a strange man on her land.

She was riding her favorite horse, Balada, along the edge of the river, checking in with her vaqueros and vaqueras, and enjoying the fine spring Alta California morning. The sky overhead was a flawless sapphire, so blue that looking into it was like falling upward into a still sea. The air was scented with sage and lemon blossoms from her orchards, the willows furry with new growth, her cattle grazing contentedly. When she encountered her forewoman, Loo-soo, the dark, muscled Kizh grinned and said, "I think our profits will be very good this year."

Antonia nodded. "I think they will." Loo-soo had ridden off then in her electric truck. Antonia preferred horses herself, but the trucks allowed her workers to cover more ground and remove any fallen trees or other large debris.

Loo-soo was right—it *would* be a good year. Rainfall had been plentiful in the winter, the grazing lands of Rancho Los Feliz were thick and cattle prices were high, and the beehives were already filling up. Her country, Alta California, was at peace with the neighboring United

States to the east and Mexico to the south, and her family's business had prospered under her management. Antonia was thirty-six and had never married, but life had brought her so many other satisfactions that she didn't miss what she'd never had.

She paused on the hillside, looking down at the river that her Kizh workers called Paayme Paxaayt. She'd heard stories of how it had flooded the Pueblo de Los Ángeles forty years ago, but gazing at its beauty now, at the rippling blue-green expanse crowded with long-necked herons and paddling ducks, it was hard to believe it could ever have been a force of destruction.

As she sat there atop her horse, looking across the river toward Providencia and the low hills beyond, she heard a rustling to her left. A grove of oaks stood there, a stand of mighty survivors several centuries old.

A man staggered out from behind one of the trunks.

He wasn't like any man Antonia had ever seen: he wore some sort of silvery suit that covered him from foot to neck, with a glass-fronted helmet over his head. At his waist hung a belt studded with instruments—one of which looked like a gun.

Balada neighed and shuffled nervously. "Easy, easy," Antonia said, patting the horse's neck.

The man saw her, and although she couldn't be sure, she thought he tried to talk. He held up his hands, a universal gesture of peace (or surrender), and then reached to latches on either side of the helmet. Undoing the latches, he pulled the helmet free.

Antonia had to restrain a gasp when she saw his face: it was covered in ugly, rippled scars, red and white, and his hair was patchy, burned away. One eye was completely sealed shut; the other fixed on her. "Do you speak English?" he asked, his voice a weathered rasp.

"Who are you? And what are you doing on my land?"

The man looked around. "Your land? I thought . . . Griffith Park . . ." He finished the sentence with a groan and then pitched forward.

For a second she was too stunned to move; then she leaped off her mount and ran to where the stranger lay unconscious.

She stood over him for a few seconds, surveying the metallic jumpsuit. Her eyes settled on the belt, on the tool that looked like a gun. She kneeled, used two fingers to gingerly pull it forth from a pocket; she instinctively knew it *was* a weapon, although she'd never seen its like before.

Running back to Balada, she tucked the gun into a saddlebag, climbed onto her horse, and rode after Loo-soo. She quickly found her tending to a steer that had gotten one leg stuck in a small crevice. Antonia told her forewoman what had happened, and together they returned to the unconscious intruder.

"*Chingichnish*," muttered Loo-soo, before asking, "What do we do with him?"

Antonia answered, "He's a human being, and an injured one. We offer him the same hospitality we would any other visitor."

Loo-soo used her portable radio to call for help. Two vaqueros rode up, and she directed them to heft the man onto the bed of her truck.

Antonia silently prayed that she hadn't just made a terrible mistake.

At the hacienda, the vaqueros hauled the man into a

ground-floor bedroom while Antonia's younger brother Abel came over to watch. Antonia telephoned her physician, Dr. Alvarez, and then joined Abel and Loo-soo as they stood over the man.

"What do you think he was doing on our land?" Abel asked.

Antonia felt the subtle assertion of power there—"*our* land." Abel always thought he should have been the one placed in charge of Rancho Los Feliz, but he lacked the management skills Antonia had demonstrated since childhood. Abel was handsome, with his gleaming black hair and perfectly trimmed mustache, good at playing the guitar and wooing the pueblo women, but he could barely add two numbers or carry on a civil conversation with an unhappy worker.

Loo-soo asked, "Do you think he's dangerous?"

"Well," Antonia said, picking up the saddlebag she'd brought in and opening it to retrieve the gun, "I took this off of him."

Abel grabbed the weapon, felt its weight, held it up to one eye. "It *looks* like a gun, but . . . where is it loaded? I can't see anywhere for bullets." After another second, he turned to leave the room. "I'm going to take it outside and try firing it."

"Abel, no!" Too late; he was gone.

Antonia and Loo-soo exchanged a look as the forewoman struggled to find the words. "Abel is . . ."

Antonia finished the sentence when Loo-soo couldn't: "Too often stupid and impulsive."

Loo-soo continued, "You didn't answer the question: do you think this man is dangerous? Should we . . . restrain him?"

"He's very sick. Even if he wanted to, I don't think he could do much. I frankly doubt he'll even survive. Just look at him." The stranger's breathing was low but ragged around the edges; he twitched slightly in his unconscious state, Antonia guessed from pain.

"You're probably right," Loo-soo agreed.

A huge blast sounded from outside.

Antonia and Loo-soo ran from the house, through the landscaped and tiled courtyard, past the tiered fountain and the intricate wrought-iron gate, to the citrus trees around the front of the house. Abel stood there, staring in wonder at the stranger's weapon; a hundred feet away, a plate-sized, smoking hole punctuated the trunk of a Valencia orange tree.

Abel looked up from the gun to the tree to his sister. "One shot did *that*." He uttered a sharp, shrill laugh that made Antonia's hair stand on end.

Regardless of what the gun fired or where it had come from, she knew that her brother wasn't responsible enough to wield that kind of power. Antonia stepped forward, extending a hand. "Give that to me."

Abel looked like a greedy child as he pulled the gun in toward himself. "No. It's mine."

"It's not—it's *his*." Antonia gestured toward the bedroom where the stranger lay, adding, "What if he wakes up and finds it's gone? What if he's got it booby-trapped, or has an even bigger weapon hidden somewhere in that suit?"

Abel couldn't argue with her logic; he reluctantly placed the gun in her extended hands.

"I'll hang onto this for now, at least until we know what's happening with him."

Abel strode off angrily, leaving Antonia to wonder how long it would be before he tried to steal the gun.

Dr. Alvarez arrived an hour later. Antonia assisted him in removing the unconscious stranger's silver suit; underneath, he wore a light one-piece stretchy white undergarment, which they also carefully pulled off.

His entire body was covered with scars, some fresh enough to be raw and oozing.

The doctor blanched. "Madre de Dios . . ." he whispered.

"Have you ever seen anything like this?"

He shook his head. "They look like burn scars, but I can't imagine what kind of fire would have created those. I'm not even sure how to treat them." As he rummaged through his travel bag, he asked, "You have no idea where this man came from?"

"None." Thinking back, Antonia realized there was something else strange about his initial appearance. "He just stepped into view from behind a tree; I don't understand how I didn't see him before that."

Alvarez frowned. "Antonia . . . for some reason this man makes me think of your father, God rest his soul."

Antonia knew what the older doctor meant; Alvarez had cared for the Feliz family for forty years, had treated her father after the Invasion of 1943, when the Japanese had landed on the shore just seventeen miles to the west in an attempt to conquer the nation of Alta California before moving on to the United States. Her father had taken a bullet to the chest; he'd been a strong man and had lived another three days—long enough to see the enemy vanquished, their few remaining forces sent home in humiliation—but in the end there'd been no way to save him. Don Alfonso Feliz had died a hero, and had left a will bequeathing control of his beloved business to his then-twenty-four-year-old daughter. Under Antonia, Feliz Agricultural had become one of the most successful companies in Alta California.

"So," Antonia said to the doctor, as he sat beside his patient, "do you also think this man could be dangerous?"

Alvarez shrugged. "We don't know anything about him." He reached into his bag, pulled out a small glass vial. "A sedative. I can give him this; it should ease his pain, and also keep him from regaining consciousness immediately."

She considered this, and then nodded. "We'll let him sleep while I make arrangements to hand him over to the authorities."

Alvarez filled a syringe, injected the man. A few seconds later, his twitching subsided, his breathing became less labored. "Bueno," the doctor mumbled.

Antonia thanked him, paid him, but knew she'd lied. She had no intention of calling the authorities (what authorities? The local police? Or the national government in Monterey?), at least not right away.

First she wanted a chance to investigate this man's mysteries on her own.

Thirty minutes later, she stepped down from Balada, threw the horse's reins around the lowest branch of a cottonwood, and approached the oak grove where she'd first seen her guest.

When she neared the trees her skin began to tingle, as if the air were charged with electricity. She heard a slight buzzing, but couldn't tell if the sound was real or just in her head. She felt light-headed, a sensation that increased as each step brought her closer to the place where she'd first seen the silver man. Behind her, Balada snorted anxiously, tugging restlessly at the reins.

Antonia reached the tree, more convinced than ever that the man must have been standing there, hidden, for some time before she'd seen him, because she would have noticed any movements.

Then she stepped behind the tree—and froze in shock.

The air—no, *everything*—behind the tree was torn, split; that was the only way Antonia could describe what she saw. There was her land, the shady grove of oaks to the left, the ground layered in leaves and sprouting weeds, and on her right, cottonwoods and buckwheat that led down to the river . . . but here, directly in front of her, six feet away, was a *rip*, a three-foot-wide and six-foot-tall window into some other place. Mesmerized, ignoring both the alarms in her psyche and the increasing nausea in her gut, she stepped forward to peer into the cleft.

She saw an urban nightmare: blocky buildings rose up through ugly vapors, their exteriors cracked and blasted. Nothing grew in that place, not even moss; the only movement was the slight swirl of purplish fog. The sunlight barely penetrated layers of smoke and gas overhead.

It wasn't only her eyes that were assaulted: she gagged at a smell like burned chemicals and scorched metal. She heard occasional distant blasts.

Once she heard screams. She was thankful she didn't see what had made those agonized sounds.

That was when she saw something that chilled her entire body: despite the buildings, the obscuring fog, the gloom that resulted from the charcoal-colored clouds overhead, *she recognized the land*. Here, a slight wrinkle in the topography; over there, the embankment that dropped away, framed in the background by the hills beyond Providencia . . .

It was her land, her beloved Rancho Los Feliz. "No," Antonia gasped.

The tingling in her skin gave way to a burning. That was when she staggered back, vomiting into the brush.

When she could stand again, she stumbled over to Balada and rode the horse as hard as she could back to the hacienda. She found Loo-soo and instructed her to assign four workers to guard the oak grove. She asked where Abel was, relieved to hear he'd gone down to the pueblo. She looked in the mirror, and saw, without surprise, that her face had turned as red as if she'd spent the hottest day of the year outside.

Then she called Dr. Alvarez and told him she needed the stranger awake.

She had to tell him to close whatever that hellish door was that he'd opened.

Despite Dr. Alvarez's efforts to wake him, the man slept for three days. During that time, Antonia saw him begin to recover: the open wounds crusted over, the swelling around the one eye receded, his breathing evened out, the twitching vanished.

Antonia paced. The workers stationed in shifts around the grove had been warned not to enter, and had reported nothing. She herself had ridden out daily to view that awful tear, but it didn't change. She was only thankful that no one—or no*thing*—had come through it.

She was at the man's bedside when he moved, groaned, opened his eyes, and tried to sit up, panicked.

"No, no," Antonia said, "you are recovering. You're in my house, where we've been caring for you."

"How long . . ." His voice, unused too long, grated until he cleared his throat. "How long has it been?"

"Three days."

He sank back down, accepting the situation. "Thank you."

Antonia shrugged. "This is how we treat those who fall sick on our land. May I ask your name?"

"Jack Parsons."

Rising, Antonia said, "I'm happy to meet you, Jack. My name is Antonia Feliz. Would you like something to eat? Maybe some simple broth, until you improve more?"

"Yes, that would be good."

Antonia rose, went to the kitchen, and returned with a bowl of chicken broth that her chef Manuela had prepared. Jack had managed to sit up in the bed, smiling as she came into the room. "That smells wonderful."

"Can you feed yourself?"

"I think so."

As he spooned the broth into his mouth, Antonia studied him. He might once have been an attractive man, although his facial scars made it difficult to know for sure. He didn't strike her as a soldier; he was middle-aged, of medium height, and there was something inherently smart in the way he studied his environs. She wondered if he'd been a doctor, or a scientist, or if he'd had a family, a wife.

"You must have a lot of questions about me," he said between spoonfuls.

"Yes, but also about *this* . . ." She bent, reached under the bed, removed a wooden box with a small lock, used a key from a pocket in her short jacket to open it, and held up the gun.

Jack stopped eating, his eyes moving from the gun to her face. "Antonia . . . be very careful with that."

"My brother fired it, so we know what it can do. Why do you carry it?"

"Purely for defense. I've been to some dangerous places."

As Antonia returned the gun to the box, she half laughed. "Then you don't come from around here, because the most dangerous place we have is a cantina where my brother drinks too much."

He took another swallow of soup before asking, "Your name—Feliz—like Los Feliz?"

"This is the Rancho Los Feliz. It has been in my family since 1795."

"Do you know the names Griffith Park or Los Angeles?"

"I don't know Griffith Park. But yes, the Pueblo de Los Ángeles is only a few miles to the south."

Jack finished the bowl and set it down. "What country is this?"

"How could you not know you are in Alta California?"

"Alta California . . ." Jack smiled and closed his eyes. Within seconds he was asleep.

Antonia was left with nothing but the empty bowl and her questions.

That night, Antonia was awakened by a commotion from outside. She heard raised voices, Loo-soo's truck approaching, frantic knocking. She grabbed a robe, belted it, and went to the front door. Abel met her halfway, his hair still messy from sleep.

"What is it?"

She answered, "I don't know," as she turned on the outside lights and opened the front door.

Loo-soo stood there; behind her, Antonio saw the truck and several vaqueros. "Ramon just got me out of bed. He was on duty outside the oak grove tonight when he heard a strange sound, and then something came out of the trees. He pulled his rifle, but it fell over before he could fire. We think it's dead."

"*It?*"

Loo-soo nodded behind her, her features stony. "Look for yourself."

Antonia walked to the truck, her chest tightening in dread.

The thing in the back of the truck was small, no more than three feet tall. It was covered in the same thick scars that Jack bore, its rear legs were stubby, the front paws curled into tight claws . . .

No, not paws—*hands*. Antonia moved its head slightly toward the light and gasped.

Behind her, Loo-soo asked, "What do you think it is?"

"It's a child."

The others around her muttered in surprise. Loo-soo said, "What kind of child looks like *that*?"

Antonio felt a rush of sympathy for the tiny, scarred thing in the truck. She swallowed it down and turned toward the house and Jack. "That's what we have to find out."

Jack awoke the next morning, and this time he was able to eat solid food—a dish of eggs and a common Kizh breakfast. "What is this?" he asked, speaking around the thick porridge. "I've never tasted anything quite like it."

"It's called *we-ch*. It's a local food made from acorns."

"Weren't the natives here enslaved by the early Spanish settlers?"

Heat rose to Antonia's face. "My ancestors did engage in that terrible practice, sí, but that was long ago. Alta California banned slavery in 1843, just seven years after Juan Bautista Alvarado led the revolt that freed us from Mexico. We share the land with the Kizh people now."

"The ranch bears your name."

"Yes, but in 1850 we returned Maugna—the original Kizh village here—to them. Those who want to work for me are valued and paid good wages, just as any other worker, and they share in our profits. Why are these things so new to you? You do not come from Alta California, obviously . . ."

Jack laughed and set his empty plate aside. "Not exactly." He was searching for words, and Antonia gave him the time he needed. Finally, he looked up at her. "Antonia, you have saved my life and I'm very grateful for your hospitality. That's all part of why I feel that I owe you the truth, as hard as this might be for you to believe."

He looked to her for confirmation to continue, and she said, "Jack, I've seen that—that *place* you must have come from."

"Ahh, of course."

"I've seen your strange clothing, your weapon. And someone else crossed through that portal last night."

Jack tensed. "Someone else?"

"I think it was a child. It died soon after my vaqueros saw it."

"Oh." He took a deep breath. "Antonia, that *portal*, as you call it, is what we call a TPD—a Temporal Phase Displacement. What you see through it is my world. TPDs allow us to investigate alternate time lines."

"I'm sorry, I don't understand."

"My world was once very much like yours. But at some point, we took divergent paths. I'm guessing technology industries are not very big in your country?"

"No. There is more of that in the United States, but Alta California's economy is mainly based on agriculture."

"Imagine a series of clocks lined up in different rooms; each clock is unique, and you can't see more than one because of the walls, but they all tell exactly the same time. That's the easiest way I can explain the alternate time lines; they're all the same place, sitting beside each other but separate, and each developed differently. In my world, we became *all* about technology. We grew very quickly, and we were poised to expand beyond our world, to move out into the stars, but there was a terrible accident. A group of our scientists lost control of a new form of energy, and it devastated our world. It destroyed the climate, the structures, most of the planet's life . . . There are only a few of us left, and we are dying."

"Like the child . . ."

"And like *me*." Jack looked down, flexed his hands, held the fingers up before his face, and Antonia was shocked to see tears streak down one misshapen cheek. "Although in just the few days I've been here, I can feel strength returning."

Something about Jack's tone unnerved Antonia; she knew she should have been proud of saving him, bringing him back from death's edge, but there was a certain calculation in his expression that left her wary. "So your world is as if someone took a right turn instead of a left in the past . . . ?"

He grinned at her. "Exactly. Is the year here 1955?"

"Yes."

"And just to the east is the riverbed, yes?"

"Well . . . yes, but it's not merely a river*bed*. It provides much of our irrigation."

Jack shook his head in wonder. "And you're in charge of it all?"

"I took it over after my father died."

"Are there many women like you? I mean, who are in charge of things?"

Antonia looked at him curiously. "That is a strange thing to ask."

"Trust me, it's not that way everywhere. Although I suspect you'd be a remarkable woman in *any* time line."

Antonia was surprised to feel heat rush to her face again; Jack saw it and laughed gently; he reached for her hand. Startled, she let him take it.

Jack sighed and gazed out on the bright red bougainvillea and many-armed cacti in multicolored talavera pots that filled the courtyard. He spoke softly, wistfully, as he soaked in the beauty. "My wife is gone, like most of the people in my world. Those of us who were left kept researching and experimenting, and, ironically, we made the most significant discovery in history: that there are infinite time lines, and that we can travel between them.

"The things I've seen! I've now visited nearly fifty of them. I've explored versions of Los Angeles that were uninhabited and wild; I've seen others that had been reduced to irradiated desert after a nuclear war. I've seen realities where the Japanese annexed this side of the Pacific Rim, from Baja to Canada. I've seen one where an attempt to secede from the United States—because yes, in that reality California was part of the US—was quashed and led the state to extreme poverty. I met myself in one reality, but it was a very different me. I've seen cities under the sway of religious cults, and I've seen cities where a movie business reigns supreme, where a part of Los Angeles is called Hollywood and the world loves their movies. But none of those versions of Los Angeles were as beautiful, as perfect, as this one."

"We are not so perfect."

"But you *are*," he said. "This whole place looks like a painting. Even your house . . ."

Antonia glanced around at the stucco walls, the warm colors of linens and draperies. She loved it all, she loved her lands and the people she worked with and her business and her country, but she'd never thought of it as extraordinary in any way.

She also realized she believed him, all of it, as impossible as it seemed. His scars, that dead child, the rift that overlooked a world that held the outlines of her land but was otherwise unrecognizable . . . what other explanation could there be? "Jack," she said, drawing his attention back from the courtyard beyond the window, "that . . . TPD, or whatever you called it . . . you can close it, yes?"

"Yes. It will close . . . when I go back."

"Oh."

Antonia rose, confused by a rush of emotions. She knew that returning to his world would surely kill him. Did she dare suggest he stay?

She turned to leave the room, but her brother lounged in the doorway so she had to wait for him to step aside. He followed her as she went to the kitchen. "I heard everything," he said to her, his voice soft but urgent. "Antonia, we have to kill him."

She turned to face Abel, shocked. "What are you saying?"

"Think: What if he's lying? What if the sickness from his world is pouring into ours right now, and he knows that? And what if that gateway or whatever it is stays open only as long as he lives? This isn't just about us, Antonia; this could be our whole world."

"No, Abel, you're wrong. We are not getting sick while he is improving. He is not bringing his world to ours, but ours is helping him."

"We don't know that."

"Which is why we are *not* going to kill a man who may be doing us no harm."

Abel considered this briefly and then placed a hand on her arm. "At least promise me that you will get him out of here and back to his own world as soon as possible."

Reluctantly, she agreed.

Abel strode off. As Antonia busied herself making a cup of coffee, she realized her world had changed, thanks to Jack.

The next day, she found Jack walking in his bedroom, slowly but steadily. He'd dressed in the soft white linen shirt and pants she'd laid out for him.

"Antonia . . . you've been very kind—kinder than anyone else I've ever known—but I overheard your argument with your brother yesterday, and I think it's time. Can you take me back to the TPD?"

She nodded, swallowed her disappointment, and left to get a truck. When she returned, she saw that Jack had dressed in the silver suit again. "I'm sorry to ask this, but . . . my gun?"

Antonia kneeled, pulled out the wooden box, unlocked it, and handed him the weapon. Together, wordlessly, they walked to the truck.

It only took them a few minutes to reach the oak grove. Loo-soo's vaqueros were still stationed there, but Antonia dismissed them. They seemed relieved to go.

Jack walked forward until he stood before the dark tear, its edges pulsing and shimmering. He removed a device from his belt that looked like a portable radio, and punched buttons on it.

Impulsively, Antonia said, "What if you stay?"

Behind them, someone said, "Oh, that's sweet."

Antonia spun to see Abel behind her, a rifle trained on them. "Abel, what . . . ?"

Her brother's handsome face turned ugly with fury. "I'm doing what you apparently wouldn't: making sure this man leaves and doesn't bring his sickness to our world."

"Abel, this isn't necessary—"

"Well, there is one other thing: he's going to leave that gun before he goes through. I could make good use of that."

"Good use for *what*?"

Abel sneered. "Maybe you should just go with him."

Antonia froze in shock. She opened her mouth to reply, but Jack interrupted: "Antonia, your brother is right—I haven't been completely honest with you." His finger hesitated above the device he still held, poised above a red button. "You never asked me why I was here."

He punched the button.

The world roared. Antonia flinched and clapped her hands to her ears, but there was no way to drown out the terrible sound that nearly forced her to her knees. Behind her, she heard Abel's rifle go off as he screamed. She looked up and saw that the TPD was *widening*, expanding, that it was now ten feet . . . twenty feet . . . thirty feet wide, one of the oak trees was gone but there were people, not a few as Jack had said but *thousands* of people in the distance, coming toward them, toward the rift, toward her world.

Antonia understood, then: Jack was a scout. He'd found a new home for the last survivors of his world. They were coming now, bringing their sickness and their science.

"Jack!" she screamed, but then she saw Jack on the ground, dead, the silver suit stained with red where Abel had shot him. Jack couldn't help her now.

A *BOOM* told her that Abel had taken Jack's gun, that he was firing at the wall of people approaching . . . But even with Jack's gun, Abel would never be able to hold back this tide.

She wished she'd had some warning; she could have prepared for this. She could have quarantined the refugees until she was sure they weren't contagious, until she was confident that they wanted only a chance at life, not theft or pillage or conquest. Why hadn't Jack just asked her? They could've worked this out together.

If she'd only had time . . .

But she knew that time wasn't hers.

DETAINMENT

BY **ALEX ESPINOZA**

El Sereno

The child returned to me by the border patrol isn't my son. My Ariel is still missing. Maybe he was left in those overcrowded detention centers. What I am certain of, though, is that this boy, the one I have, he's an impostor.

He's wrong.

I want *my* son back.

He looks just like him, right down to the birthmark he has on the back of his left arm. He even has the cluster of three little moles on the side of his neck.

"Máma," he said the moment he laid eyes on me, tugging at the arm of the social worker who'd traveled with him. "Máma."

"Sí," I said, sobbing, "soy yo. Máma!" I stood in the airport terminal with my cousin Licha, her boyfriend Juan, and the attorney named Grace Lopez-Hull. I gripped the teddy bear I'd bought him—a large brown thing wearing a bright red bow tie with yellow polka dots.

"That's your mother," I heard the social worker state. "Mercedes."

"Máma. Mercedes," his voice echoed.

He even lisped the way my Ariel did, pronouncing my name Mer*th*edes like he always had.

Grace shouted at the reporters and the police and the airport security in their puffy jackets and dark boots to move aside, to give me some room. Let the woman go to her son, she implored. They've been separated long enough. The photographers and the reporters smiled and snapped pictures of me as I made my way to him. Then I hugged my boy and I pulled his black hair back and brought his face to mine and said, "Look at me, Ariel. Look at me. It's your mother. Do you remember?"

He nodded, rubbed a few tears from his eyes, and said, "Yes. You are my máma." He pressed his finger against my collarbone, and I felt the jab penetrating my skin, warming my blood because here was my son again. There were more pictures, and a handful of the reporters sighed and gripped their microphones and I could hear one saying into a camera positioned near us, "We're reporting live at LAX where five-year-old Ariel Tomás Garza has been reunited with his mother. The two were separated for months after being detained by ICE. They were part of the second wave of asylum seekers stopped at the border."

"A tearful reunion after a harrowing separation," I heard another reporter say.

A woman speaking into a tiny tape recorder said, "I'm witnessing Mercedes Garza and her young son finally together. As I stand here in an unassuming LAX terminal this cold and rainy evening, I am reminded of the bond between a mother and her child, how strong and yet fragile this bond is. Who knows how many other mothers out there are missing their children? The current administration's policies are literally ripping families apart. We have no idea what the psychological ramifications of a traumatic experience like this could have on these individuals."

There were questions, so many questions, and my head was spinning, and all I could do was grip Ariel with the same force I had exerted when the officers tore him away from me. Grace Lopez-Hull answered the inquiries in English, and I could only make out a few phrases: ". . . not for six months," she replied to one reporter. "If you have kids, imagine not knowing about your child for six long months."

"I feel like a piece of me has been recovered," I told another reporter from a Spanish-language newspaper. "We gave up everything to come here. We were only seeking asylum. We just wanted to be safe." My hands shook, and Ariel looked away. "At the border, they questioned us. They separated me from my boy. I have not seen him until now. I didn't know where he was, if he was alive. Nothing."

Grace, Licha, and Juan led us out as the reporters followed, a long mass of people trailing behind. It was like a pageant. Exciting and terrifying at the same time. All I heard was the consistent snap of pictures, the endless murmuring of questions, and Grace shouting at them to stop, urging them to leave us alone. There would be more time, she promised, but now we needed some peace, my son and me. Because we were going home.

In the car, I kissed his head and cheeks and each eye. I felt his hands, checked his arms and legs for bruises or injuries. It wasn't until Licha turned the car light on that I was able to notice that he looked taller, his limbs dangling down the seat bench like limp tree branches. He was wearing different clothing—a red jacket with a hood, a striped undershirt, tan trousers, and brand-new shoes with different-colored laces.

"You're safe," I said. "Seguro," I said, again and again.

Licha maneuvered the car out of the airport, and we started on the freeway toward their apartment.

"Let's get you some food, yes?" Juan said from the passenger seat. "Hamburgers and fries."

"Does that sound good?" Licha asked. After switching lanes, she reached around and squeezed his foot. "Your mother said you asked about me before the migra took . . ." Her voice trailed off. "Anyway, aren't you happy to see me?"

He hardly said a word, though. He just stared out the window, the teddy bear resting on his lap. I thought, *Shock*. That's likely what it was. *Shock*. After all, this was a lot for a child to endure.

Licha and Juan cracked jokes, tried engaging him, but Ariel was so aloof and distant. Not like him at all, they whispered. He would talk and talk for hours. He had always been so curious, my boy. This child was silent, almost brooding. The whole car took on an air of unease. It was immediate. What had they done to him in there? I wondered. How long would it take for my Ariel to be himself again? I had to be patient, to love and reassure him. But when I reached out across the car seat to hold his hand, he recoiled.

He then turned and asked, "Why are you doing that?"

"What do you mean?" I said, my voice meek. "I haven't seen you in months. You are my son, and I'm so happy to be with you again."

He placed his hand out and said, "Go ahead then."

His skin no longer felt like his skin. It wasn't soft like I remembered. It felt like holding a doll, plastic and hard.

Was I losing my mind?

We'd been through a lot, I thought, as we continued on toward the apartment. Here we were. Finally. After everything. After all the walking and the sleeping in muddy ditches and on the cold steps of the few churches that offered us clemency, us looking like a band of marauders with plastic bags draped over our shoulders to protect us from the torrential rains.

I sighed. Things were fine. We were the lucky ones. We got out of that infernal country, and now we were here. We would start over. In Los Angeles.

In a neighborhood named for peace and serenity.

El Sereno.

At the apartment, I watched him pick up his french fries, take tiny bites of his hamburger, then rub his nose and eyes. He must be tired. Licha and Juan had retired to her bedroom. I took the sheets and pillows from the hall closet and made up the couch.

"Here is where I've been sleeping," I told Ariel.

He looked around at the small living room—its oversize television and mismatched chairs, the broken tiles of the entryway, and into the kitchen where the crumpled fast-food bag sat, bloated and empty. I bathed him, using an old margarine tub to splash water over his head and body. I rubbed soap over his distended belly and across the small crevices along his back. I felt the bones of his spine, little lumps connected, one after the other, like smooth river stones. He stood in the middle of the bathroom, shivering. I pulled strands of his wet hair back, wiped his face, his body, and dressed him in the pajamas I had brought with us from home.

I wanted to ask where he'd been. Where they'd kept him. Had anybody hurt him? Was he afraid? Did he know I had spent the weeks after I was released racked with guilt and anger? That I blamed myself for this? That I thought it would have been better had we stayed put, never trying to make the journey to the United States? There was danger back home, of course. He was getting older. It was only a matter of time before the gang would come into town again, rounding him up like they did so many others, and take him into the jungle, never to be seen again.

There was so much I wanted to know. Instead I picked him up, cradled him in my arms, and walked him down the short hallway and back out to the living room. He was already asleep; I could hear the familiar whistling of his breath as it passed through those small nostrils. *Not even an ant could wiggle through them*, my mother would say before she died.

Tomorrow, I told myself. There will be time for questions tomorrow.

I undid my braid, let my long hair tumble down my back and across my chest. I held my son tightly against me, rocked him even though I knew he was fast asleep, even though no amount of my moving would ever rouse him. This is what a mother yearns for. To be with her child like this. In the serenity. No bullets piercing the night sky, rattling the trees, disrupting the movements and rhythms of the spirits they say roam the darkness.

Tomorrow there would be an opportunity for questions.

·

Between the gangs, the drug cartels, the corrupt military and politicians, where could someone like me turn? I watched whole communities burn to the ground, saw countless men and women and children slaughtered, their bodies tortured and disfigured, left to rot and fester in mass graves. It was the stuff of nightmares. I need no proof of the existence of hell; I have lived there. Hell is where I came from. Hell is what I was determined to leave behind. For the safety and well-being of my son.

The handful of us that were left cowered in fear whenever we saw the trucks. We watched as they took turns on us—soldiers one day, drug kings the next, then the pandilleros. They would descend into town, gather us in the main square, and make us watch the public executions or tortures. We watched as they hauled the young girls away, raped them, then returned them to us, shattered, their eyes vacant, their mouths quivering.

One of those was my comadre Amparo's daughter, Venacia. I remember the day. How could anyone forget something like that? I stood with Amparo under the shade of a guava tree washing clothes and hanging them out to dry on a string we'd tied across the front of my house. It was weeks since Venacia had gone missing, taken by a group of soldiers. She was destroyed. Her skirt was torn, her legs scratched and bruised. She only wore her green sweater, the school's crest over the right side of her chest frayed. There were leaves and bugs in her hair. But it was her face that made us both gasp, that caused us to turn away. She'd been beaten badly, and her nose had been fractured. Her eyes were swollen and there was a large gash running down the side of her cheek. She screamed when we tried touching her, when we tried getting her out of the filthy rags she was wearing. There was dried blood caked on her underwear, inside her thighs, and along her back. Bite marks and cigarette burns dotted her breasts. This is what happened to our children. They would come back broken, forever changed.

* * *

I loved Ariel's father very much. He read books and believed in the ability of people to rise up and change things. Daniel wanted to fight. He wanted to take back the country and overthrow the crooked politicians and mercenaries, the drug lords and gang members. He thought democracy could one day return to the country, that we would live to see the moment when everything would be restored once more.

"A utopia," he once said to me.

"A what?" I asked. This was in the days when we'd just discovered that I was pregnant with Ariel.

"A utopia," he repeated. "A place where people live communally, where everything is shared, and where everyone has a purpose."

He saw hope in everything. That's what I loved so much about him, my Daniel. His courage, his faith that was endless, a faith that indeed made me believe that things would change someday. But, in fact, they got worse.

After Venacia returned—and was never again in her right mind—and once Ariel was born, more factories closed down, more people lost their jobs, and everything was teetering toward complete collapse. Paper money lost all value; a few street vendors started stitching together shirts and jackets out of bills. It was a sight to see a purse made of hundreds and hundreds of thousand-peso notes selling for less than a pack of cigarettes. The supermarkets ran out of food. Teachers went on strike, hospitals closed down, and the police simply stopped caring. My husband grew more and more desperate and angry. He took to pacing back and forth. He cursed the wealthy and those who supported the president and his crooked administration. I tried calming him down, but it was useless. He was frightened. He had me and Ariel to worry about. What kind of future would there be for our son?

The protest happened on a warm Saturday afternoon. First it was a few campesinos. Then somebody showed up with a bullhorn. Then more people came out. A hunger strike was called. Some of the men, including Daniel, sat down, linked their arms together, and demanded justice. Then we heard a loud rumble, a slow groan coming deep from the bowels of the earth. People scattered when they saw the tear gas canisters fly through the air and hit the ground. Daniel and the others held firm, though. They didn't budge. They wrapped handkerchiefs over their mouths and noses and remained there, even when the gunfire began. I heard fast, sharp whizzes, smelled smoke; one of the buildings was on fire now.

I watched the soldiers descend on the square. A woman gripped my arm. Daniel shot me a look, those wide eyes of his cutting through the smoke and bullets. *Go*, he was telling me. So I ran, following the stream of women shouting and crying, all of us scattering like torn strips of paper. There was no Daniel. No Horacio. No Miguel. No Antonio. No Justo. No Mario. All our men were gone. We waited a few days. A body turned up, splayed across a pile of boulders beside the river with a note attached to his chest. It was a warning. I had no time to mourn him, no time to remember my beautiful man. Soon they would come for the rest of us. There was only one thought: *Leave*. So, we gathered our things, those of us who were left—the women, the children, the homosexuals, the elderly, the sick and disabled—and we formed a caravan. We walked for days, addled by the heat and hunger. Some of us died or got lost along the way.

"May God be with them," we said, erecting crosses along the roadside.

We arrived. Somehow. We arrived. We declared ourselves at the border, told the agents we sought asylum. This was when they separated me from Ariel. They took him and the rest of the children. We were sent into a giant room with green cots lined up along a cinder-block wall. There was one bathroom, a handful of tables, and a television. All of this was enclosed behind a metal fence, and guards with guns paced back and forth along the outside perimeter.

I don't know how long I was there. I was allowed only one call. Thank goodness Licha was home. It took them a few days, but she showed up with Juan and the lawyer, Grace, who argued and argued with the government officials, and I was released.

"She's a real chingona," Licha said.

Juan nodded. "Don't mess with Grace."

I told her about Ariel. I pleaded, said I would not leave the facility without him. We had come too far, I explained. We had lost so much.

"The children were sent to another facility," she told us. "And I don't know where that is, but I promise you I'm going to find out."

"She owes us a solid," Juan said. "Isn't that right, Gracie?"

She balled up her fist and gave him a soft punch in the arm. "Yes. Anything for Licha. She's like family." Grace glared at Juan. "You, on the other hand—"

"Stop joking," Licha said. "This is serious. How do we know the boy will be okay?"

"Because he has to be," Grace said. "I promise you that we will find your Ariel and get him back."

Weeks went by. There were phone calls. There were forms that needed to be filed. There were meetings and interviews. An endless parade of men and women in suits and ties who scrutinized me, who asked me why I would risk so much, why I would take such a dangerous trip with my young son. Wasn't I afraid that something terrible would happen to him along the way?

"Yes," I said. "But I was also afraid that something terrible would happen to him if we stayed back there."

Weeks became months. I cried a lot. Licha and Juan tried to distract me. They took me places on the weekends. The beach. The mountains. We saw celebrities' houses, large structures as ornate as birthday cakes. The weekdays were the hardest, though. There was no one to keep me company. I found myself wandering up and down the street. I went to the El Sereno Park just a short walk from the apartment. I sat there for hours watching the children play. My heart longed only to see them jump and laugh and run around. I imagined my Ariel there, among them.

More time. More waiting. Nothing.

It was agony.

Then the call came. Grace had located him. He was on his way, from where we weren't told, only that he was safe.

I cried. Licha and Juan clapped and shouted.

He was coming back to me. At long last. The only piece of home I had left. A reminder of my husband. I would feel complete again.

Hot dogs sliced into little pink circles and cooked with eggs. To drink, a glass of chocolate milk. That was his favorite meal. Always. Without fail. Only, the next morning, when I cooked this and offered it to him, he refused it. He sat at the table and stared and stared at the food.

"What's wrong?" I asked.

He shook his head. "I'm not hungry."

"Try," I implored him.

He played with the food for an hour. He moved the hot dog circles to one side of the plate, stabbed the eggs with his fork, and tapped his finger against the glass of chocolate milk. I sensed an unease in him, a restlessness.

A few hours later, as I was in the kitchen cleaning up, my back to him, I heard a sound. Movement. Like furniture being dragged across the floor. I turned the water off and found him standing in front of the television. Just staring at it.

It was turned off. His eyes were vacant, his mouth wide open, like he'd seen something awful and was about to scream. I tapped him on the shoulder, but there was no response. I shook him. Nothing. I snapped my fingers right in front of his face. Still nothing. I picked him up, carried him to the couch, and shouted his name, over and over. It was only a few seconds, but it felt like an eternity before I saw movement in his eyes and his face.

"Ariel," I said, "what happened?"

He paused, opened his mouth, and recited a string of numbers in Spanish: "186543379-675-344547."

"What?" I asked. "I don't understand."

Then he looked at me and said, in a voice that was clear and very stern, "I'm fine now. You can return to what you were doing"

"But, Ariel—"

"I'm fine."

Water, he said. He needed water. I poured him a glass,

and I watched as he gulped the entire thing down in a matter of seconds. He demanded another. Then another. In total, he finished four large glasses, then sat on the couch and smoothed out the wrinkles on his shirt from where I'd grabbed him.

"What is there to do here?" he said.

He didn't talk like my son. His words were elevated, clear, almost like they'd been rehearsed. "What do you mean?" I asked.

He tilted his head to one side, squinted his eyes, and repeated it: "What is there to do here?"

I pointed out the window. "There's a park."

He rose slowly off the couch, zipped up his jacket, and said, "Let us go there then."

I put the dishes away, grabbed my sweater, and we headed out.

Fresh air will be good, I thought as we made our way down the steps and toward the street. *He probably wasn't allowed outside where they kept him and the others. Poor children. They need air and grass and trees.*

Still, I tried convincing myself that the feelings of unease and dread cascading down and around me were just figments of my imagination. At the park, instead of playing, instead of running around or climbing on the playground equipment, he sat down on a bench and just watched them, watched the other children. When I asked him if he wanted to walk over, maybe talk with some of the other kids, he said he was fine.

"Do you just want to sit here?" I asked.

"Yes," he replied. "It suits me fine."

The sun was warm; a bright white light bathed everything. I looked out across the street, watched ravens circle in the sky over the railroad tracks running parallel to Valley Boulevard. We just . . . sat there. I was on one end of the bench and he was on the other. He perched at the edge, starting intently like an animal stalking its prey. He flinched when I reached out and tapped him on the shoulder. It was getting cold, and the clouds were gathering. I was afraid it would rain.

"I don't mind the rain," he said. I noticed a few drops fall on his jacket.

"You'll get soaked," I explained. "I didn't bring an umbrella."

He didn't budge, though.

I stood, stretched my legs. Nervousness had settled in my stomach. I took a few steps away from the bench, turned around for just one second, and then he was gone. I called his name, but there was nothing. My eyes scanned the playground, the trash can near the bathrooms. No Ariel. Where was he? Then I caught a sense that someone was watching me. Standing in front of a cluster of low bushes was my son. At first, I thought the light was playing tricks on me, and I approached slowly. The few drops of rain turned to drizzle as I bent down toward him. I couldn't see that it was a dead raven at first; all I could make out through the drizzle clouding my eyes was a clump of black feathers, oily and slick as tar. The bird's beak was ash gray, dusted with a white film that looked like chalk. Its yellow eyes were still, bulging out of their sockets, as if the poor creature had been startled or choked.

"He was making too much noise," Ariel said, holding the animal's limp body. "He needed to be quiet. He needed to obey. If you break the rules, you get punished severely."

I looked on in horror. "Put that down," I finally said. "Please, Ariel. Put it down now."

He said nothing to me, though. He simply tossed the dead bird on the ground; it landed with a light thud on a muddy patch between our feet.

The rain was falling harder now. I reached out to scoop him up in my arms. I gripped him, and I ran down the street, past the tire shop and the liquor store, across the parking lots riddled with empty bags of chips. A man with stringy blond hair holding a dog on a leash was coming out of the coffee shop. I almost knocked him over, and I apologized in my best English.

He nodded, said, "It's okay. No hay problema."

The dog wore a silly pink knitted sweater. Those big, moist eyes looked up at us, but the animal concentrated its stare on Ariel. Then it growled and barked, baring its teeth, its nostrils flaring. When the man reached out to pet the dog, speaking to it in a soothing voice, the animal lunged forward, biting his arm. It broke skin, and I saw fat sores starting to form, then bleed across his hand as he dropped his coffee and yelled, "Rufus! What the fuck?"

On I ran. Past the run-down motel with its coral-blue walls and rusted iron gate, past the little shop with the purple doors selling nopalitos in glazed pots. The puddles on the sidewalk widened and grew deeper. The drops falling on the roofs of the houses and the shops sounded like bullets. My breathing became ragged. I couldn't see very well; strands of damp hair fell over my eyes. But I held onto my Ariel, and we ran and ran and my skirt was soaking wet and so was my sweater and my feet and my arms were sore and my legs were trembling and by the time we reached the front of the apartment door, I was heaving and crying and I was wet and angry and I couldn't figure out why. And my son, there in my arms, he felt light as air. It seemed the tighter I held him, the thinner he became.

Inside, I took off his wet shoes and hurried him into the bathroom. I grabbed towels and placed him inside the tub and told him to remove his wet clothing. First his jacket and his shirt, then his pants and underwear and socks. I noticed a strange patch of raised skin across his waistline as I reached over to pull a pair of freshly washed pants on him. A cluster of perfectly round bumps. I touched them and asked if they itched.

He shook his head. "No," he said.

"Do they hurt?"

"No, it's fine. You don't need to worry."

The raised bumps didn't go away. They never spread. He never complained about them. If I asked him to let me see them, he'd raise his little shirt. I'd push the elastic band of his pants down, and there they'd be. Always the same. I rubbed ointments and lotion on, but they never went away. They never worsened. They just were. I was confused. Were they an inoculation? Maybe someone had hurt him in there. How long would they last? Would they ever go away?

Then one night, I was awakened by a strange voice. It sounded like a man speaking. Through the haze of half sleep, I rubbed my eyes and focused. Yes, it was a man, I was sure of it. The voice was gruff and deep. At first, I thought maybe it was Juan; he was spending the night so he wouldn't have to drive back home to Fontana after his long shift at the factory.

The voice speaking, though, was closer. It wasn't coming from the bedroom. I turned my head. Through the light of the streetlamps outside, I could make out Ariel's profile. I could trace the dark outline of his forehead, the small ridge of his eyebrow, his nose, and then his lips. They seemed to be moving, like he was talking in his sleep. It was his voice that I was hearing. Low and sinister. It wasn't my son. That wasn't his voice. And the words he was speaking. It was like he was talking in another language. An endless string of words I couldn't figure out. But he only knew Spanish and a little English. Finally, after about thirty minutes, he stopped. He just . . . stopped talking.

The next morning, as Licha and Juan got ready to leave, Licha turned to me and asked what I'd been watching the night before.

"Me?" I looked at her confused. "Nothing."

"I heard the television on. Voices."

"Me too," Juan said. "Like a conversation."

"Oh," I said. "It was just . . . I couldn't sleep."

I lied. I also said nothing about the strange marks on his body and the dead bird.

I didn't want them to think I was crazy. It would all pass, I thought. Little by little.

We walked to the library up on Huntington Boulevard. There, we gathered a stack of picture books, and I asked Ariel to sit by me and look at them as I turned the computer on. I didn't know exactly what I was looking for, but there had to be something to explain all these odd things. It took awhile, but slowly certain similarities began emerging. A mother in Texas reported that her daughter had grown very depressed and moody ever since she'd been returned. The girl refused to go outside and spent all day in her bedroom, the curtains drawn. She turned very pale, and her hair started to fall out in clumps. Another woman reported that her son had become increasingly violent, harming himself and others; he had beaten up a classmate and pushed him down a flight of stairs. Another mother from Arizona was so sure her daughter had been replaced by a robot that she began cutting the little girl's arms and legs to see if she bled. The little girl nearly died before the mother was arrested and her daughter placed in a foster home.

All of these children had been separated from their parents after crossing the border. Just like me and Ariel. None of it made sense. I watched Ariel flipping through a book on dinosaurs. He was so unfamiliar to me now, so distant and far away. No matter what I did, I couldn't break through to him.

I remember my mother and grandmother telling us stories about duendes, small creatures that lived in the forests and caves around the village. They'd roam the countryside at night and steal laundry and food, vandalize the barns, and rouse the chickens and roosters.

"I saw one once," my grandmother told me when I was a girl. "A little thing. It looked like a child scurrying a few feet ahead of me as I was coming back from the río one evening. In the moonlight, I could see that it walked funny. As I approached, it turned to look at me. Its eyes glowed bright green. And when it grinned, I saw a set of sharp yellow teeth. It had long fingernails, and its skin was covered in hair."

The truly sinister ones, though, did more things, awful things. They butchered animals for food, skinned their hides to wear. They disguised themselves and walked into houses, caused mischief; some even reportedly lit a woman's home on fire as she slept.

They would also steal babies and children, replacing them with look-alikes in order to trick the parents and cause more mischief. When I asked why they did this, my grandmother sighed and shook her head.

"They're just bad," my mother replied. "They only do it because they are evil. There's no other reason. They are bitter and foul things with hate in their souls."

Maybe politicians are duendes disguised as people. I don't know who this child is, but he is not mine. I am not crazy. Even after all that I've been through, I've remained fully intact, fully aware of myself. I am of sound mind, as the Americans say. I look at this boy now, this mysterious little life lying next to me, sleeping. The rash on his waist has changed now. After the blisters broke, scabs formed that scarred, leaving a series of marks on his skin, dark lines like those found on the backs of packages with tiny letters and numbers:

Grace took notes in her pad and snapped a few pictures. She said she'd get to the bottom of this, though I have little faith now. Things are getting worse. They say on the news that more caravans of migrants are on their way. It seems governments everywhere are unraveling, and the only choice people have is to leave. Such is the will to live. Part of me wishes I could tell those mothers I see on television not to come here. To stay where they are, that the lives of their children aren't worth it. That this process changes them, that they will forever be plagued by irrevocable damage, that our babies will be lost to us.

But I can't stop them. And even if I could, I wouldn't. Because at least we are alive.

My child is out there somewhere. I'll find him.

I'm a mother and, like all mothers, this is what we do.

PEAK TV

BY **BEN H. WINTERS**

Culver City

On the day the streamer ordered a second season, Jack Avril went ahead and bought his kid a dog.

Little Jayden had been asking incessantly for at least six months, at least since his friend Paulie Weisberg got a little corgi for Hanukkah, but Jack had thus far maintained his position on the dog question, which was, in essence: hard pass. He was busy as hell with work, basically all the time, and his wife Angel was pretty tied up with all her charity stuff, plus the tennis. And Jayden, at the tender age of seven, was nowhere *near* old enough for the responsibility. But Jayden would not be discouraged, he really wouldn't, even going so far at one point as to present a PowerPoint called "Why I Should Get a Dog."

Jack had held the line, though, even when Angel got a little wobbly sometimes. "Maybe . . ." she would say. Or, "Maybe just a *little* dog . . ." Jack, somehow, stuck to his guns.

But after today? After the meeting, after the good news, Jack felt like, basically: let's do it. And forget about a *little* dog. Let's blow this kid's mind.

Jack was flying—he was on top of the universe.

A trio of execs from the streamer had made the pilgrimage to his offices on the studio lot in Culver City, bearing the big news along with a box of blueberry donuts—his particular favorite and the subject of a long-running in-joke between himself and the suits. It was silly, but the gesture warmed his heart. Everybody shook hands. They ate the big messy donuts, and laughed and took pictures, everybody grinning.

Of course, Jack had been 99.99 percent sure that a Season 2 order was in the works. His agent had told him to expect it, and so had his lawyer, and in truth he hadn't needed to be told. *The Bleachers* was a hit. Not a beloved-but-little-watched critical darling, not a buzzed-about cult thing, but an honest-to-God, out-of-the-park *hit*—and not a hit twenty years ago but a hit *today,* a hit in "the current environment," where between network and cable and streaming and YouTube Red and friggin' Facebook Watch, there were 400-odd pieces of original programming being aired on *some* kind of air every year, and twenty times that number in development at any given moment. It was such a huge volume of television shows that the average viewer had never even heard of most of them. In that context, the kinds of numbers *The Bleachers* was posting had guaranteed Avril a second batch of episodes.

But it was nice to hear the words. Nice to get the donuts. Nice, in a career so full of disappointed hopes, to experience on a beautiful blue Tuesday afternoon a genuinely life-changing event.

So why not roll that happiness down the hill?

Jack stopped at a breeder on the way home, a place on Doheny in Beverly Hills called Four Legs Better, which had been recommended by an old friend named Chick Stuart, who he'd worked with for a season on *Justified* about a million years ago. "You know, the whole thing with the breeders, it's kind of an ethical gray area," Chick had said, when

Jack called for the name of a place he remembered him mentioning. "What animal people would say is, you know, go to the pound and get a rescue dog? But with a breeder, you know what you're getting. And the experience—you pay for it, but it's just *easier*, you know?"

Jack didn't sweat the ethical gray area. He valeted his Lexus at Four Legs Better and found the place exactly as Chick had described it: all very professional and schmancy, all air-conditioned and clean, with each dog's stats and pedigree on display, like they were prize fighters. He pointed to a big handsome Dogue de Bordeaux named Augustus Caesar, and the guy explained how, despite the size of the thing, it was actually a perfect dog for a young kid, a stalwart and loving pet. The animal cost a goddamn fortune, but what the hell—Jack could afford it, right?

For the next bunch of years, he could afford whatever he wanted, or wanted for his only child.

When they brought his car around, Jack wrangled this big beautiful animal—122 pounds is what they told him, at just two years old—into the backseat of the Lexus. In the car, Augustus Caesar looked even bigger.

At a stoplight on Santa Monica Boulevard, Jack turned and examined the newest member of his family: sleek chestnut fur and curving lips, slightly parted, and gleaming teeth, each a perfect white dagger. Small gray eyes that stared back at Jack, curious and calm.

He'd never been a dog person, really. He just loved his kid.

"He's awesome, Dad!" Jayden kept saying, over and over, wide-eyed with excitement, panting with delight. "He's awesome!"

He and Augustus Caesar became fast friends, right from go. The dog had bounded right in and bowled the little guy over, like something out of a cartoon movie about dogs, and Jayden had bounced up and wrapped his new pet in a big tight hug. "He's *so* awesome!"

Angel came and wrapped her arms around Jack and stood behind him with her head buried in his neck. She was happy too, of course; as soon as he'd texted her about Season 2, she'd texted back and asked if this meant they could remodel the downstairs. Winking emoji. Kidding, not kidding.

"You're a good dad," she said into his back, and the two of them stood watching Jayden wrestle the dog.

"Oh, hey, guys," said Jack. "The breeder called him Augustus Caesar. But we can rename him if you want. It's up to you."

"Jayden?" said Angel. "What do you think?"

"I *like* that name," said Jayden, enthusiastic, guileless, full of love. "I *really* like it."

And so Augustus Caesar he remained, and it made a certain sense. The dog was majestic. A dog of stature. An emperor of a dog.

Jack yawned, satisfied with the happy ending to his happy day, and walked toward the kitchen to pour himself a Scotch.

Augustus Caesar set its steely small eyes on Jack and bared its teeth as he passed.

The Bleachers was a show for teen audiences about the soul-searching, grief, and social realignments at an elite private high school in suburban Maryland, in the wake of a popular student's suicide.

Jack Avril was the showrunner, executive producer, and cocreator, but the show had not, strictly speaking, originated with him.

It was adapted from a young adult book called *Hummingbird High* (terrible title—that had been Jack's first note), the debut novel by a woman in Michigan named Genevieve Jackson. The book had pubbed in 2010 or 2011, made no ripple, and disappeared—except among some ultrasensitive book nerds, including a Vassar sophomore named Jessica Bailey—who, fast-forward three years, is a baby writer, repped at UTA, staffed as a room assistant on a Disney Channel show but hot to develop. Her UTA agent, a minimally talented clown named Benny Rocco maybe six months out of the mailroom, gets the book to a producer named Janet Ko, who has a deal at Fox on the strength of a briefly beloved family sitcom she'd developed called *Lunchbox Sam*. Jack Avril, at the time, was in the twilight months of a fruitless overall at Fox, and he was feeling a distinct lack of momentum. He fielded an incoming call from Ko, who basically said: "This girl Jessica has this book, it's maybe something, but we need an adult in the room. You busy?"

Jack was not busy. He did a pass on Jessica's pass, ditched the title and sexed up the character palette, moved the inciting suicide to the *end* of the pilot outline, and they took the thing to the town. Verdict: six no's and one very soft yes: the streamer took a flier, said show us a draft and write the Bible and let's see what happens.

And what had happened? They shot the pilot, they made a series, and the series exploded.

And suddenly, ol' Jack Avril, ancient at thirty-eight, everybody's favorite affordable EP, veteran of a thousand one-season stands, is the showrunner on this streaming YA thing turning the world upside down. People *love* the thing. Gen-Xers, millennials and post-millennials, and even—miracle of miracles—the actual target demo: young adults. They eat *The Bleachers* for breakfast. They're dissecting the dialogue on Twitter, they're setting up Instagram accounts for the characters, they're doing podcasts where they argue about the show's racial politics.

And yes, okay, there were some suicides.

The first one had been a girl, in Tampa, Florida, named Valerie Escobar. Well, actually, Valerie Escobar was the first one that people explicitly connected with the show, although there had been some concern, in some quarters, before the show had even aired; all the usual hand-wringing about the danger of vivid dramatization of self-harm, especially in entertainment aimed at young people . . .

But look, you couldn't even say for *sure* that Valerie's suicide had been directly related to *The Bleachers*, let alone inspired by it—although she was clearly obsessed with the show, as was attested by all her friends and plainly evident on her socials. There was also the unsettling fact that her suicide note had quoted heavily from the monologue Jack had written for Norman Dyson, the football player who hangs himself under the bleachers at the end of the pilot.

Inevitably, with the suicide of Valerie Escobar, there were more articles and more questioning, and even, from some quarters, outright condemnation. But with so many other outrages clamoring for the public's attention, concerns about *The Bleachers* remained fairly muted—until the second suicide. This time it was a boy named Luke Worth, from Midlands, Texas, who snuck onto his school's football field in the middle of the night and hanged himself under the bleachers with a bedsheet, just like Norman, on the show.

For fuck's sake, Jack thought, when they called to tell him, though he immediately felt bad for thinking it. *A little on the nose, kid.*

After that, the streamer had felt compelled to add a Parental Advisory note at the beginning of each episode, along with a list of hotline phone numbers at the end, and they'd issued a somber statement, complete with a quote from showrunner Jack Avril: *Our hearts go out to the Worth family. We at* The Bleachers *are proud to be participating in an important conversation about the pressures faced by today's young people, and we urge anyone feeling suicidal . . .*

And so forth. Something to that effect. Jack had approved his quote without reading it super closely.

What he felt, in his heart of hearts, was that a kid who was going to kill himself was going to kill himself. TV show or no TV show.

He felt bad, of course. Everybody felt *bad.*

One aspect of the whole thing that Jack found pretty interesting, which he had been told in confidence by a drinking buddy inside the streamer, was that the controversy attending the suicides had been one of the drivers of the show's continuing popularity.

They had let Jayden stay up an extra hour or two to play with Augustus Caesar, and to set up the doggy bed in a corner of his room. Then Jack and Angel had celebrated properly, first with champagne and then in the bedroom.

Jack was yawning and humming and sipping coffee from his travel mug when he approached the studio lot the next morning, past the cluster of six or seven protesters who were gathered across the street as usual, marching in their silent circle, holding up their signs with simplistic, handwritten slogans.

They watched him as he turned right off Washington Boulevard onto the lot, beeped his security badge, and waited for the gate arm to rise. But Jack didn't think they knew who he was—with a few exceptions, showrunners do not have known faces. The only thing that was better than fame and fortune, Jack thought, piloting the Lexus to the space with his name on it, was fortune on its own.

"Well, I'm gonna be honest with you," Jack said, smiling as politely as he could, sipping a cup of coffee. "I don't *totally* get it."

Jack was taking pitches today. This had been a big part of his life the last few weeks, and would continue to be for the next few, until the writers room opened up for Season 2. Written into his first-look deal with the studio was the expectation that he'd bring in projects he hadn't created, but to which he'd be attached as a producer; an above-the-title producer whose name attracts talent, and money, and—eventually, knock on wood—viewers.

So his agents had been sending him writers hustling projects of their own, who would sit in his office, reading from their pitch docs with various levels of nervousness or animation or plain terror, trying to get him turned on by their ideas.

Which were, sadly, generally, pretty terrible.

So, for example, right now he was listening to a very thin man named Todd something, who gesticulated alarmingly while he presented his drama about a family of trapeze artists, one of whom keeps getting badly hurt.

"So—you said it's an hour, but this is a *comedy*, right?"

"No," said Todd whatever, absolutely aghast. "Absolutely not! *No*."

Jack texted his assistant Beth under the table: *Next?*

Diversity was in vogue, so a lot of the pitches had it, generally in transparent and superfluous ways, tacked on at the end like a tail on a Halloween costume. "Oh," the writer would say toward the end of the pitch, "and I should mention that the couple we're talking about is interracial." Or, "It's important to note that the chief of the fire department is out and proud."

"Ah. Sure."

Next.

During lunch Jack wandered into downtown Culver City for a bagel and cream cheese, and to watch a little video that Angel had texted him of Jayden and Augustus Caesar cavorting in the backyard. God, it was really such a big animal. So much bigger than the kid. In the clip, which was only a few seconds long, the dog launched himself into the air at Jayden, who stood with his arms extended, delighted by this huge monster about to crash into his chest. The clip cut off before the dog landed.

Jack watched it again, and there were tears in his eyes when the video was interrupted by a text from Beth: *Need you back.*

The last pitch of the day was from a woman named Darla Nunez, and it was a very cute, very meta idea called *Peak TV.* Nunez, heavyset and bald-headed, with big hoop earrings and jangly bracelets and a big nervous smile, explained that *Peak TV* was about floats.

"Floats?"

"Floating spirits of retribution. When one person causes the death or pain of another, that person's spirit floats into another dimension, where it is washed—"

"Washed?"

"Yeah. No. Not literally. It's like a spiritual washing—"

"Okay—"

"And then the floater returns to our dimension, where it seizes a physical entity in our dimension, so it can wreak havoc on the offending person."

Peak TV, said Nunez, was about a misogynistic television producer who steals an idea from a woman—this was the meta part—who then ends up poor, and a junkie-slash-prostitute, and gets killed by a john, and whose soul then returns as one of these floats.

"So the floats," said Jack, "they're basically ghosts?"

"No," said Nunez. "Floats."

"It really sounds like they're just ghosts," said Jack, and Nunez smiled nervously.

"Well," she said, "if I called them ghosts, would you be more interested in doing the show?"

Lord Almighty, thought Jack. This town. What a bunch of hacks.

That night he met a movie star for drinks.

This was the sort of thing you got to do, Jack was discovering, when you were the genius behind a hit show. People wanted to meet you, even people with substantial clout of their own. They just wanted to see what else you were working on, see what was in the pipeline, see if there was any kind of alliance to be formed.

So he and the movie star, as astonishingly good looking in person as on screen, even with his hair buzzed close for the role he was currently playing (the Navy SEAL who killed Osama bin Laden), met at Soho House and shared a bottle of very expensive whiskey, for which no one ever asked them to pay. Jack diplomatically heard the star out about the show he wanted to develop, and star in, and write (oh God!), which was "a *Bridges of Madison County* kind of thing," except set during the Mexican-American War.

"Well, huh," Jack said, a lot of times. "That is really—huh."

Then Jack drove his Lexus home unsteadily, weaving slightly up and then down Benedict Canyon Drive, and opened the door and was slammed against the wall of the foyer by the dog.

"Whoa! Jesus!" shouted Jack, confused, pinned under the huge snarling weight of Augustus Caesar, whose face was down near his, mouth open, bared teeth like a forest of knives.

Jack managed to get one hand free and pushed the dog's face away from his, realizing as he did that he was still holding his keys in that hand, and now his house key had pierced the side of Augustus Caesar's face, just above his mouth, and the dog, enraged, snapped his head back toward Jack's.

Only at the last instant did Jack bring his other hand up to protect his face, and he felt a sting as the dog sank its teeth into his wrist.

"Oh! Shit! Shit!"

Jack kicked out and connected, his foot landing squarely in the dog's thick midsection. Augustus Caesar tumbled backward, paws skittering on the tiles of the front hall, and Jack looked down at his arm. It was throbbing, with bright red blood blooming in a ragged line and oozing out ugly.

He struggled to his feet and stared at the dog, who was staring at him.

"Dad?" Jayden's voice, tremulous. His little body in his white briefs, at the top of the stairs.

"Be careful, honey. Stay right there."

"Are you okay, Dad?"

Jack looked down at his arm. It was actually barely bleeding. "I'm fine, I'm okay. Just . . ."

Augustus Caesar, meanwhile, was trotting up the stairs to Jayden, gently nosing his great head into the boy's stomach, all nuzzly and fond. Jayden bent automatically and hugged the dog around the neck.

"It's okay, Auggie. It's okay."

"Jesus. What *happened*?" said Angel, from the top of the stairs, completing a tableau: dog and boy and mom. She had gathered her bathrobe to her chest and stood holding it in place.

"Nothing," mumbled Jack. "We're good. All good." Embarrassed. Tipsy. It wasn't a big deal. "I surprised Augustus, I think. He nipped me a little."

"Poor thing."

Jack wasn't sure if she meant him or the dog. But then she went to the bathroom for gauze, and came down and cooed over Jack. No rabies shot would be necessary, he knew. He had all the animal's papers—it was clean.

But when Jayden had gone back off to bed, Augustus Caesar trotting sweetly at his heels, and he and Angel were in their own bed, the whole strange incident replayed in his head. He might have to go back to that breeder and raise a ruckus. He hadn't paid five hundred bucks for fucking Cujo.

"I think that dog has got a screw loose, honey. I really do."

Angel didn't answer. She'd taken a Xanax. She was already asleep.

There were new protesters today. A lot more.

The streamer hadn't put out a press release about season 2, but somehow or other *Deadline* had picked it up, and done a piece, with the predictable tidal wave of reaction on social media—excited, enthusiastic, and not so enthusiastic.

Among the several dozen people now across from the studio, marching in a quiet circle, was an older couple, plainly dressed, both holding giant poster-board photographs of Luke Worth: the boy in Texas who had killed himself under the bleachers of his high school with a bedsheet, just like poor Norman.

Those were his parents. The man very thin, gray-headed; the woman holding her poster with trembling arms.

Jack knew this, instantly. They had the radiant sadness of people who had suffered.

Jack drove past them, eyes straight ahead.

In her small office outside his larger one, Beth was reading an article on her computer. The picture with the article was the same as on the posters outside: a young man, fit and broad-shouldered, looking at the camera. All his sadness coiled up inside, hidden. Luke Worth. Tough, masculine, doomed.

Jack scowled. "Don't read that," he told Beth. "What are you reading that for?"

"Someone sent me the link." She cringed. These assistant jobs were very easy to lose. "I'm really sorry."

"Coffee, please," said Jack, and walked past her. "I need coffee."

* * *

That weekend Jack was unexpectedly blessed with a Saturday afternoon all to himself.

Jayden had been invited to a three-hour birthday party, and Angel had volunteered to bring him, and then take him to dinner with a friend of hers who had a kid the same age.

Which left Jack happily alone, sitting down in his home office, ready to start kicking away at Season 2.

No time like the present, right?

His MacBook screen glowed back at him. It wasn't like he needed to do all that much. In a couple weeks he'd have twelve eager beavers gathered around a long table scarfing snacks and trying to impress him. All he needed was a broad outline for Day One.

He knew that the main character would still be Elle, the dead kid's big-hearted ex-girlfriend, who at first had been widely blamed for his suicide, but who by the season's end was understood to be the one person who very nearly kept him alive.

So what happens now? Jack asked himself.

What if *she* kills herself now? The girl—and what if it's a copycat thing: she goes out to the bleachers, and then everyone blames Norman for having inspired her, just like some people were blaming Norman's TV death for inspiring real-life ones?

Too much? Too "clever"?

Or maybe just kind of . . . awful.

Maybe the whole thing was kind of awful, after all.

Jack tilted his chair back, looking thoughtfully out the window at the pool.

The door of his den rattled in its hinges, and Jack jumped.

The door rattled again. Fuck. Jesus. He didn't even remember having closed it. He got up, walked slowly over, and pulled open the door

It was the dog, of course. Augustus Caesar, staring at him, cool-eyed and big and sleek as a freight engine. Back on its haunches, the mouth slightly parted, teeth showing.

"Yeah?" said Jack. Absurdly, he realized, he was trying to sound tough. To what purpose—to impress the dog? "What the hell do you want?"

But the dog kept staring; the small hint of a snarl at the back of the mouth, yellow in the corners of its eyes.

Float. Jack didn't think the word, really, it just appeared in his head. A visitor from another dimension.

That's what she called them, that lady. Nunez. The writer. The spirits, they float. They get washed, so they can come back for retribution.

Oh shut up, he told himself, and then he said it out loud: "Shut *up*."

Then he took a deep breath and leaned down and grabbed the dog by the collar. "I'm not scared of you," he told Augustus Caesar. "If that's what you're thinking."

The dog didn't try to bite him this time. But neither did it submit pliantly to his grip—it wrestled and fought the whole way, as Jack dragged it away from the door of his den, and then slowly, laboriously, up the stairs, one by one, up to the second floor and then down the hall to Jayden's bedroom.

"Come on," said Jack, huffing and grinning, lugging this massive beast while it bristled and twisted its body away. "Come *on*."

He pushed the dog into the kid's room, where Jayden had set up a whole little area for it: a couple of fluffy pillows for nighttime, a water bowl, and a poster of puppies on the wall. Jack pushed the dog in and slammed the door closed. He breathed heavily, with his back against the door, listening to the dog scrabbling against the door and howling.

Panting, sweating, he stomped back down the stairs to his home office, and sat heavily back on his chair, and then turned and screamed.

Augustus Caesar was on the other side of the office. Majestic and upright, staring, teeth slightly bared, eyes narrowed to slits.

"Hi, Ms. Nunez?"

"Yes?"

"I have Jack Avril for you."

"Oh. Whoa. Okay, great. I'll take it!"

This was not a nice thing to do, and Jack knew it. Darla Nunez would be over the moon that he was calling—on a Sunday morning, no less. She would assume this meant she'd hooked him, and he wanted to talk turkey about her show.

What was it called again? *Peak TV.* Yeah. No. No thanks.

"Mr. Avril," she said, and he could hear the nervous smile in her voice. There were kids in the background, at least two of them—Sunday morning at the Nunez household.

"Listen," he said, "I have a question for you, about your pitch."

"Absolutely. What can I tell you?"

Jack cleared his throat. He'd been up all night. He did not feel great.

"This thing, about the floating. The spirits of retribution. Is it real, or what?"

"What do you—what do you mean?"

"Does it come from a real thing, or did you just make it up? Where does it *come* from?"

"Oh. Um . . . so . . ."

There was a long silence. She was probably afraid he was going to steal her idea, which, the way the town worked, was not the craziest fear.

"Well," she said finally, "there are a lot of myths like this, of course. The Greeks had something like it. So do the Koreans."

"Right, right," he said, feeling suddenly stupid. This was useless. This would do him no good. Jayden was outside in the backyard, with the dog. They ran together along the narrow strip of lawn.

"But as far as this thing," she said, "I guess—well, I had a professor in college, I did a lot of anthropology, and I had a professor who told us about this idea of floaters. I wish I could remember. But it was definitely from South America. Or Central America, maybe. I just never forgot it. I never stopped thinking, *This would make a good TV show*."

"Okay, but, Ms. Nunez . . ."

"Darla. Darla is—"

"How do you stop it?"

"Oh. Well, okay, so in the final episode of the first season—and this is totally provisional, I'm totally open to feedback on this—"

"No! Not in your show!" Jack was shouting. He heard himself shouting: "In life! How does a person stop it, if it happens in real life?"

"Oh. Well . . ."

A long pause She had no idea, this lady. She had no earthly idea.

Jack had a picture of Luke Worth up on his computer. Gray eyes, staring straight ahead, football helmet under his arm like a severed head.

Augustus Caesar was outside his office window. Jayden was throwing a ball and catching it, and his dog was staring through the window.

"You know what? It's okay. Thanks," said Jack.

"No problem," said Darla Nunez, uncertainly. Somehow in her desperate aspiring-writer's heart, she still thought this was a business call. "So shall I have my agent reach out, or . . . Mr. Avril? Hello?"

Jack blinked. The dog was on the other side of the lawn, beside his son.

So what do you do?

Jack lay awake in his bed.

He hadn't slept.

He couldn't sleep.

How could he sleep?

It was two in the morning now, Monday morning.

Nothing else to be done.

Let it float on then. Let it be freed to float away.

He had a gun. Since the presidential election he'd had it under the bed, convinced by a conspiratorial anarchist friend of his that some kind of political violence was imminent. But it hadn't happened yet, and Jack had never learned to shoot the thing. Didn't even know how to hold it.

He had a bat, though. The bat was easy.

He could hear the dog somewhere in his house, prowling and pacing. Nails clicking on the tile.

It was right outside his room. Or in the kitchen.

Or both. It was everywhere.

He laughed. Angel muttered and turned over. She'd taken a Xanax. She slept through everything.

The dog—that's not what it was, it was no dog—it was *floating* around. In his house. In his life.

I didn't kill anybody, he thought. *We're just—we're contributing to a dialogue. We're asking urgent questions about the way children live today.*

It didn't work. Those kinds of sentiments, they hold no force. Not in the middle of the night, with a dog on the prowl in your house. All those kinds of words blend with the shadows on the wall and disappear.

The bat was in the closet. He got out of bed and opened the closet door, as quiet as he could, and put his hands on it.

Fine then, dog. Augustus. Luke. Fine. I killed you.

I'll fucking do it again.

Augustus Caesar was at the bottom of the stairs. The tile in much of the first floor was an unappealing beige. One of the things Angel wanted to fix in the remodel.

The dog sat on the tile, in a shaft of moonlight, staring up at him.

Jack screamed and ran down the stairs, swinging the bat.

The bat smashed into the hallway wall, and the wall exploded in a cloud of plaster and dust, and Jack felt the shock roll up his arm. But the dog, the dog, the dog was—

Behind him. At the top of the stairs, staring down.

He screamed again and dashed up, and it was running away, that coward, coward dog, bounding down the hallway, toward the bedrooms, Jack loping after, trailing the bat along the shag carpet like a caveman's club. Shouting, hoarse.

"Come on, Luke! Come on, you bastard!"

It stopped outside Jayden's room, big brown dog breathing evenly, just staring back at him, taunting him, and then he rushed at it and it disappeared and he slammed into his son's door, wheeled around and saw the dog by the door to the master suite.

"Dad?"

The other bedroom door, behind him now, was creaking slowly open.

"Daddy?"

"Go to sleep, Jayden." Not turning to look at him. Keeping his eyes fixed on the dog, at the other end of the hall.

"I'm gonna get you. I'm gonna get you, you son of a bitch."

"Dad? Are you okay?"

Then the dog came running.

Racing down the hallway in great leaps, one leap and then two, and then it bounded into the air, and Jack put himself in front of Jayden and swung the bat, hard and fast, and connected with the dog's head with a terrible *crack*, and the giant body dropped out of the air and landed with an ugly thud on the thick carpet. Blood pouring from the broken head.

Then silence. Jack heard himself breathing. He heard his heart pounding. He was exultant. He was trembling. *Motherfucker*, he thought.

Jayden was silent beside him.

"Sweetheart?" Jack said softly, and turned. The boy was staring at his dead dog, his eyes wide. Jack crouched slowly.

"Jayden, I don't . . ." He let the bat drop, and gripped

the little guy by both shoulders. "I don't know how to explain this. But that was not a dog, okay? That was *not* a dog. That was the—it was a spirit, son. There was a boy named Luke Worth, and he—he—no—I . . . son, I . . ."

"No, Mr. Avril." Jayden's voice was different now. "That was Valerie."

"What?"

"I'm Luke. That was the girl."

And then Jayden was gone, and was behind him.

PAST THE MISSION

BY DENISE HAMILTON

Encino

Talina pulls in at the trailhead and turns her wheels dutifully against the hillside. Night has fallen and cars already line both sides of the road. She applies the emergency brake, kills the engine, and flips down the mirror. Taking a small earthen pot from her purse, she daubs on lip gloss, careful not to touch the inside of her mouth. She rarely wears makeup, and it feels wrong, greasy and thick as pork fat. Plus there's that residual bitterness from the herbs she's pounded in.

From the mirror, a painted, nervous stranger stares back. Talina frowns and hardens her eyes. Then she scrubs her red-stained finger with a wipe until no trace of color remains.

Can she really do this? Should she? What will it accomplish? The skeleton of the past has been picked clean, bones cracked, marrow sucked, leaving only shards buried in time.

And yet.

A word in a dead language, the smell of raw spirits, the toll of a bell—any of these things can send a dagger through her heart.

And just like that, memory swamps her. Her lower belly contracts. Rough wool chafes her skin. A weight pins her to the ground like a splayed insect. Talina grips the steering wheel, hands slick with moisture. She starts to dry them on her skirt, thinks better of it. She can't do this. It was stupid to come. She will start the car and drive home.

Outside, a shadow streaks across the windshield, a tree branch snapped by the warm winds that Santa Ana has sent blustering down her canyons tonight. Then Talina sees the outstretched wings, the dense tips of bristling feathers.

Intent on prey, it hurtles past with a blood-curdling cry before silence descends once more.

The owl is a portent, infusing her with strength.

Enough to see this through.

It's time. It is her time. She has felt the quickening all around her, the rustling of nameless voiceless multitudes urging her on, buoying her, leading her here, tonight, to this.

Talina presses a hand to her cleavage, feels the reassuring bump of the tiny cobalt bottle nestled there. She climbs out, locks the car, and follows the fire road until it branches onto a narrow footpath. The night is dark, the stars just beginning to glow, but she's always liked the dark, has no problem navigating. Her eyes adjust and soon she sees in a different way. Another half mile and she'll be there.

Talina hears the music first, a faint hum floating on the night air. Then she sees it in the distance, an adobe structure so old and weathered it almost blends into the hillside.

It disappears as the trail descends, only to wink back into sight as she peels off the main path onto an animal trail that leads through the scrub and around a bend. No one knows who built the Old Bar. It may have always been there, squat and brooding, an earthen clay adobe tucked into the eastern spur of the Santa Monica Mountains.

Talina has reconnoitered the entrance and exit, outhouse and cellar, the river rock fireplace whose iron tools could double as weapons. She has sat at the long bar of burnished wood, sipped red wine from forgotten Pueblo vineyards, chatted up bartenders. She knows the hidden room in the back, wallpaper stained brown from cigar smoke, where secret treaties with Spain and Mexico were signed; where Mickey Cohen played poker with the Brothers Warner; where police chiefs and bootleggers hammered out clandestine deals and cash-strapped moguls auctioned off nights with their leading ladies.

Now a new generation has discovered the Old Bar. Undeterred by the long hike, they come—drawn by something indescribable and haunting about this spot where time seems to eddy and pool in strange ways.

Upon arriving, they leash their ratty rescue dogs to ancient hitching posts, the animals' coats dusty from the trail, their brindled necks draped in faded bandannas. Near the stone water trough stand the horses of patrons who ride in.

Talina makes her way to the horses, lets their tawny animal heat wash over her. She strokes velvet muzzles, whispers equine blandishments, feels soft nickers and warm exhaled breath on her neck. They greet her as a friend and she draws strength from their patience, a skill she's worked so hard to cultivate.

As she musters her courage, raucous laughter and shouting leak from the Old Bar. Then Los Lobos comes on the jukebox. It's a song that always stirs the melancholy in her—those strumming guitars and hitched beats set against David Hidalgo's mournful croon.

The man in the song is torn between the outlaw world and his love for a girl, and it's killing him. Suddenly the front door blows open and a couple staggers out, arms wrapped around each other. A horse paws the ground. A dog lifts her head, looks at Talina, then sets it back down on her outstretched paws.

Go now.

She weaves like a shadow along the horses' flanks, moving closer to the entrance. Then she runs across the dirt lot and slips past the iron-strapped wood door before it creaks shut.

Inside, the noise and music and perfume and mingled sweat clobber her senses and she blinks to adjust her eyes, though the lights in the Old Bar can in no way be considered bright.

Orange-and-black bunting decorates the bar. Chili-pepper lights line the eaves. Giant shellacked tumbleweeds sit atop acrylic plinths. Many patrons still wear their Halloween finery, as if they'd partied all night and never gone home. Or maybe they dress like that all the time, not just on All Saints' Day. At the Old Bar, such things are strictly your own business.

The crowd splinters into jagged prisms—a glass raised high, a mouth cranked open, a jeweled hand carving the air. Some patrons wear wigs, masks, hats, crowns; carry canes, scepters, whips, lassos. Talina, too, has cloaked her identity. Under the snorting approval of the horses, she'd veiled herself in the black lace mantilla of a high-born Spanish doña.

Now she makes her way to a pillar, where, partially obscured, she scans the crowd until she finds him.

There.

An old monk with a creased leathery face wearing a threadbare brown robe sits at the bar, bald except for white wisps encircling his skull. His mouth droops as he considers his drained highball glass, staring into the melting ice as if it might foretell his future. Or provide a portal into days past, when Russian fur traders plied the California coast for otters and Native Americans moved silently through the land. As Los Lobos sings about a man torn between two passions, Talina can almost read his thoughts. In the early days of orange groves and missions, this monk, too, had dangled between worlds, forced to choose what kind of man he'd become.

As Talina watches, a thump to his back almost knocks the elderly monk off his stool. He grabs the bar to steady himself.

"Nando! *Qué tal, compa!*"

The monk named Nando turns and beholds the smiling face of another monk.

They beam at each other, their teeth too white, square, and mail-order perfect. Pretending to study her phone, Talina inches closer. The monks are halfway across the crowded room, but her senses have grown acute. She sees each detail. She smells oiled leather, musty wool, and the fragrant sagebrush they wear called "cowboy cologne." She hears their conversation, shouted over the din of the crowd.

"Gabe! You came," Nando says, as his friend slides onto a stool and adjusts his cassock.

"Haven't missed one yet." Gabe looks around. "Are we the first?"

Nando nods. "Maybe the only."

"Do you think the others will make it?"

Nando shrugs. "There's been a mudslide along the coast, so Santa Barbara sends her regrets. San Diego fell and broke his hip. San Juan Cap says surf's up, gnarly southwest swell, so he's out. San Charles Borromeo's trying to get his script to Clint Eastwood in Carmel. The others haven't responded."

That's because their time is over.

The thought fills Talina with satisfaction. She knows that Nando spends his days slinking around the dusty barrios of Arleta, San Fernando, and Pacoima, hauling bags of aluminum cans to the recycling center for a few coins, and not gold reales either. At sunset, after the schoolchildren have clambered back onto their buses and the echo of their high, clear voices fades, he creeps back to his mission to patch cracks in the old plaster. Later, in his unheated bedroom cell, he keeps a solitary vigil, his only companions the Good Book and a dirty futon he dragged in from the alley.

None of this displeases Talina.

"How was traffic this year?" asks Gabe.

"Can't complain," Nando says. "I took the bus from the mission. Hopped out at the Narrows and followed the river to Santos Stables in Burbank. They had my horse saddled and ready to go in no time."

"Bus to the Gold Line to the stables for me," says Gabe.

"I heard it's been bad in your dominion."

Gabe grimaces. "I spend my days visiting the sick, sabotaging new housing developments, and urging the bears and pumas to stay in the mountains. But the drought is terrible and the swimming pools draw them. Your dominion isn't exactly thriving, Nando. What about those brush fires? Foreclosures. That guy who killed his family?"

Nando tosses back the last of his melted ice. "Each day a new test of faith. But tonight, we set the year's troubles aside and celebrate."

Gabe nods, then waves the bartender over. As Talina listens, he grills the man about grand crus from long-gone vineyards that gather dust in the cellar below. The bartender goes off to retrieve a bottle.

Gabe winks at his compadre.

"Sommelier, that's me. Know a thing or two." He taps the side of his head. "Tried for a job at that downtown winery by the freeway, gave them my bona fides. They shooed me away. Said I could get a hot meal at the mission down the street. *My good man*, I told him, *I AM the mission. One of them, anyway.* Things got a little heated after that, and they called security to escort me out."

"No respect anymore," Nando shakes his head.

Cry me a river.

Now that she's finally here, at the culmination of her plans, a strange prickly lethargy washes over Talina. She's both keyed up and unable to move, to shatter the spell of their old-fashioned, petulant voices.

As the bartender sets drinks before them, they sigh and reminisce.

"Those were the glory days, eh? Tending the trellises of our missions, testing for sweetness and must, teaching the neophytes to prune, fertilize, and irrigate. Shame they rejected their lessons and fell asleep in the fields."

"Too exhausted from sneaking out at night for their own harvest rituals."

"Wayward children, they were."

"Needed a firm hand."

"Didn't we give it to them."

At this, red spots dance in Talina's eyes and she steps forward. Suddenly, a girl with bobbed hair wearing a cocktail dress lunges toward the padres and Talina freezes.

"Great costumes," the cocktail-dress girl slurs, grabbing the carved cherrywood rosary that dangles from Nando's neck as she nearly tumbles into his lap.

Nando reddens. Placing his large, work-roughened hands around the girl's cinched waist, he deposits her back onto tottering heels.

The girl giggles, swipes Nando's drink, and staggers off to rejoin her friends.

Gabe elbows his compadre. "Enough to make a man forego his vows, eh, *San* Fernando?"

Nando looks annoyed. "Speaking of vows, my dear *San* Gabriel, what's this I hear about your Chinese Girl Friday in Monterey Park?"

"We must be ever vigilant in stamping out gossip, *San* Fernando. Like that scurrilous rumor about you and the Indian maiden back at Los Encinos with Father Serra."

At this, Talina startles.

"At least she was a maiden. What about that Native warrior? Teaching him catechism, were you?"

Gabe winces. "Monkish vices in a moment's weakness that I soon put behind me."

"Five years later when he died of smallpox," says Nando. "Still, we've all got our skeletons."

"Skeletons," drones the bartender. "Here ya go, friars, one for each of you. Press this button and the eyes light up. Tequila company's giving 'em away, swag for their fancy new agave. We'll have it in stock all week. Bottles made of artisanal glass, set you back $160 a pop. And at those prices you damn well better see visions. You fellas with that studio wrap party?"

Not waiting for an answer, he continues down the bar, handing out little light-up skeleton pins that say, *Happy Dia de Los Muertos 2020*.

Sheepishly, Gabe and Nando affix the pins to their robes. The front door blows open again. It's just the wind, but as gusts of canyon air billow into the bar, Talina makes her move.

In preparing for this moment, she chose each item of her costume very carefully—the skirt of cormorant feathers and sandals of soft deerskin. The ropes of cowrie shells that hang from her neck. Instead of the usual ponytail, her long hair hangs loose. She watched in the bedroom mirror how it rippled down her back, black as the bubbling brea from the tar pits. Behind the lace mantilla, she knows her large eyes shine luminous against her skin.

As Talina walks toward the monks, a girl sings on the jukebox, a sad piano canción about doomed love, missions, and prison towers. Sensing something unusual afoot, the patrons clear a path. She feels their eyes on her, trying to decide if she's a young girl or a mature woman, knows it's hard to tell, knows that there's something ageless about her.

Aware of some disturbance, Nando and Gabe crane their ancient tortoise heads.

Talina pulls off the mantilla and drops it to the floor. She steps on it, trampling it with sawdust, leaving it sticky and filthy from spilled drinks. The exquisite lace tears.

"Over here, Pocahantas," a voice calls out.

An embarrassed murmur starts up, but Talina doesn't seem to notice.

"Now there's a gal who knows how to make an entrance," a man calls out. "Somebody oughta get her a screen test."

Everybody laughs, except for the cocktail-frock girl, who climbs unsteadily onto a table, cheeks flushed, eyes flashing. "Shut it, you sexist, racist pigs!" she yells. "Do you live under a rock? You can't talk to people like that. I'm calling you all out!"

"Amen, sister," a woman says.

Talina has reached the monks. She stops and stands silently before them.

Nando clutches his chest. His mouth moves but no words come out. Lunging for Gabe's wine, he guzzles it. "You," he says at last. "After all this time. I never thought . . ."

Talina tilts her head, as if she can't quite believe it either. "Yet here I am, Fernando."

"How'd you find me?"

"I've been following you."

His voice quails. "You have?"

"I know your habits, the places you go, I know when you get up in the morning, the taco truck where you buy lunch, what time you turn out the light at night."

Nando shreds the edge of his cocktail napkin. "That sounds m-more like st-stalking. Of course, your people were always good trackers."

In the long ages since they last met, Talina has learned to roll her eyes.

"I'm just messing with you, Fernando." She pauses. "Or maybe not. Still, everyone knows you and your com-*padres*"—she stretches the syllables like poison taffy—"gather here every year on this night."

He fixes her with a guilty, worried look. "I suppose you'll want money." Reaching into the folds of his cassock, he pulls out a battered leather purse. He fumbles for coins, but she stops him.

"I don't need money. The casino revenues have left us well off."

Nando rubs his chin. "Casinos, yes. I've heard something . . . We're a little cut off, you know, at the mission." He glances sideways at her, drawn to her painted lips. Slowly, he licks his own.

She sees him struggle to tamp down his secret thoughts, bring himself back to the present. If only he'd shown such resolve when . . .

"You're still beautiful," Nando says. "My Little Teresa of the Flowers."

Talina's nostrils flare. "That was never my name."

"It was the name I gave you." Nando's voice drops to a whisper. "At your baptism." His right hand rises trembling in midair and traces a palsied cross.

Talina makes a dismissive motion. "Say my name, Fernando."

"But I have. Teresa. Mi Teresita. And it fit you. So small you were, and delicate as a flower."

A spasm moves through her.

"My name is Talina."

"That's not the name I called you when—"

"Say it." Her voice, usually so lilting, is rough and pitted as a millstone. "Say my name. My *real* name."

Conflicting emotions play over the old padre's face. Talina sees a shadow brush ashen wings of doubt across his mind. Watches him banish it.

"If you wish," he says, "though I like Teresita better. Tere . . . Tele . . . Tale . . ." He grimaces with effort. "Tah-leena. There," his voice rises in triumph.

Talina crosses her arms and considers something in the middle distance. She feels, more than sees, Nando's eyes devouring her.

"I see you've gone back to the old ways," he says.

She can almost hear what he's left unsaid: *Except for that tawdry lipstick.*

Talina shakes her head, and the cormorant feathers whisper against her thighs. "I never abandoned them. You only saw what you wanted."

"But it's the right thing. I see that now. Those high-necked dresses never suited you."

"This?" Talina touches a feather on her skirt. "This is regalia for ceremonial occasions. Also a cultural signifier."

"I don't—"

"Most days it's jeans or yoga pants. We live in a split-level in the Encino Hills. I made sure it overlooks the sacred spring and we built a sweat lodge in back. But there's a Prius in the garage. I shop at Macy's. Bend like the willow, you know?"

"Why, then, after all this time . . . have you come?" He swallows. "Is it the . . . is something wrong with," his voice breaks, "the babe?"

An explosion goes off in Talina's head. She no longer stands in the crowded bar. The world telescopes down to a panting, sweating girl squatting by the riverbank, grunting and biting down on a stick of green wood while the women pull something from inside her that begins to mewl.

The midwife holds up the newborn.

Hoping against hope, Talina looks.

Relief floods her. All her prayers, the offerings, have worked.

The midwife wipes off the blood, the slick birth layer. Carefully, she compares the color of the infant's skin to hers.

"A healthy boy," she says, her voice drooping with resignation. "But not ours."

You fool. How could it be otherwise?

"I'll snap the neck," another woman says.

"No." Talina struggles up. "Give him to me."

The midwife places a hand on her arm. "Sister, all of us here have felt your pain."

They stand around her, the truth of it visible in their eyes. A girl who was led off by Spanish soldiers at night and returned two days later, mute and bleeding, bangs her head against a tree.

"The People must survive," the midwife says, as the others murmur assent.

"He's mine. I'm keeping him."

"He is not of our blood."

"He is of *my* blood."

My blood my blood my blood.

Her empty arms ache.

Her spirit rises and she floats, unmoored in time, lost between worlds.

She thinks of how much blood has been shed down the generations. More will be shed tonight. And for what? Her mind is dizzy with jumbled memory and sensation.

"Get your skeletons," intones the bartender.

Talina flips.

There are wooden planks beneath her feet, not earth.

The air no longer smells of green willows and metallic blood, but of chemical perfumes and spilled hops.

The circle of women has retreated back into the multitudes that live inside her head. Only the padres hunch beside her, raggedy brown crows who watch with weak, fearful eyes.

Talina trembles with rage and hurt and love for the child who arrived when she was but a child herself.

My blood my blood my blood.

It's time to finish the business that lies between them.

"Our son is dead, Fernando," she says.

Nando covers his face with his hands. Strangled birdlike cries rise from his throat.

"Our daughter, who came the following year, survived."

Nando lifts his head.

"I hid her from the world until it was safe," Talina says.

"How is the . . . this . . . this girl child?"

"She is long grown," Talina says, exasperated. "She lives up in San Jose's dominion, where she restores the old sites and builds virtual new ones. She's smart and kind and funny and deeply moral." Talina lets the contrast sink in. "Too bad you never met her. But that would have meant confronting a truth you'd rather forget."

"I am a father twice over." Nando's voice is hushed with wonder.

"Not in any sense of the word, Fernando. But our daughter had an excellent father. Jorie Webweaver adopted her when we got together, and then we had two more. Jorie's a good man."

"Webweaver?" A disparaging tone creeps into Nando's voice. "Since when do your people name children after spiders?"

Talina sighs at such ignorance. "Jorie's a tech guy. He built the Nativenet, used by all the sovereign nations. The concept of a shamanistic interface was revolutionary, even Zuck was interested."

"I'm not familiar with the Nativenet," Nando says, stroking his rosary beads.

"That's because you live in a crumbling mission with only mice and lizards for company, Fernando."

"You're happy with this Webweaver, Tere . . . Talina? Do you ever think back to the time when we . . . ?"

"I was fourteen years old. You bewitched me with your white skin and your gunpowder, your mirrors and sugar and fine cloth. I thought you were a god."

She has pictured screaming these words, spraying him with spittle, her nails gouging bloody furrows down his cheeks. But now she's curiously inert, as if recounting the story of a stranger.

"We loved each other, didn't we?" Nando is almost pleading. "I never mistreated you. I wasn't like the soldiers, drunk and vile as beasts . . ."

Talina struggles to make sense of the sounds that emerge from his mouth, but it's like he's speaking some incomprehensible language and she must first translate the words, then assemble them into a sentence she can understand.

When at last she does, it still defies comprehension. "For that I should thank you?" She snorts, then explodes in bitter laughter that trails into sobs. How can such black absurdity exist? Clasping her sides, she convulses helplessly like she's having a fit as Nando looks on in bewilderment and dismay.

Slowly she composes herself. Straightens. "You tore me from my family and brought me to the mission to serve you. Then you called me Jezebel and sent me away. But you crept back at night, begging me to forgive you, your shoulders oozing blood from your flagellations, resigned to burning in hell if it meant holding me again. At dawn you'd be back in the chapel, asking your god's forgiveness. I wanted to kill myself. Instead, I ran away with our daughter and made sure you couldn't find me. And yes, I'm happy with Jorie. He completes me, as you never could."

Nando looks stricken. "Then why—"

"It was so long ago, but it was also yesterday You stole part of me before I could even put a name to it. But the world has changed, and I've come to reclaim what's mine. And to hear you apologize."

"I've spent years atoning."

"Not to your god. To *me*."

"Yes. You're right. Tonight I'll pray for you. I'll kneel until dawn."

"Mortifications of the flesh. Bread and water. Suffering and abasement and nights of sleepless feverish prayer. You'll do it all, won't you, Fernando?"

"Yes," he says. "I will."

A small cold pleasure runs through her at the thought of his suffering. She is astonished to discover this chamber of cruelty hidden in her heart. Was it always there, just waiting to be kindled? Or had he twisted and perverted something inside her all that time ago?

It doesn't matter anymore. But Nando's god is a bloodthirsty one, and the monk will perform his penance too eagerly.

It is not enough.

"I don't want your prayers, Fernando, I want your apology. Right here, right now. You wronged me. Look at me. Say my name and tell me you're sorry."

She wants to hate this decrepit old man who once held such power over her. Who now lives like a haunted ghost amid his derelict mission that reminds him daily of how far he's fallen. But hate is too facile, too pure a word for the rich loamy churn of emotions she feels.

The old monk's hands twist and writhe like snakes. "I am sorry, Talina. I never meant to hurt you." Stoned on memory, he sways. His voice drops. "But you see, I thought we wanted the same thing."

Talina's head jerks, and she stares at him, disbelieving. She'd been wavering, but now she makes her decision. With great deliberation, she steps closer to the old padre.

Filled with joy, Nando throws his arms around her and covers her cheeks in clumsy kisses. Talina struggles to break free, then feels her body go limp as the muscle memory of nightmare floods her, of making herself small and remote and perfectly still so that it happened to someone else.

With difficulty, she claws her way back from the edge of madness. She must focus. She has come here with a purpose.

And with that, resolve fills her and she presses her thickly painted lips against his. Again the faint waft of bitter herbs hits her. Working its way in. And with that, the thing is done.

All around them, the bar patrons applaud.

"Get it, Granddad!" yells a barfly.

"San Fernando, your vows," cries Gabe, scandalized. "Release her at once."

Talina steps back, breathing heavily, and wipes her mouth on her sleeve. Then she places her open palms on Nando's chest. Eagerly, the old friar leans in, and Talina shoves him hard. He staggers and falls backward.

"Too much for you, pops?" someone yells.

"Gonna give the old buzzard a heart attack."

"At least he'll die happy."

Talina watches the padre convulsing on the ground and gasping for breath.

With one foot, she prods the coarse wool cassock, shiny from wear, patchy from clumsy darnings.

Gazing up at her, his face turning purple, his mouth smeared red like a clown from her lip gloss, Nando glows like he's experienced a miracle. "You trembled in my arms just now," he rasps. "Your heart b-b-beat wildly, like a little bird, just as it used to, mi Teresita de las Flores . . . and then I knew that you . . . you still loved me just a little."

The triumph in his eyes makes her sick. He will go to his death unrepentant, believing his web of lies. An empty defeated taste fills her mouth. She presses her hand against her heart, feels the tiny cobalt bottle.

In the surge of emotions, she'd almost forgotten.

But there it waits. Silent and ready.

And she understands that it doesn't have to end this way.

That today she is the one who holds the power.

"Should I call 911?" asks the cocktail-frock girl, who has followed every move from her perch atop the table and now stands, thumbs poised over her phone.

"He'll be fine," Talina says.

She drops to one knee, and her hair ripples like a stage curtain to block the crowd's view.

Using his cassock, she wipes his mouth clean of the garish gloss. Then she pulls the tiny cobalt bottle from her bodice, unstoppers it, and brings it to his mouth, cradling his head.

Nando's distended lips part. The grizzled throat moves up and down.

Talina lays his head back against the wood floorboards and takes a long swig from the bottle herself before putting it away. Their eyes meet in strange communion. Something wordless passes between them, and the fervor in Nando's eyes dulls as he finally understands.

"Goodbye, Fernando," Talina says.

Nando shuts his eyes. A deep shudder moves through him. When he opens them, she is gone and Gabe is pulling him to his feet.

"Are you okay?" Gabe asks.

"I'll live," he says, and the despair in his voice is palpable to all.

Stalks of lavender and rosemary lash Talina's legs as she walks to her front door in Los Encinos. The night has drained her. Even the voices in her head have stilled to the murmur of drowsy bees. But as the fragrant oils rise in the air, a wave of memory crashes down and pulls her out to the drowning sea.

"What is the meaning of this?" says Doña Luisa, her voice clipped and angry. She dangles the hand-sewn doll between them like a soiled handkerchief.

The doll has long black hair snipped from Talina's own head and and carved-acorn eyes. Talina has sewn a tiny dress from bits of rags and stuffed the body with dried lavender petals for the child she has hidden away.

"I . . . I just wanted to make something pretty."

All day, Talina moves silently through the cool hushed adobe, cooking and cleaning for the household. She tends

Doña Luisa's garden and sews sachets of sweet-smelling herbs to tuck into the linen closets. That's what gave her the idea.

"This is a heathen idol, is it not?"

Eyes downcast, Talina shakes her head. Her wool dress is too tight, and its coarse fiber scrapes her skin raw with each step. The muslin doll would be soft against her daughter's cheek, a fragrant pillow to clutch at night when her mother has to work late. But Talina cannot reveal this child to Doña Luisa any more than she can name its father. To the family she is a young, innocent girl. The truth would spark disbelief, dismissal, and worse.

Doña Luisa crosses herself and recites a prayer. Her mouth sets in a grim line as she tears the doll apart. Dried lavender petals fall like purple snow and cover Talina's bare feet.

"Sweep this up immediately. And let there be no more abominations."

Doña Luisa's long skirts swish angrily away.

But Talina is determined, stealthy. She collects more lavender, thread, muslin, and a needle. When Doña Luisa discovers these things in her pockets, along with bread she's hidden to take home for the child, she tells her husband. That night, Don Felix assembles the entire rancho. He delivers an impassioned sermon against thievery and graven idols, then administers a whipping. Talina leaves the rancho in disgrace, her wages withheld to pay for the clothing that she strips off, bloody and shredded, and burns when she gets home.

The voices swirl and echo around her.

We're sorry We're sorry We're sorry.

It is a fall evening in Los Encinos. The sunbaked flagstones release the day's heat and warm Talina as she comes to. Pushing up onto her elbows, she grabs handfuls of lavender and crushes them violently against her neck, her bare arms, her cheeks.

"I'll make a hundred dolls from these petals, do you hear?" she roars at the night sky. "I'll eat an entire loaf of bread with my daughter, washed down with good wine and Spanish cheese and tiny olives, and by the gods, just you try and stop me."

No one does. The suburban streets are empty as usual.

Talina struggles to her feet, brushing plant debris from her skin and clothes, and makes her way inside.

"Hi, hon," Jorie calls from the kitchen, plugging in the rice cooker. "How was your day?"

"I settled a very old debt," Talina says.

"Don't tell me you paid off the car."

"Nothing like that." Talina opens the fridge and pours herself a glass of sun tea. She takes a sip, considers. "Actually, it was way bigger than that."

"Oh?" says Jorie, getting out the cutting board.

"I thought it would free me. That my heart would soar like a hawk. Nope. Not at all." Talina can hear how strange and shaky her voice sounds. She plucks a miniature candy bar from the plastic orange pumpkin they offered to the trick-or-treaters the night before, rips it open, and crams it into her mouth.

Jorie regards her with concern. He comes over. With soft moth fingers, he flicks bits of lavender off her cheek. She gulps down the half-chewed chocolate but it catches in her throat and she almost chokes.

"What's going on?" Jorie says. "Your eyes are red and there's lip gloss all over your face and—"

"Allergies," she mutters.

"Since when do you have allergies?"

She shrugs and won't meet his gaze.

"Soak in the springs?" he says after a moment.

"Maybe later."

He leans in to kiss her, but she pulls away and runs to the bathroom to gargle and scrub her mouth until it hurts.

The cold water revives her. Slowly she eases back into her skin.

"It's probably overkill," she calls from the sink. "But I have to get it all off. I don't want to take any chances."

Jorie stands in the doorway, his broad shoulders filling the frame. He frowns. "So *that's* the kind of debt it was. I was wondering . . . You're not a lip gloss kind of girl."

Talina takes the tiny pot from her purse and hurls it into the trash. Then she goes to Jorie, lips chapped and swollen. She wraps her arms around his waist and buries her head in his chest.

He strokes her hair. "Did you say the prayers for the dying?" he asks.

"No," she responds, her voice muffled against his chest.

Alarmed, Jorie pulls back. "Hey now. We always . . ."

Talina's cheeks are wet and streaked. She reaches into her blouse and pulls out the cobalt bottle, holding it up and turning it until it catches the light.

"Whoa," Jorie says. "Getting pretty low."

"I brought him back."

"You changed your mind?"

Talina shrugs. "For so long, I wanted vengeance. It ate away at me until I was so brittle and hollow that sometimes I thought I'd shatter when you touched me. When I finally confronted him tonight, I was terrified, but then . . ."

She pauses. "I don't know. It was nothing like I thought. He was pathetic. So old and shrunken. He'd lost his lands, his power, his titles. Then I destroyed his last illusion."

"It's wrong to destroy a person's faith."

"Oh, I'm pretty sure that still hangs by a thread." She exhales heavily. "I mean me."

Jorie's mouth twitches, but he says nothing.

Talina reaches for the memory. Again and again, she replays it, just as she knows Fernando will, for eternity, as he haunts the halls and walls of his ruined mission. She recalls the anguish in his voice, the desolation in his eyes, the despair as his last, most intricately constructed illusion shattered and slipped away forever.

Her heart surges, and she isn't sure if it is hardening or softening.

"I want him to live."

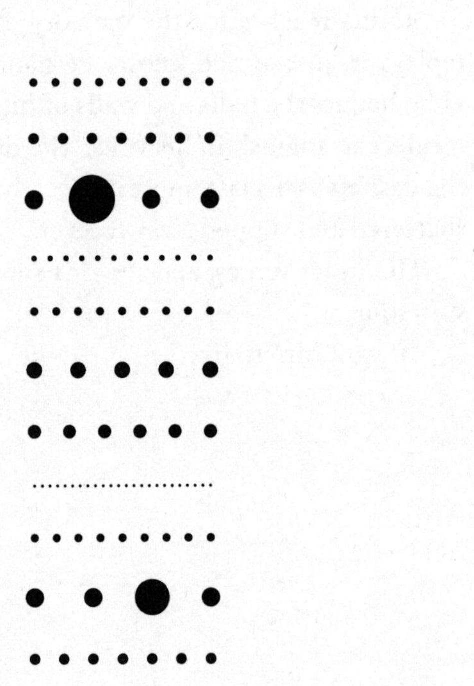

¤ ¤

PART II

STEAMPUNKS, ALCHEMISTS, AND MEMORY ARTISTS

¤ ¤

WHERE THERE ARE CITIES, THESE DISSOLVE TOO

BY S. QIOUYI LU

La Puente

Inhale. Strap on your helmet. Exhale, one long stream between pursed lips. Gloves on, goggles adjusted. Seat belt strapped tight. The chomper rattles and groans as it creaks, accordion-like, into a standing position. By now, the jostling throwing you from wall to wall on imperfect suspension is a comfort in itself.

Your chomper is Gundam-like, individual plates laser-etched with golden filigree that gleams against the chomper's deep-red paint job. With your chomper at full height, taloned feet gripping the packed dirt beneath you, layers of still-unexcavated garbage underneath, you rise to a height of nearly twenty feet. From here, you can see how the path to the arena carves through the landfill, a poorly lit, narrow road that branches off the main thoroughfare. Tangled string lights daisy-chained into a fire hazard pull electricity from an off-grid generator, illuminating the makeshift arena with humming, flickering bulbs.

Everything stays off the grid. Chomper battles are an underground sport, born in the heart of the San Gabriel Valley, in Los Angeles's biggest landfill, hidden in plain sight and known only to a few like you. You are Winnie Su, better known by your chomper's name, Lady Danger. But the spectators have a different nickname for you. In the Spanglish patois that arises around the arena, you are La China Cochina. It's a badge of pride, to be known for your ruthless battle style: Double tap. Show no mercy. Don't celebrate until the match has officially been declared over.

Your opponent today is more formidable than the rookie you slaughtered last week. Figuratively slaughtered, but some of the matches still come dangerously close. There are paramedics on site and an ambulance on call, but injuries can still be nasty.

You know that firsthand.

Even though your opponent doesn't look too intimidating, you can't let down your guard. You've seen tricked-out chompers get taken down by modest-looking scrap heaps.

The chomper opposite you is named Quetzalli. It's well-designed, more symmetrical than the average chomper, as if some thought had gone into envisioning its assembly, rather than being an ad hoc collection of parts and modifications. Not the challenger's first chomper—a mark of experience, collective in this case. Las Basureras run an auto repair shop off of Valley in City of Industry, and the way Quetzalli bounces from leg to leg, hydraulics pumping, shows off their mastery in lowrider hop contests. The rooster-like chomper's body is similarly sleek as classic muscle cars, art deco–influenced lines and chrome hiding gnashing teeth and bladed wings. The body clanks against the chassis as the chomper springs from leg to leg, frame gleaming, banners streaming from the crest of her head. Shadows dance through the arena. Any other sport would have floodlights to bring the whole space into sharp relief, but floodlights here would be visible from nearby freeways, exposing the match to their steady hum.

The overwhelming stench of the place filters through to your tiny space. Diesel. Garbage. Methane. Roasting meat. Spilled beer. Piss. Sweat. Smoke. Fire. Each breath feels like swallowing poison, though you have no choice but to inhale—carrying oxygen would only serve to make Lady Danger that much more flammable.

The audience crowds in. Several spectators are eating foil-wrapped burritos or paper trays of tacos, meat freshly grilled, cilantro and onions fresh and crisp. The vendors are out toward the dump's parking lot, a herd of food trucks with neon lights flashing red and green, proclaiming in scrolling text, *TACOS AL PASTOR CARNITAS CARNE ASADA CERVEZA AGUA FRESCA HORCHATA* . . . Another truck has signs in English and Chinese with twenty types of boba and several tea-marinated snacks and bowls. Beside it is a banh mi truck, then a Korean-Peruvian fusion truck. The whole parking lot smells like garlic and onions, the scent thick enough to penetrate through the dump's constant smell of rotting garbage, making the dilapidated surroundings seem almost hospitable. On the makeshift benches, cobbled together from sheets of ungalvanized metal and wobbly patio furniture, several people have coolers open with sweating glass bottles of beer. Others are tailgating and laughing raucously as they knock back oysters with twists of lime and dashes of Tapatío. To one side, a chain-smoking group of Mandarin speakers gathers around a mahjong table, betting pool growing as they keep one eye on the chomper ring.

The rules are simple: Three rounds, five minutes per round, one minute rest period in between. One perimeter. Win by knocking an opponent out of bounds. Or win by utterly disabling your opponent at any point in any match. No repairs or adjustments allowed between rounds.

There's money exchanging hands, masked by clouds of cigarette and marijuana smoke. The odds are decent tonight. If you take down Quetzalli, you'll get a hefty cut of betting profits. Makes it well worth it to participate.

But, as the announcements come on and the referee counts down to match start, you know that money was never your motivation here. You pull a lever to your right, swinging Lady Danger's left arm around in a hook. Lady Danger is a collection of limbs and prosthetics with an uneven, loping gait like a three-legged rabbit. Yet, despite her imperfections, Lady Danger embodies grace in your hands, with you as the maestro in her cradle. There is no exhilaration that can come even close to the power of conquest, the mad glee of destruction, the soul-feeding satisfaction of complete annihilation. It sickens you sometimes to see how much you get off on tearing people's prize machines asunder. But the pleasure destruction brings you, the brute recklessness that you can't get anywhere else, provides a catharsis for your id, an outlet that far supersedes any concerns for your own soul.

You plow a claw through Quetzalli's left wing, ripping off several panels to expose frame and wiring. The move unbalances Quetzalli, but isn't enough to disable her. You swing back around, swaying and quick. Quetzalli bounces from one foot to the other before hopping high into the air, clearing Lady Danger easily. She knocks you off balance when she crash-lands into you. A flurry of blows between the two machines leaves dents in both, scuffing up Quetzalli's beautiful paint job, smearing streaks of red from Lady Danger into the gouges on Quetzalli's frame. Quetzalli is the first to retreat as two of Las Basureras bow their heads together from the side and talk last-minute strategy to their teammate in the cockpit. Quetzalli's windshield is tinted, preventing you from seeing what the operator looks like. In a way, that's better. Easier to rip a chomper apart when its operator is anonymous.

You take the retreat as an opportunity. You've been stomping on this battleground for a while now, and you know its quirks. The ugly stink of cow farts has gotten more intense. There's a PVC pipe creaking a few paces to one side, its joints swelling and settling, shuddering and rattling. You stride over and spark a pilot light, launching yourself off a perfectly timed burst of methane piping out of decaying refuse. The blast is a spectacle, bright and sudden, launching you straight toward Quetzalli while the crowd whoops and cheers.

You tear a devastating gash through Quetzalli, setting her aflame with the last of the fire propelling you.

It's a humiliating loss for Las Basureras, whose prize fighter is now a pile of sparking and smoldering scrap, the operator hauling herself out of the wreck, coughing as she limps through the smoke. But a chomper is as ephemeral as the trash it's made from: useful only for a moment, its final home a heap of garbage hidden in Los Angeles's suburbs.

Lady Danger shudders as she lowers back to the ground. You disembark from the chomper. People congratulate you as you stride by, offering high fives, fist bumps, and bro-hugs. The vast majority of spectators are men. You've learned their body language to reciprocate their appreciation and thump people back just as heartily, even if you're half their size.

You make your way past ahjussis wreathed in clouds of cigarette smoke and over to the bookie. He nods at you, shouts over his shoulder, then goes back to distributing wads of well-thumbed cash to a mostly drunk crowd. There's a makeshift shanty behind him, all rusting tin roof, cinder block, tarp, and pallets. Someone steps out from it, counting under her breath as she flips through bills.

"The legendary Lady Danger," she says, looking you up and down. Round-framed glasses sit on her nose. She wears a mustard-colored beanie over her hair, which is braided into two pigtails, sleek and raven dark over her shoulders. She has the kind of rosy skin that reminds you of a white peach, its flesh pale and luminescent, hiding a secret core of red, a flash of brightness as rich as sex. The lights have her partly backlit, limning her flyaway baby hairs and the fuzz otherwise invisible on her cheeks.

"You know, I've been wanting to meet you for a while," she says.

"Is that so?"

She's stepped closer to you, her bubble of personal space brushing up against yours. Your heart beats a racing tattoo against your solar plexus as you inhale, exhale. She hands you your cut of the pool. When your fingers brush against hers, you could swear a shock of electricity turns your nails into claws that dimple her succulent skin, leaving crescent moons in their wake.

It's a momentary illusion, one that leaves you breathless with want.

"You're quite the name around these parts. The boss may handle most of the cash, but I keep the accounts. Nothing digital or online—all paper and abacus calculations that we destroy after each match."

She grins, her teeth slightly crooked and turned in—the rabbit teeth so coveted in Asia.

"I see how much you're pulling in. Every figure."

You imagine her fingers dancing over the abacus, beads clacking like stilettos on hardwood, her fingers feather-light. How keen her eyes are as she murmurs numbers like incantations.

"I'm Agnes," she says, blurs of orange light reflecting off her glasses.

"Winnie."

You hook your thumb into your belt, if only to quell its thrumming.

"Winnie," Agnes repeats, making your skin break out in a ripple of goose bumps. "Fitting." She shifts her weight to her other leg, her stance casual, hip cocked to one side, hand resting on top. "I'm not going to waste your time, Winnie. Keeping the books here—I get a decent cut for helping out and all, but you and I both know we're not here for the money."

She smiles at you again. It's charming, the way her full lips hold high the apples of her cheeks. But under the twinkle in her eyes lies something fierce: a reservoir of wickedness, one that draws you in like a lighthouse in a storm.

"I want to operate a chomper. I've got some designs drafted, but I need someone to help me make the chomper a reality, and someone to coach me through matches. Who better than the incredible Lady Danger?" Her face shines with fervor, full moon plating the world in silver. Agnes comes close, her pigtails brushing against your shoulder as she murmurs into your ear, "I'll make it worth your while."

You have no anchor to throw overboard, nothing left to pull you back as you agree. Nothing left to ground you as you crash into the waves, welcoming how her presence drowns you.

The mornings after matches always feel unreal. You return to the same landfill for your day job processing waste, but the sunbathed crags of garbage are an alien landscape compared to the landfill's evening counterpart.

You didn't exactly aspire to this occupation. Your father had wanted you to be an engineer, so you'd complied, having never given much thought to your future. But, by some fluke of Asian parenting, you ended up enjoying engineering after all. Mechanical engineering, electrical engineering, fluid mechanics—you're adept at them all.

But what you like the most is creating. Envisioning a thing that doesn't exist in this world and then *making* it exist, as if you straddle a portal between dimensions, importing visions.

You get a position at a lab in Caltech and expect to stay there for the rest of your life, researching automation and manufacturing techniques.

Then, amid escalating anti-immigrant sentiment, the Chinese Exclusion Act is renewed and a complete trade embargo placed on China.

The head of the lab, a Chinese professor, is falsely charged with spying for the Chinese government. A good two-thirds of the grad students there are on student visas. They are all promptly deported, and the lab disbanded.

So you go into industry, intending to work on automating waste processing to minimize municipal landfill usage. However, with the nation no longer able to ship hazardous electronic waste to China for processing, nor able to purchase raw material or cheaper recycled imports, you are flung into the new world of waste mining.

Bulldozers break through layers of earth at the previously full Puente Hills landfill to get to the rotting piles of garbage underneath. You help develop the first chompers—machines built to take in trash and digest it, extracting useful materials like metals, rare elements, plastics, anything that can be repurposed to meet domestic demand.

By day, you are quiet and mild-mannered as you oversee blueprint development and the latest figures while people drive chompers through the decay and muck, digging trenches into the archeology of humanity's excess. Others clear and reset methane piping in their wake, ensuring careful venting of the disturbed burial mounds.

You envy those who can work so closely to the heart of the dump. It is a living thing to you: breathing out methane, gurgling and shifting, quaking with the earth, pulsing with its own ecosystems. It is the teeming id of Los Angeles, dismantled to bring new opportunity.

Certainly, you are one of the few with the knowledge and training to work in research and development in this area. You cannot leave your post. But the longing to be swallowed by abyssal waste is there still, powerful as magnetism, all-present as gravity.

So you return to the dump at night, to the craters and cliffs carved into the hills, to teetering pallets and tarps dripping garbage juice, to the choking hiss of methane as sharp as laughter.

And there, you come alive.

Agnes invites you to a cafeteria-style spot called Kang Kang Shau May, where everyone minds their own business as the two of you share beef rolls, buns, and pickled cucumbers. Agnes places her tablet on the table and shows you her sketches.

"This is Kill Switch," she says.

You chuckle. "Hang out in the import scene much?"

Agnes looks over the underbody lighting scheme, turning mechanisms, and decals as she grins. "How could you tell?"

You pan through the notes, nodding to yourself as you take in the plans. They're feasible and only need some small adjustments. "So, we'll go for both speed and agility. Good for feinting and quick recoveries. Maybe a couple tricks up the sleeve."

You get to work building the actual chomper at a salvage yard owned by a friend of yours, who gives you free rein to use the place for a modest fee. Agnes welds a prototype of the chomper's frame, sparks magnesium-bright as they fall. You haven't needed to buy new parts. Not even more solder. It amazes you, what kinds of things end up at the landfill. You'd expect scarcity, when the truth is that entire towns could live off the dump's intake.

Agnes learns quickly. Her hands are slender, the lines of her wrists elegant, but you know she has hidden strength. Her grip on the torch is steady. Even though the mask conceals her face, you can imagine how intense her gaze is with its scrutiny.

Then, Agnes puts down the torch and lifts her mask. Her smile is disarming. You want to believe that she's genuinely excited to see you, and maybe Agnes senses that. In two steps, she's come right up to you and draped her arms over your shoulders. She's so close that you can feel the heat radiating off her.

"Winnie . . ." she says, as if savoring your name. Your breath catches in your throat.

You want to hear your name on her tongue again, and again, and again. So when Agnes presses her lips to yours, you welcome her.

You have never been known to have restraint. You and Agnes burn like a wildfire, brilliant and all-consuming, as terrifying as it is awe-inspiring. You are the Santa Ana wind stoking her, urging her on, pulling her to your breast, wreaking a trail of havoc through her.

The two of you do, of course, continue to work on the chomper. It's beginning to come together, and its progress becomes a blur of days: Agnes, in steel-toed boots and Daisy Dukes tinkering with the engine, her thighs smeared with grease; Agnes, on her knees, her half-lidded eyes asking you for more as she submits to you; Agnes, hopping into the body of the chomper for the first time to test the controls, sinful delight written in every line of her body; Agnes, her back arched as perfectly as the golden spiral as she gasps, opening for you, more than she ever thought she could, her heartbeat thrumming through your fist, as if you hold in your palm the very core of her; Agnes, lit by strings of lights, pearlescent with sweat as she takes on her first matches with your voice murmuring directions into her ear, her trust in you as powerful as surrender; Agnes, blood trickling from cuts red as danger, breathing sounds of pleasure at your care and silent attention as you patch her up.

You wonder if this love, too, is dangerous. Whether the swelling in your chest as Agnes leans against your shoulder, asleep, is just an illusion.

There's a part of you that loves to see Agnes lit with

the adrenaline of the win. How she teeters on the cusp of brutality like the most elegant of ballerinas en pointe, primal catharsis in her every delighted laugh.

But when Agnes takes a hard blow during a tense match and cracks her head against the dash, knocking her unconscious, you can't help but feel responsible. After all, you are the one who challenges Agnes with increasingly difficult battles, the one egging her on, placing her in riskier and riskier situations to see how she reacts.

You are at Agnes's bedside when she wakes up in the hospital. You're shocked by the relief you feel when she meets your gaze and smiles, a sunrise slanting through redwoods, her ferocity momentarily tamed. You reach out for her hand. She wraps her fingers around yours.

"Thanks for being here," she says.

You bark out a laugh.

"Of course. I'm the one who landed you here."

Agnes waves you off as she makes a face. "I may be younger than you, but I'm not a child. I can make my own decisions." She raises a finger, silencing you before you can protest. "I'm not delicate," she says, serious, before grinning slyly. "You of all people should know how much I can take."

She has you laughing, dispelling any argument left in you. You lean in for a kiss. Even now, in a sterile hospital room smelling of rubbing alcohol and the unnameable scent of something deeply human, even under fluorescent lights that wash the color out of everything, even while alarms go off around you and nurses run to and fro tending to emergencies, Agnes can still take your breath away.

"Win," she murmurs. You blush when she calls you that; she's the only person you'd allow to use this nickname. "I'm okay. Really."

Agnes is discharged an hour later, her head wound requiring only a few stitches and her concussion mild. You pull her in extra close that night, sucking bruising kisses into her breasts, pushing her to the brink, to just shy of both your safeword limits, as if to prove to yourself that she's still here, that she's more powerful than you think. That maybe, as your hands leave fingerprints on her skin, she needs you too.

You dream of pomegranates, seeds glistening and full as clitorises, bursting wine-red between teeth, tart and sweet. You dream of your skin pulling back to reveal rivers, deltas, highways. You dream of climbing a peak and brushing your fingertips against the moon.

You dream of Samson.

He comes to you sometimes like a premonition, or perhaps an omen. "Don't get attached," he says, his voice warm like hypothermia, undressing you with its paradoxes.

But you do. Even as you tell yourself that your intimacy is rented, that he only wants you around for what you can provide to him, you get attached. It's a mistake, but you open yourself to him anyway. You allow him to infiltrate you, to leave his impressions on your synapses like a ghost in a machine.

"Don't get attached," he says, cupping your cheek, kissing your fingertips, as he slams skin-to-skin against you, tearing cries from your throat until you come undone against him, trembling as he buries your face in the sheets.

You drift on a sea of desire, a river of stars splitting you in two. Samson slips through your fingers like grains of sand, each counting down to absence. You tell yourself to stay cool and collected, an astronaut untethered in the zero-gravity of space.

But you have never loved lightly, even as you brace yourself for inevitable separation.

Your dreams take you further back sometimes, to the landscape of a country you know only through brief trysts, as if she were a mistress to keep hidden from your main allegiance. You remember flocks of bicycles a hundred people thick; you recall a city dense with blocky buildings and diesel, bursting with people: in alleys, in corner stores, at bus stops, on steps and balconies.

You remember an apartment, claustrophobic with its compactness. Firm, bead-filled pillows, beds stiff as planks. A television set on the floor playing cartoons. A figure whose face you can no longer picture, but whose very silhouette imbues you with a sense of safety.

When you were a year old, you were sent back to China to be raised by relatives. A satellite child, not unlike other Chinese-American children, set adrift between two coasts before settling on one. A year later, you were returned to your parents in the US. Your mother tells you sometimes that you were crying for your uncle as you returned, inconsolable.

She tells the story as if it were amusing. But you find more and more traces of separation as you grow older: hollows, absences where safety should be, where fear replaces love. Where attachment is to be guarded, hoarded, so that it becomes unreal if you ever do find yourself moored.

Don't get attached.

Samson crosses the border between the dream world and your waking life. You see him in the corner of a coffee shop one day, his nose in a book. Shocked, your head going light, your hands going clammy, you duck and pivot on your heel, walking away as briskly as you can while not drawing attention to yourself.

You see him in the crowd, eyes dark and watching, at your next chomper battle.

He'd told you that he was moving away. You figured you were simply something too short-term and casual to justify the energy of keeping in touch over distance. But whatever took Samson away appears to have brought him back. He returns several times a month to watch matches.

You have no idea if he's still battling. But you know that, despite everything, your heart still remembers your limerence, betraying your shaking body.

Agnes notices the tension you're carrying before you do. She manhandles you onto the bed and kneads your shoulders, drawing long groans of pleasure from you.

"You've been quiet lately," she says as she straddles your waist and works her way down your back. "Other than now, that is."

All you can manage is a soft *mmph* in response.

"Really, though," Agnes says, her hands slowing to rub circles on your skin. "What's wrong?"

You turn your face away from the pillow and look up at her with one eye. She's trying to play it cool, but there's a hint of genuine concern in her eyes, so tender it could make you weep.

But you don't.

"My ex is back in town," you say after a moment. Funny, how your relationship with Samson had been so multilayered, so all-consuming, and yet it's now so easily glossed over with the single syllable *ex*.

"Didn't part on good terms, then?" Agnes says.

The laugh escapes you before you can contain it. "He left me bleeding and bruised in a wrecked chomper," you say, your stomach turning at the memory. "Lucky there was an EMT at the match who could help out before the ambulance arrived."

Agnes goes still. You close your eyes, but when you feel Agnes shaking against you, you open them to look up at her again.

You call them flashbulb memories, the way a fraction of a second, a single sight, can imprint on you so strongly that it shines clear over a murky haze of memory. Agnes impresses on you like that now, her hands balled into fists, her face a lightning bolt of fury.

"I'm fine," you say. Agnes's brief *ha* doesn't break her expression. "Really."

"Sure," she says, then lets out a long breath and runs a hand through her hair. "Okay. I'll believe you."

Some part of you wants to spring up, to hurl her off of you, to let yourself become feral and wild as you snap at her. For what, you're not sure: for her condescension, you'd say; her insolence and her assumptions. But there's a deeper part of you, still bruised, wounds reopening, that's furious because she's right.

Of course you're not okay. You woke up to strangers around your bed, asking you question after question and taking whatever samples they needed, while you asked for Samson again and again, only for him to never appear. The recovery afterward, lonely and aching—gathering the nerve to call him for some kind of closure, only to find that he'd disconnected his number.

The ghost of absence inhabits your very marrow. Despite it all, you still love battling, even find solace in the thrumming womb of a chomper. But seeing Samson once more, unchanged, unrepentant, chokes you with waves of unparsable emotion.

Samson's face superimposes itself on others' faces, sometimes even on Agnes's face, so that you have to blink and recompose yourself, remind yourself of where you are, *when* you are. PTSD is a perpetual engine that powers you across space and time at the cost of splitting your being in two, astral-projecting one half while anchoring the other to a touchstone of trauma.

Don't get attached.

You coach Agnes less and less as she grows into herself as a fighter. These days, you make only the occasional comment, and usually only on technical details.

"I want to do a solo match," she says. She stirs the boba at the bottom of her cup with her straw before sucking up several of them, the two of you walking down Alhambra's main street, Agnes sipping on Hokkaido milk tea, and you on Tieguanyin oolong milk tea.

You've discussed this with her before, having her battle without your voice in her ear guiding her. Last time, she wasn't quite there yet, but now, you have confidence in her ability to react on her own.

Still, something stabs at you when you imagine watching her from the sidelines without a channel open to communicate with her. But it's no use holding her back with your fondness for her. The greatest mentors know when to let their students go.

On the night of Agnes's solo match, you walk down the winding path through garbage, finding solace in the sensory overload. Stink clings to your skin. You pass cathode-ray televisions, your skin crawling as you notice that the glass in the tubes is, thankfully, unbroken. You make a note to come back during the day to properly dispose of and recycle the leaded tubes. Closer to the arena, the dump's excavation is less orderly, a relic of the experiments you undertook with prototypes.

Your legs go weak when you round the final cascades of garbage into the arena and see a familiar sight, one that throws you straight from your body into a stratosphere of dread befitting the chomper's name.

You should have expected this long before you stepped into the arena. Should have realized the instant Samson appeared in your life again that there was no way he'd ever find another outlet for his aggressions.

Dreadnought.

You hope there's a mistake. That maybe Kill Switch isn't up against that monster. But when you take the final steps into the arena, Agnes catches your eye and waves.

You don't get a chance to wave back. Samson's across the arena, solid as a mountain face and just as unscalable. Even though he's wearing a button-down flannel shirt, you know that tattooed on his left shoulder is the Rising Sun.

You remember being stunned by it when you first got into bed with him. You run your fingers over it, your heart thudding not with arousal, but with a surge of fear.

"What does your tattoo mean?" you ask, deciding to give him the benefit of the doubt.

He turns his head from the pillow just as you'd done with Agnes and says, "It's a Japanese symbol. For my mom's side."

You don't know how to respond to that. Why the Rising Sun, of all symbols, to represent Japan? You tell yourself that maybe he doesn't know its meaning. How seeing it is like having a hand around your throat, squeezing, constricting, collapsing your larynx, plunging you into silence, reminding you of a broader history you're from, even if you only have secondhand memories of it.

Seeing Samson here now is like the shock of that discovery, striking quick as a punch to the chin and just as disabling.

Agnes follows your gaze. You don't know what you look like now, whether fear shows in your features, or whether you've thrown on the mask again, seeing through the world around you to a point beyond the horizon.

Thunderclouds of rage gather over Agnes's face. She's always been smart. She puts two and two together. The moment she does, she clenches her fists until her knuckles are white as dolomite.

"I . . ." you begin, then catch yourself breathing too shallowly as your throat thickens. "I can't let you go solo against him. I can't let you go against him at all."

But that only seems to encourage Agnes. She stands up straighter and meets Samson's gaze from across the arena, her eyes narrowing into a glare. "No way. I'm taking him down."

Tectonic plates strike against each other as the violence of impact slams into you again. The sounds around you muffle as you stare at the single word *Dreadnought*.

There's so much you want to say to Agnes. So much in your heart that you've never told anyone: the sting of being snipped away like an inconvenience. Detachment that spreads through your whole consciousness until it manifests in your veins, your arteries, your retinas, until the very sight of yourself in the mirror is foreign, an uninhabited land. How you weave absence into a cocoon and use it to tell yourself that your very core is unknowable to anyone.

But some metamorphosis has occurred in you, with Agnes as the catalyst. She fits into you like water, opening your heart to hers. You have osmosed into her, membrane to membrane, and she into you, traded in heated kisses that fog up her glasses, your qi and hers as one. She knows you in a way no one else does, even though it hasn't even been a full year since your relationship began.

But you don't know how to vocalize that, or to say how much she means to you, how your spirit soars when you're with her. How you dare to imagine a future with her: possibility is, to you, far more terrifying than oblivion.

Agnes's expression softens. She touches your shoulder. "Hey," she says, turning you to face her. She cups her hand against the base of your skull and touches your forehead to hers.

Warmth suffuses you, grounds you. You feel steady against her. Rooted.

"Breathe with me," she says, voice loud enough for only you to hear.

You want to panic. But Agnes breathes in for eight measured counts, holds for a moment, then lets out a steady exhale, her breath hot against your cheeks, pulling you back from a racing spiral of thoughts.

One. Two. Three. Four. Five. Six. Seven. Eight. Hold. Exhale. After a few rounds, you've returned to the present, your thumb rubbing circles into Agnes's other hand.

"Thank you," you murmur, your voice going hoarse.

"I'll be okay," she says. "Trust me."

You do. You trust that she can get through the match,

even as you send her off with your eyes into Kill Switch, knives digging into every pulsing chamber of your heart.

Samson doesn't bother to speak to you before the match. He keeps himself at a distance, looking at Agnes with the same predatory gaze you've seen dozens of times.

Agnes and Samson step up to each other in the center of the ring. Their mouths are moving, but you can't hear the words being exchanged.

Samson climbs into Dreadnought and Agnes into Kill Switch. Unlike others who take a more Transformers approach to turning chompers into fighting machines, Agnes preserves the chomper's original form: the treads, the claw, the epiglottis, the various chambers into which raw materials are sorted. But she's added her own touches to the design. Blue LEDs outline the treads, creating an otherworldly underbody glow. The machine is far more compact than the typical chomper. Agnes's streamlined design has even inspired you to make the next generation of chompers more energy-efficient and compact without sacrificing power. Kill Switch's lightness and multitread system allow her to turn quickly and pivot corners faster than most chompers you've seen, even ambulating ones. And instead of storing materials in the gut chambers, Kill Switch is filled with extra battery cells for boosts of power and speed. Kill Switch is a clean machine, one that fills you with pride, even as Dreadnought roars with anticipation.

Dreadnought is more juggernaut than machine, capable of crumpling flimsy chompers on impact. Without Agnes grounding you, you're floating again, two visions overlaying your sight: one of the present, and one of the past. Dreadnought, shrugging off your blows and charging you, Samson's leering grin visible through the windshield; Dreadnought, shaking debris down from towers of garbage with its might, even as spectators shout and shield themselves from brittle showers of sun-bleached plastic, unidentifiable sludge, old packaging, and bits of metal; Dreadnought, jumping up to close the distance between you and Samson, crushing Lady Danger into twists of metal; you, hysterical with adrenaline, shaken, the roof of the body caved in to an inch above your head, airbags punching bruises into you, realizing only when blood trickles into your eyes that you have gashes all over from where you collided into Lady Danger's frame; Samson, declared winner, flashing you a sharp-toothed grin as he walks away to collect his winnings.

You're the one who'd helped him develop a propulsion system powerful enough to give Dreadnought the lift to execute its devastating moves. You'd even prioritized developing Dreadnought over Lady Danger, because Samson would lavish you with the praise, attention, and validation you never gave yourself. He was the one who brought up facing off against each other: proof of concept for both machines. You agreed, thinking of the match as an exercise.

But Samson never pulls his punches.

The buzzer sounds, starting the timer for the first round. Agnes stays nimble, dodging Dreadnought's blows with a wide margin while trying to punch through Dreadnought's armor.

But if Dreadnought had been armored when you faced Samson, she's even more so now. Blows that would have torn through others as if their hulls were made of tissue paper leave only shallow gouges in Dreadnought's steel plates. You wonder if Agnes will have the mental fortitude to persist through Dreadnought's defenses—the game is as much about being levelheaded and sure of yourself as it is about brute force.

You don't sense Agnes's energy flagging, though, even as Kill Switch and Dreadnought end the first round in a stalemate. But you can tell that Samson's getting aggravated—that he'd intended to take down Kill Switch viciously and quickly during the first round. Dreadnought has an agitated energy about her, and, when the second buzzer sounds, Samson comes at Agnes with even more force, barreling at her with such energy that the ground trembles. Agnes leaves less and less of a margin when Kill Switch dodges Dreadnought.

It pains you that you're only able to watch from the sidelines—that you can't hear Agnes's panting, or the moments when she takes a deep breath to center herself. You can't whisper encouragements to her, or hear her curse when things don't go as she expects. But maybe that's for the best—you can't trust your voice to not shake as you speak to her, or trust that you can keep yourself collected as you hear Agnes's cries, knowing that Samson is responsible for them. He puts up such a front of impenetrability that you can't afford to introduce anything that would compromise Agnes mentally or emotionally.

The crowd winces together when Dreadnought sideswipes Kill Switch, knocking her off-balance. Kill Switch's gyroscopes engage stabilizers that extend from her body to keep her upright, yet as Agnes steadies Kill Switch, Samson comes in for another blow, one that Agnes doesn't have time to dodge. Kill Switch crashes hard enough to rattle the trucks parked around the arena, empty glass bottles of beer clinking together as the ground quakes.

Kill Switch's stabilizer hydraulics pump madly as her arms scrabble for leverage to rock upright.

Dreadnought retreats several feet. Someone less familiar with the machine and her operator would think that perhaps Dreadnought is giving Kill Switch the room to get back up. But your heart plunges like a stone from your throat to your stomach.

You know what Samson is about to do.

"Agnes!"

The roar of Dreadnought's engine drowns out your cry, her jet boosters filling the arena with the tang of ozone and exhaust. Dreadnought pulls from her reserve energy to propel herself into the air, clearing enough height that, when she lands on Kill Switch, folding her lighter frame like an accordion with a massive quake, the bookie's shanty collapses and several strings of lights come tumbling down from their posts, sparking a fire on the edge of the ring.

You don't hear the ref calling the match. You've already darted down from the makeshift bleachers, past people trying to contain the fire, and broken into a sprint toward Kill Switch. Samson climbs out of Dreadnought's cab like an astronaut stepping out of a vessel after a successful space mission.

It takes everything in you to face Samson. To hold his gaze and not back down, even as he triggers a cascade of images and memory so thick that you almost lose sight of the present in the deluge.

You've never allowed yourself to imagine what you'd say to Samson if you ever saw him again, because you never wanted to see him again.

So you don't say anything.

Samson smiles as if he hasn't just crushed a machine and possibly a person, as if the sport were no different than a game of tennis.

"Winnie," he says. The sound of him saying your name sickens you, curls your lips back into a snarl.

"Get out of my way," you hiss, trying to push past him to get to Kill Switch. Agnes still hasn't appeared.

But Samson grabs your arm, his fingertips digging into your flesh. "You know her?" he asks, nodding at Kill Switch. "She seems sweet."

With Samson holding you back from Agnes, something snaps. Anger replaces shame, replaces hurt, replaces fear. You yank your arm away from him so hard he's thrown off-balance. Then you swing your fist around, landing a punch square against his jaw, making him stagger back and collapse against Dreadnought's frame.

"If you show your face around here again, I will fucking destroy you," you say as Samson's eyes swim in and out of focus. "That's a promise."

You leave him as he left you. You don't have the time for vindication or satisfaction. Knuckles throbbing, you dash over to one of Kill Switch's doors. It no longer fits flush to the frame, both the door and the body creased like balled-up paper. A mere tug won't do. You find a position where you can leverage your weight against the door. Even as your muscles burn, as pain floods your whole body, and you feel like your head could burst with the strain of it all, you will yourself to keep pulling.

Finally, you work a gap large enough that you can reach inside. Agnes looks hazy, blood trickling down her neck, staining her clothing, which is already damp with adrenaline-laden sweat. You fumble around until you can unbuckle her seat belt and pull her from the wreck. Her breaths are shallow, but at least she's breathing.

The whiplash of emotions makes you feel manic, as if you're about to break out into wild laughter. But when Agnes opens her eyes again to meet yours, when she smiles at you, firelight dancing in her eyes, you find tears falling before you can stop them from spilling over.

"Win," Agnes breathes.

You sob with relief as you hold her close.

You live in a palimpsest, people and places double-exposed in a spatiotemporal pocket where layers and planes merge. Time is distorted here, long stretches compressing into incomplete montages, micromoments blooming into eternities, whole years hauled to the surface of your mind in an instant.

Dragging Agnes out of Kill Switch becomes another shadow impressed over the negative of your memory, exposing panic in your bones. Even when she recovers with little more to show from the incident than whitening scars, you find exposure after exposure layering on her aura, making you fall silent as she asks you what's wrong.

"I told you," Agnes says, the two of you under the covers, your hands twitching with want for her even as your mind stops you from acting, "I'm not delicate."

You allow yourself to cup her cheek. It's true—she's been resilient and strong, keeping both of you afloat.

"I know," you murmur, then pull her close and say into her neck, "but maybe I am."

Your face is wet with tears that soak into Agnes's shoulder as you clutch her closer, willing her not to leave.

"I'm okay," she says.

"I'm not," you whisper in reply.

"I know."

Agnes pulls back enough to look into your eyes.

"I love you, Win."

The words shoot through you like a star you could make a wish on, like something you could pin a hope on. You entwine your fingers with hers.

"I love you too," you say.

Agnes touches her forehead to yours. She is a safe harbor in the sea of possibilities that the two of you are drifting on, anchored to each other with a red thread.

Come what may. As you look into her dark eyes, you see Agnes, and only Agnes.

IF MEMORY SERVES

BY LYNELL GEORGE

Echo Park

I tried to get to the ocean today. We all have predilections, bad habits. Things we like to keep locked deep, even to ourselves. This one is mine.

Again no luck, even with auxiliary plans, the barter, workarounds I've cultivated over time. It's impossible now (or they want you to think), with the ways the roads work (and don't). The "freeways" are now roads reserved mostly for emergency vehicles or autonomous vehicles for dignitaries. Then, too, the sorting out of pass cards and tokens for passage. You're done before you're through.

I don't dare entertain even the notion of the train—going underground. The whole enterprise "a tourniquet for a hemorrhage, all kinds of ways wrong," my father used to rant. The subways fall apart, infrastructure collapsing into itself, fluorescents wavering like a wild eye tic with each shudder over the old webbing of track. There's grab-and-dash crime and the annoyance of wandering eyes and hands. "I'm not so soft," I snapped back at Calvin one morning, a month or so ago. "You've got talk skills, Alondra," he tossed back, and snatched up his knife kit and scooted out the door. That was the last I'd seen of him.

It is not untypical for Calvin and me to go days and weeks without seeing one another face-to-face. We try to keep a standing date in reserve around which to schedule commutes and job duties. Though, truth told, I didn't need the external reminder—this morning, my handheld signaled that today is one of those days.

Calvin relies on pedal power to move from kitchen gig to kitchen gig around the county. He's cultivated iron-pipe calves and quads from the miles and hills. I rely on my feet and the occasional GIPSI—Geographical Interactive Passenger Sharing, Inc.—splurge when I've gathered enough change from my tips: I work physical therapy and memory coaching—a cluster of jobs that pushes me across the city's expanse. The GIPSI is the best way to close impossible distances, the best way to press quietly across borders, but you need time and a zoned-out-to-nothing face. "You got that, girl." My ear held on to Calvin's echo, the gears and tires, down the stairs, trying to figure out if I heard teasing or tension in his voice.

The Pacific really exists. I tell people who have never seen it. You just can't get to it. Not *everyone* can get to it, I should say. Transportation. The choked roads—that's just one hurdle. But decades ago, when I could still access it, the broad stretch of slate water was visually fenced away by high-rise LuxLive buildings standing as blank-faced as twenty-four-hour guards. The memory I retain of that sector—closer to the ocean—swings back sharply, an intrusion sometimes. I want to forget it, to stop making something out of nothing. Brackish. The salt of the water—the water now so much warmer so sea life is "spoiling" much like a bunch of leafy greens left forgotten in your crisper if you're absentminded, or wasteful. You don't let things turn to ruin when so much is scarce, but here we are. Imagine: a drifting riot of decomposition.

In another lifetime, it seems, I drifted into a dingbat squat in Venice near where the pier once collapsed into jigsaw pieces in the water after a nightmare fire flashed through the night sky. We watched it, kids then, in shorts and canvas slip-ons bundled into Bajas, those wool patterned pullovers rough as burlap to the touch, feeling a thrill loop through us collectively. It was heartbreaking, certainly, but startlingly gorgeous too, this firelight in the sky at the crescendo of its burn. Yet another attempt at a Venice Pier now husks and ashes. As it attracted too many daytrippers from outside the sector, it would be, no doubt, the last attempt at a replica.

Maybe that was the end of it, that story of the city that I knew, or the city that I understood as "home"—like weeds jutting out of paved asphalt. That fire, in its warring coppers and persimmons, was some sort of epic overture to what was next. LA has burned for centuries—in riots and wildfires and arsons that grabbed neighborhoods away from early settlers and then "urban pioneers"—to be remade by those who could afford the cleanup and rehab. Fires, both propelled and conjured by theatrical winds that people don't want to call by "that saint's name" any longer—don't taunt them, don't stoke them. "Don't talk them up," as the elderly I counsel still say. If you grew up in my generation, you don't romanticize the winds. They are a cliché of this place. The winds are like a too-long hem that catches and drags detritus, kindling—sycamore and oak leaves, what's left of the palm fronds, sharp as blades as they crash to the ground from on high.

The fires, often ignited by the winds, are no longer seasonal but mercurial and thirsty. Temperamental in their out-of-nowhere fury. They claim territory. They're a secret weapon if they can be controlled—a secret weapon of privilege.

Like those fires, I'm restive—as predictable as I am unpredictable. My thoughts jump across space and time. I can't seem to corral or control them. Sometimes I don't want to. This bus won't come. Dead end this time: East Hollywood. Those of us clustered at the lip of the curb lean into the road, nearly into the flow of traffic, hoping to catch a glimpse of orange headlights, the shimmer of heat from the engine. The sky is the pink of artificial roses—too pink—like a rose-colored-glasses filter, or the altered "blooms" you can buy or barter for at the kiosks on street medians, long stems, rose with a hint of lilac at the edges. Sometimes the color at this time of day gives me a headache. The pink sky always seems to be pressing down on me. There's an urgency to it. To stave off the panic, I always have to remind myself to squint through the haze, until gloaming and then finally nightfall. I watch the others once again lean toward the sigh of air brakes, staring into the crowded distance. A bus hums toward us, but when it pauses, it doesn't open its doors, I glimpse a crowded grid of brown faces looking out through the windows. We look back. It's a mirror: brown faces looking in and out, regarding one another. Over and over and over. I have no other cheap way to get back across town, down Sunset, alongside the edges of the fenced-off canyons where, from the street, you used to see flora—threads of ivy and seasonal bursts of bougainvillea; then through Beverly Hills and West Hollywood; then spilling into Hollywood and finally back to the neighborhood—too far for my feet alone to carry me on an especially hot day like this.

I've been trying to sock away change. Every bit of it. So much is so see-through lean of late. But I had this notion about the beach, that big water, and trying to go back to my old neighborhood to see if there was anyone or anything left, maybe some off-path roost to crash in like the old days. I've been cycling through opposing emotions, feeling hemmed in and yet adrift. How do you get from A to B if you don't remember where A *was* or wonder if A even existed. You learn your sense of direction simply enough—a recognizable starting point, then move outward, from A to B to C. Connecting the elements, "*See*, this is your story," I coach my clients: "*This* is the shape of your story." We peel away the husk. "Keep in mind," I recite, week after week, "we're not remembering days, we are remembering moments." I see recognition flicker in their eyes, a pilot light wavering in there, somewhere.

Time moves. Very fast here. It always has. I've always felt caught—or forgotten—in the hot rush of that slipstream, backward and forward at once. Once there were hills and mountains and an ocean to situate you even if you tripped off course, but no longer, at least for me.

Landmarks bulldozed by deep-pocket developers, natural features hidden by high fences always too heaven-reaching to see above or around. My old Venice street, Brooks Avenue, was tough even at its loose ends near the calm water. For decades it resisted change. I continue to feel that old urge—childhood devotion—to see that ramshackle row of Venice bungalows drenched by the crashing sunset. "Why do you keep *trying* to go back, Alondra?" Calvin always asks. "Nothing there for you anymore." He sings it like a blues, trying to keep it light. I'd toss him steel: a menacing no-way-in glare, because, as always, it is impossible to answer his very simple question.

I give up on the bus and press my code into my handheld's keypad. When the GIPSI arrives, the driver will ask: "Where to?" I never know exactly where to say, I don't have a set/traditional address anymore—that used to embarrass me, less so now. More, I am happy to have the excuse for a magic-carpet GIPSI ride, eastward along the big curves of Sunset, back to my cohab slip—a podshare in Echo Park—in time to meet up with Calvin to discuss the future: near and long-term. That queue is long too, but more reliable. The GIPSI is the last of the human driver ride-hailing services left. All else is autonomous. GIPSIs are for the rest of us. Those of us who are poor. Those of us who run on fumes or hope. I'm trying not to count the days, to obsess over the hours as they drain with the sunset I can no longer see slide into the ocean that's now obscured by honeycombs of luxury.

I should have never called my little slot *my* or *mine*. This morning there were acid-green *Notice to Quit* signs taped to some of our doors. Again. Mine among so many this time. Something big is in the works, it seems. Change comes fast and total here in Los Angeles. Like the fury of the fires. Month-to-month is really week-to-week: Just four months in, I'm on the lookout again for some other place with a roof and space to set up a bed.

I should feel more rooted. I have dogged and hard-fought-for family history here. I am named after a grandmother whom I never met, but family lore—apocryphal perhaps—attests that she was named after a freeway exit, her mother fresh out of names, fresh out of gifts, fresh out of goodwill, maybe even hope. *Alondra* flew by on one of the green-

and-white freeway signs and my grandmother's mother said it aloud, once and then again, to test its music, its loft.

Nobody bothered to look it up. To see if it had deeper meaning. A family name or christened homestead. Spanish for *lark*, I knew that from being in school and worrying through language classes, but what did it signal and carry with it? This name that flowed like water. Later, in middle school, I looked it up: *defender of mankind* in Greek. I was deflated. For some reason, I had hoped for something more.

I'm next up at the GIPSI stop, flash my token when the driver floats up along the curb, and I'm in. His sound system is loud—electronic pulse tone. I wince my hello and, bless him, he reads it for what it is and lowers the volume with a voice command.

He doesn't speak beyond a faint greeting that comes with a head nod. The car smells of miscellaneous dank—not bad, but heavy with bitter eucalyptus that I suppose was intended to mask something else. I shut my eyes and shut down my thoughts and settle into a ride that I know will be two hours and change, maybe three—a day trip in my grandmother's day, out to Santa Barbara or down to San Diego, I'd seen digitized images floating on mantle screens. I sleep in this car like I sleep in my slip, shallow but steady, grateful for the break even if it's brief.

The light has dimmed some by the time the GIPSI drops me at my neighborhood stop, on Sunset Boulevard where Silver Lake meets Echo Park, an indiscernible boundary, where a concrete bunker straddles the "line." It has high walls covered with "native" grasses, succulents/cacti, scrubby little do-not-disturb tokens of unappreciation.

They warn, *Don't lean here. Don't even think about loitering. Keep stepping.*

The long walk home in my thin sandals reminds me just how hot it is. Humid too. I can still feel the concrete's vivid heat radiating through my soles. It also reminds me that seasons don't matter, seasons as something fixed or expected. It's January and the temperature rarely dips below eighty after nightfall.

I have some time to kill before Calvin turns up, or it becomes apparent that I need to search him out. I am not sure which, given our parting. I walk the long block east down Sunset Boulevard toward my own honeycombed, plain-faced complex. I can see it from the distance, painted pine green to be nondescript, to blend quietly; its facade like a toppled cheese grater. This stretch of Sunset's sidewalk is jammed with the afternoon street vendors hawking everything from fake IDs and forged scrip to bitter, watery mood boosts and tonics and handmade soap. I smell garlic and onions circling somewhere in the near distance; the twinge in my stomach reminds me that I haven't made time to scrounge up some sort of meal today.

As I approach my building, even at street level, I count more acid-green signs on doors. More misery behind them, I know. This whole complex will be gone soon. This is how it always goes. In waves.

I'd found this outpost, this ragged wedge of land, not far from Elysian Park, years ago, by chance while visiting a client, Mr. Thibault, a loquacious ex–city servant, now deep into his nineties, who spoke English with a plush Quebecois accent. His memory was mostly intact, just tipped a little askew, allowing that his essential day-to-day tasks were sometimes performed in scattershot fashion.

His stories helped me form a map that connected a complex past to a quickly vanishing present.

I wind up the narrow spiral concrete staircase four flights, pass the communal bathrooms and kitchens, and take the metal catwalk toward my unit. Calvin's bike isn't parked in the corner lock unit I'd installed to make him feel safer about leaving his bike outside when he's here overnight. I input my security code; the door slides open. Behind it, just my disarray as I'd left it. Two orange canvas butterfly chairs. A wooden daybed. Stacks of books and notepads and my work handheld resting on my small multiuse table. My special lamps with their old-fashioned bulbs. Highway and street maps tacked to the white walls. "This is what you call decor?" Calvin never fails to say. At least, I comfort myself, my eyes calculating what must be done, packing will be easy.

No sign of Calvin.

He's been finding work all over the county, dreaming up and preparing meticulously wrought meals in the styles to which the neighborhoods cater. He's an alchemist, a quick study of people and palates, and it will keep him afloat as long as his strong legs can carry him.

My gigs are more flexible. I group clients by territory. In the sessions, we verbally walk through their distress, untangle their memories. My job is to keep their stories orderly in my head, help them back onto the right path when they waver. I am a living memory repository. Irony is I can't rely on my own.

I know I won't be able to sit still, to let my mind race within open-ended time. So I drop my day bag on one of the butterfly chairs and head straight back down to the noise of the street. It's still in the low hundreds and the sun has finally dipped, burnishing the sidewalk and walls a dull copper. I move with the sun in my eyes for a few long blocks, then make a sharp right at the opening of what looks to be not more than a driveway: this walk is a calculation of precise steps—a stroll by rote. What I concretely "remember"—or *was* familiar from one corner to the next—is gone, long gone before you can form a connection, make a memory. Ritual also makes memory, sears an image into the "story" of your life, but that doesn't happen as much anymore. I float through time and space, trying to staunch longing.

Some people drown in drink, or the latest apothecary's potion, to try to push down memories—I am the opposite. In this moment, I just want consolation for today's beach misadventure. Now, I must not float, but focus: That small opening off Sunset gives way to earth, then up the hardscrabble hill with crabgrass jutting through the cracks in concrete. Torn edges of chain link are strewn like mussed blankets on hard dirt perforated by old tree trunks, rows and rows of them. The old private roads up there are gray, soft heaps of old asphalt sprinkled with shards of shiny matter—glass mixed with rusted metal bits—soft as trail sand. Nothing has been tended to here for a generation at least. Potholes riddle most pathways, rendering them impassable—and that's what has saved this tiny stretch of a hill hidden away from the twenty-four-hour hum on the boulevard, this perch high enough to just hear the white noise of traffic and see the stadium lights, but not exposed enough to attract notice from below.

There are times I worry that he won't be there, that the shop will stand empty; its windows vacant as unfocused eyes; the piled-up junk mail and fast-food flyers in a swirl on the sidewalk, filthy with old waffle footprint marks and all the other ways we can measure time.

On the way up, I pass more anonymous concrete facades fronted by corrugated steel fences rolled out parallel to the curb. The sameness of everything, like the white noise below. I count my steps, keeping an easy rhythm, and finally the pile of wild brown shrubs and dusty bougainvillea reveals itself. Penn's tumbledown bungalow is hidden in a tangle of junk and rubble. I quick-tap on the heavy glass of the house's side window with the tip of my index finger on the spot between the words *by* and *appointment* in tiny hand-painted white script. Inside I see stirring. Penn huddles in his spot, just out of sidewalk eye range. His head pops up into my line of vision, he pushes his chair back, then ambles to the door, his upper body's shifting suggesting that there is a bit of a maze to traverse. He props the door open with a foot. "Again. You," he says, his voice cheerless. "So soon."

His generosity surely isn't boundless, even though his time for me seems to be. He can be difficult to read, but I also know he doesn't want to draw attention to frequent visitors. "Is now a good time?" I stare into his lineless face, his head shaved to razor stubble.

"For you, I have no choice."

I started stopping in at Penn's some months ago, when neighbors told me he had a collection of incandescent lights from the 1980s along with the corresponding fixtures and converters to run them. These warm lights that made our slips feel less like a perfunctory-between-stations triage center and more like a home. They also allowed me to sleep; they provided quiet golden light to drift off to.

Once inside, I saw he had squirreled away much more. And this was the beginning of something—something else—that I couldn't quite control. It calmed the urgency in me.

Along with vintage hardware, tangled extension cords, old street atlases and folding maps, and piles of frayed newspapers and magazines, Penn kept a spinner rack of old photo cards detailing the many faces of the city through the decades: Family prints—sepia-toned—fashioned into a heavy card that could be mailed for a penny or two. Others were linen cards with careful hand-tinted scenes of buildings (churches or theaters), pastel vistas or the old two-lane, gently curving, near-empty parkways.

Baffled by their purpose, I had to ask. "Postcards," Penn said flatly. I didn't recognize any of the locations, nor any of the names (so much of LA now goes by acronyms or are enclaves that have been retitled by their investor blocs). I would look into the frames of these cards and see things I'd never glimpsed as I moved across the expanse of the city. The rows of palms had been replanted decades ago with trees that provide shade for our perma-summers. Palms weren't native, but they looked regal and magnificent if you were set-dressing your fantasy. Why wouldn't you choose the very thing that mirages seem to always require—sky, water, and the gentle arc of a listing palm tree?

The palm trees dried, became frail, then brittle, victims of fungus and infestation. "Beetles," Penn explained. They arrived as stowaways on trees during the post–World War II housing boom. "Trojan horses. Imagine that." He paused. "All those headless palm trees of my childhood. I always wondered why they didn't take the whole thing down." I'd seen them too, scattered across the landscape. Even still. Blunt as omens.

Then the create-your-own experience "Neighborhood As Lifestyle" overtook the Los Angeles story. Even when my mother was a child, families entered lotteries to gain entry into vapid gated communities with stern-faced tract homes that looked like 3-D copies: *Come! Make it up as you go!* Back then, though, Penn told me, people would augment themselves—adapt to their surroundings—to occupy an existing backdrop: *You* fit into *it*.

Now the money men topple twenty-first-century backdrops over and over again; all struck like the scrims they were; transforming them into the latest fad, or a particular buyer's fervent aspiration. "Fewer and fewer," says Penn, "come for the wonders of the flora and fauna and the air, that place to change themselves." So you didn't achieve your last-city dream? Come here: claim your New York, mile-high, high-rise, or a Nantucket cottage in a row of others, or a San Francisco gingerbread Victorian, or a Midwest farmhouse next to neighbors who wanted and lost out on the same. Just make it happen *here*.

Behind all those fences were once neighborhoods. Now they are "experiences," theme park–style controlled environments. Those are the folks that Calvin pedals all over the grid cooking for, creating yet another layer of verisimilitude.

Much like the disorder I move through daily, Penn's archive has no system. Also, to be clear, he wouldn't call it that. It's just a casual collection of castoffs he inherited from an old man named Jake who ran a bookstore here for decades and let Penn move in when he could no longer afford a slip. Jake maintained the shop primarily not to sell things, but to provide a meeting spot. "Cohesion," Jake told Penn. "In a landscape that is fragmented, formless."

One day Jake didn't show up to clear away the debris and open up the finicky front door. As far as Penn knows, Jake is still out there, sorting through "tiny treasures," as he called them. Penn lifts and stretches that first syllable in an exaggerated lilt, summoning Jake into the room. I don't ask for details. He offers nothing. But we're both intrigued by letters that still arrive addressed to Jake in the once-a-week government mail. Handwritten on lavender paper, no return address, just a name along the back flap: *Victoria.*

Since coming to the shop, I've learned bits and pieces about Echo Park and Edendale and Jake's rough conviviality. There's a mysterious dome that peeks over one of the tall walls at the corner of Clinton and Bellevue near Echo Park Lake that I'd long been curious about. Penn told me it's called a *cupola* and was once part of a structure that housed the School of Success, founded and operated by a man named Victor Sengo. A Los Angeles charismatic. "Charlatan," Penn translated matter-of-factly, unpacking boxes of fresh finds—old waterlogged mass market paperbacks, wooden packing crates, garishly hand-painted figurines of cherubs. "He told people he could read palms and sort out your 'energy.' Something he called 'Mentalism.' The idea was if you got your head right—or *he* got your head right—your brain waves on the 'right' frequency, success was yours. You just needed to pay him, naturally. He did well. Very. Well enough to build a fancy center with many cupolas."

Penn's story about Sengo had hovered for days, weeks. One evening, when I couldn't sleep, I searched online—

the school, the man, the aftermath. He was heat-seeking the forlorn and estranged. The vulnerable. *How about interpersonal relationships in general? Do you feel as if you relate satisfactorily to other people, that you have a niche in the emotional ecology of your environment?* Deep into the night, I checked off hundred-year-old boxes in my head: *No, no, and no . . .*

I can't afford Jake's and Penn's postcards, these little windows of light. Clear views. I probably can't even afford the time it takes to look at them—the time away from my crosstown hustle—but I am transfixed. Within them: women in rumpled cotton dresses at work in their gardens; men in slouchy fedoras, arms akimbo, conversing on their bungalow porches or in front of automobiles—all spheres and gleaming fenders. Even in the muted softness of these cards, you could edge them end to end and create an old neighborhood, the way you would link a train—and these images could take you there. Not necessarily a place, but a moment.

It's not the past, per se, that I'm longing for. This isn't nostalgia. It's antecedents.

This lingering, pausing over street names and houses, and gardens and dayscapes, is more powerful than any drug I know because it takes me somewhere real, not fantasy or simulacrum. There is something about the structure of a story—history. I see it in these front yards—some full of rocks and raked dirt, others sturdy grass and tightly coiled garden hoses; I see it in the children standing in a driveway on what looks like the first day of school, and I can make out, in the background a row of domiciles, different shapes and sizes, no fences, no walls, then, too, space and sky. There were fruit trees—apricot and peach. I couldn't identify them myself, but the descriptions in the postcards tell me. (*Please visit. Come see our Garden of Eden!*) I keep hoping for a faded rectangle depicting my old neighborhood. Not the pier stretched across the water, a scene rendered in sunset shades of pastels—that's a sad memory. I want to see the little survivor cottages on Brooks, the tumbledown fences, the sun-faded walls, but Penn warned me when I first got started, "They didn't make postcards of that."

My cohab slip is a no-man's-land. It sits on fraught territorial boundaries that have been in dispute—not just who owns what but how much of it. I've heard from locals that this unit supplanted an encampment of transients—*people living out of doors*, as they called them. They created complex shanties that looked strikingly similar to our cohab honeycombs. I felt particularly sensitive to the women who marched the perimeter of the collective squats. I'd see them in other parts of this sector after their encampment had been bulldozed away. They piled on layers of clothes to obscure their bodies. To be less of a target on the street. Sleeping outside even in winter isn't a problem now. The nights, with the lingering heat, are nearly as warm as the days. But there is much else to be tuned in to and wary of.

This sector, though, curled up in my imagination, because it still retains features of a neighborhood. Just a few. Porches and yards. Broken fences. Volunteer flora pushed up in the crabgrass. And here, there's still a token cluster of palm trees that trace the incline and curve of road up to the sports stadium, not too far from a neighborhood that locals still sometimes refer to as the *forgotten edge*, one that some of Penn's postcards and street atlases identify as Victor Heights. The neighborhood was a shape-shifter, "moved like a spirit," my client Mr. Thibault confided. "If memory serves, it wasn't always set down on maps. Some years there. Others, not."

Whose sleight of hand? I tease Mr. Thibault: "Do I trust the story? Do I trust its teller?" I'm surprised to feel a little wave of worry move through my body. What if he doesn't show? Calvin. This place Calvin thought we could be lost together in the forgotten edge. This has been a longer run than usual. He goes to where the jobs are and he never says no, but this city takes a lot out of you. Calvin is about as sturdy as they come. He has a thousand-watt smile, but LA breaks him in ways and places he can't always articulate or explain. Our slips are miles apart and distance often makes rifts for others, but for us it has worked until now. I feel the little fissures, the chill running through them; also impatience, wariness. Calvin is now forever picking up debris in the street—gum wrappers, crushed paper coffee cups—trash, pure trash, telling me I should give it to Penn. That's the only time I vibe just a hint of jealousy—perhaps, more plainly, his insecurity. Penn is a larger-than-life figure trapped in skin, a myth to Calvin, a man whose story I'll never really know and I've come to realize doesn't matter.

Even if I had a little extra in reserve, I can't indulge. No money for purchases, not even a foldout map on "clearance," I'm staked out on the sidewalk now, hearing Calvin's voice in my head, louder than an alarm clock: *Better not make me wait, Alondra, snooping at dead people's business.* Once I reach the edge of the park, I balance myself on this poor excuse of a bench, a long metal pole turned horizontal, set into a stack of bricks, near Laguna Avenue, and wait to hear the gears and whiz of Calvin's tricked-out bike. I told Calvin I wanted to try to take a walk down to Echo Park, near the spot where you can see Sengo's cupola, since I wouldn't be in my slip much longer. Maybe we could bring some of the leftovers he stashes away—the ends of baguettes and what's left of the wheels of gooey cheeses and greenhouse fruit from his latest "Napa County" enclave gig. Perhaps we could make a picnic, if we don't get busted for loitering. I am 1,000 percent certain he will bring up moving together, away from here. North to Ranch Tejon, where at least we could live closer together, perhaps even share a slip. There you still have a sense of land and can orient yourself by the rise of hills and sky. Calvin says, "C'mon, Alondra. No future here for us. You have to *afford* a future here. Existing isn't living."

He's right. These buildings have their backs turned on us, with their neat wooden or stucco fences stretched high. They are worlds unto themselves. Edens, I am sure, of this moment.

I don't want to "leave" Los Angeles, but I'm not sure what that means any longer. What, specifically, am I lashing my soul to?

I have practiced many ways to say, *No, I can't go,* or, *No, you go without me, and we'll see,* to Calvin, but can't find the right note to hit, because I know the damage it will wreak. But my ambivalence is surely worse, a slow-release poison.

What did people one hundred, two hundred years ago see in Los Angeles, when they first set foot in it? This is not meant as a flippant question. I'm mining for some truth. I even sometimes ask clients as a way to tease out pins in the map toward their pasts, toward who they were and now are: "What about your home means the most to you?"

Maybe it wasn't just the physical, that "Eden, " I know, I long for. That "lushness" was constructed—embellished too; a power of positive thought and willful manifestation.

"What's more radical and powerful than money?" Calvin always quizzes me.

"Imagination," I reply with little affect.

"Now *you*, Ms. Memory, remember that."

Early morning, when it still feels like night, Calvin and I sometimes hike down to the tiny part of the lake's shore that is still accessible to "visitors." It's for all purposes a pocket-park patch of grass and pond-size slip of water laced with algae and drifting lotus pads. Sometimes beyond the topiary hedges, I can glimpse just the crown tip of a pedal boat swan skimming the surface. It is in some way the only piece of vintage Los Angeles that I can easily travel to—that looks like the rectangles in Penn's shop. Even if it is now just a miniature of what the landowners behind the fence see. We pretend that it is ours.

I wonder if a too-large part of our discussion this evening will be about the time I spend with Penn. It isn't Penn that Calvin is worried about, though; it's me. Not Penn drifting into me, but me away, just like all of these sojourns to the Pacific to see what I can see. You can get hooked on a yearning. What is it that is so powerful in me that I can't put into words?

When I step back far enough, remembering my own memories, I can see where we come together and where we're fraying—where we pull apart: Calvin's job is to feed the rich whatever they desire, for which he draws a pittance. It nourishes him because it is the ritual that brings him pleasure. My desire—hunger and what it takes to satiate it—is more abstract.

I don't have the words to tell Calvin this. He's a man of certitude and science: measures and temperatures, technique and time—that all add up to a tangible result. My trips to the ocean, my yearning for and obsession with and connection to Penn's shop, have nothing to do with Penn but rather with Jake. With his spirit. I understand this predilection, the attempt to order chaos, to provide context. To reach for what feels real. Solid.

Calvin, I know, wonders what it must be like to be filled up with other people's busy random thoughts, their piecemeal recollections: the dreams and disappointments, the night terrors, the old telephone numbers, former addresses, routes to work, paths to the market, a life of small duties and pleasure. We need our memories, good and bad—they warn us and they guide us. And often, they comfort us. "Sometimes," I say to Calvin, as a way to let him in, to help him understand, "people will hand you their heart."

Once a week, when I sit across from Mrs. Lau and her disarrayed brain, braiding and unbraiding her memories, I understand this most acutely.

We talk in the deep amber light of her tiny room—a delicate windowed space cut from one larger bedroom in an old grand boardinghouse in Hi-Fi (at one time, Historic Filipinotown, as she still adamantly calls it; the one thing that sticks). Even still, the curved staircase up to her room, adorned with bright patterned tiles of another century and accented with a looping black iron handrail, looks like the flourish of signatures I see on the backs of Penn's postcards.

The north side of the room features a faux fireplace with a simple tiled mantelpiece, upon which her own family photos collect the fine ash from the fires and exhaust and seasonal bad air. They are not cards from a curiosity shop; they are her *own* people—feet sunk in the sand of the Pacific, a dozen flash-lit faces squeezed around a small but food-laden table—whether or not she can always remember them. Adjacent to the fireplace, she has installed a cooking surface and a small sink with intermittent running water. She always asks if I would like something to eat. I always decline. It's her way, I know, of staving off what may or may not come back to her.

Mrs. Lau is frustrated, frequently moved to tears. "You'll help me remember?" Her voice, thin, flutters like a distant transmission. It halts and trembles, as if we are going to venture across a tightrope, or dive into the depthless ocean. It must truly feel like this. Acknowledging grand loss once more. I am patient; I keep my voice even but full of warmth. When she stumbles and can't recall, which is always and often, we take it all down—like a building—to the studs, a frame with empty rooms. We start again. It's slow work: Person. Place. Thing. Her face relaxes, she can see the contours of a profile or the bend in a familiar road emerging as I keep nudging her toward her clear view. She *has* memories and they are distinct and they are rooted in a real place and time, detail upon detail, that I recite back to her again and again. They are here. We are here. We struggle in the dark water together. I swim in the chaos, in the jagged ruin of jigsaw pieces. For her, I will retrieve what I can't for myself. Not even in maps and stories and postcards. Always, I'm ready to risk the depths—the tumbled-down past—for the light of life for her.

LOVE, ROCKET SCIENCE, AND THE MOTHER OF ABOMINATIONS

BY STEPHEN BLACKMOORE

Pasadena

Diane wakes in a cold sweat, the image of James lying on the floor of his apartment, blood cooling underneath his shattered head, is as vivid as the day it happened. She used to play it back in her dreams every few nights, then weeks, then months. A way to cling to her rage and despair. Then it was to help her mourn. Finally, she had to admit that she was just punishing herself.

So she stopped. Copied it into long-term storage. Almost ten years on and it had gotten blurry, fuzzy around the edges. Couldn't quite bring herself to delete the file, though. Like an ex-smoker who keeps that one cigarette in her pocket to remind herself she can resist.

She thought she had moved on. Wanted to move on. She'd cut professional and personal ties, got out of the business, used her expertise to build a security consulting business where she operated under a different name.

She was out. She was done.

Until an AI search she'd set up so long ago she'd almost forgotten it got a hit. The surveillance footage from around her building that night, the footage that had somehow all disappeared from the street cameras. That was three years ago.

She sits up in the single bed, slides a command over to the window to open the blinds. A hazy yellow light fills the studio apartment. First thing every morning, she does what everyone does—she checks her messages. Three phone calls while she slept shunted to voice mail, icon blinking in her left eye.

One call each from Pam and Indigo giving her the green light. Indigo bitching about bandwidth at the site, but Indigo's always bitching about bandwidth.

Then there's one from Peter. Peter the Partner, Peter the Broker, Peter the Knife in Her Back. He's a charming man, Peter is, with an easy smile, smooth voice, and slicked-back hair. Hadn't seen him in years, but got in touch with him a few months back. She's back in the game. Now she's ready to play.

"I found a buyer for you." His voice sets her teeth on edge. She pushes it down, forces herself to listen. "Buyer wants to see that sample. Meet me at Curb Stomper tonight. Seven o'clock. Oh, and it's good to be working with you again."

He didn't have anything for her then, and she knew he wouldn't. That wasn't the point. She just needed to be on his radar long enough, nonthreatening enough, that when she dangled the bait he wouldn't look for the hook.

Diane sends a thumbs-up emoji to him. He responds with a heart. She takes a deep breath and tries not to rip her own eyes out in anger.

You want hearts, motherfucker? She's happy to oblige. After all, he tore hers out and left it bleeding out on an apartment floor.

* * *

Bank district, Downtown LA, a withered old lady, broken but dignified, surrounded by the young, the hardy, the terribly tall. Skyscrapers loom over this three-block patch of dead businesses, ancient facades, shitty bars.

She sips her drink, a poorly made, overpriced Manhattan using rye that's never seen the inside of a barrel. The walls are floor-to-ceiling, corner-to-corner, 3-D panels, scenes changing every five minutes with a fidelity greater than the human eye can detect.

But they're so old and the programming's so jacked that they're out of sync. Part of the bar is a vibrant beach in Mallorca, next to it stand redwoods towering into the sky, vivid trees, snow falling in whorls. Two more are nothing but jagged static that makes Diane want to vomit.

So she focuses on the bartender, the only appealing thing in this place. His shirt is threadbare thin, all the better to show off his six-pack abs. She wonders if they're store-bought. These days most things are.

She feels Peter long before she sees him, before he even exits his Uber. He knows how to blend in, go unnoticed. But ten years on Diane can still feel his passage through a room by the void he leaves in his wake, a null space that closes up behind him like the collapse of a wave function.

Peter slides into the seat next to her, opens a tab, throws her a receipt. She does the same. Now there's a big, fat digital stamp that will show anyone who looks that they were in the same place at the same time.

Tit for tat, of course. It's as much insurance for him as it is for her. Diane has prepared for this. She sends Pam a quick text. A thumbs-up pops up in her vision a few seconds later. Pam's copied Diane's digital footprint at the bar, and erased her from the system.

Something happens to Peter, she was never here. Something happens to her, her data slides back in and a big red flag gets sent to a security firm she's hired, just in case.

"How's your evening treating you?" Peter says. He orders an old-fashioned, winces at the taste.

"Impatiently." She smiles, forcing it to reach her eyes. She's done this before. Every woman has done this before. Smile at the man and he won't hit, shoot, mock, belittle. Smile the lie that says everything's fine.

But tonight, hers is a predator's smile.

"This drink's shit anyway," Peter says. "Shall we?"

Outside, the heat hits Diane like a brick. Summers keep getting longer, winters shorter. Here it is February and the thermometer's cracking at a hundred and change with a low in the nineties. The Santa Ana winds are an almost year-long phenomenon now. Worse, in fact. The high buildings channel it, focusing the dry, blazing heat, scouring the streets like a wind-powered belt sander.

The heat bakes in the smell of homelessness, urine, brake dust, overheating batteries, while the wind carries it on to assault everyone who takes a breath. Windows above the street are dark. Historic buildings converted to luxury lofts and bought by offshore companies to hide their money. They sit empty, unused. If it weren't for the high-priced security in place, they'd be filled with squatters by now.

LA isn't a city that grows. It's a city that swallows, bloating ever fatter off the neighbors it subsumes. It accretes. Layer upon layer upon layer. History like coral. Skyscrapers lie on two-hundred-year-old foundations, ancient buildings gutted, leaving nothing behind but the facade.

LA likes to forget its history, but it never can. It's always there, slathered over with spackle and steel like it's pancake makeup, an aging Norma Desmond so desperate for her close-up she'll do anything to get it.

Peter hails an Uber with a wave of his hand. The stubby, driverless car pulls up to the curb, door sliding open. He requests a preloaded sightseeing route that will drive them aimlessly through Chinatown, up to look at Google Stadium, and back down again.

He pulls a small tube that looks a little like lipstick out of his pocket and thumbs a button on the side. Diane feels, more than hears, the high-frequency buzz of the device that momentarily futzes the car's transmitter to the network, wipes its memory of the last three hours, and deletes everything as it's recorded. When they're done it will be as if they never existed at all.

"You said you have a buyer?" Diane says. She considers killing him right then and there. Put a bullet in him and damn the consequences. But where's the poetry in that?

"If they're what you say they are, yeah. What do you have?" Peter asks.

Diane doesn't blink at the lie. She knows there's no buyer. She pulls a flat, 3-D-printed object from her purse. Rectangular, small. At four-by-five inches it's half the size of the real thing. Its topography is exaggerated to show details, false colors indicate actual height and depth, like a map of some distant planet.

"LIDAR image?" Peter says.

"And MRI. It's sitting behind a wall inside a box. Had to hack a surveillance drone to get the scan. Took a lot to clean the image, but it's definitely one of the tablets."

"How do you know?"

Diane takes the tablet back, points out the trenches, the ridges. Runs her finger along cliff tops, dips it into canyons. "It's Enochian," she says. "Language of the angels, according to John Dee, personal astrologer to Queen Elizabeth I. This one only has four symbols" She touches each one in turn. "Mals, Gon, Un, Mals. Spells *piap* of all things. Means *balance*."

"You're fucking kidding me," Peter says.

"Nope. It's all bullshit, but it's verifiable, historical bullshit. And it fits. Parsons wrote on slate tablets by dragging lines through his, um, particular medium, with a stick."

"Particular medium?" Peter takes back the tablet, peers closely to make out the letters. Diane has to give him credit. He's good at looking ignorant.

"Jizz," Diane says, and Peter drops it, a look of surprise and disgust on his face—Diane can't help but laugh. "Parsons rubbed one out over every single tablet and used a stick to run through a puddle of come to make the letters."

"How many are there?"

"No idea. From the dimensions of this one and the box they're in, it could be two or three, or twenty or thirty. I've matched them against records of another group of tablets that came on the market about ten years ago and then went missing. I'll know more when I get to it and get everything scanned. Honestly, I think it comes down to how hydrated Parsons was."

"The client wants the originals. That's the contract."

"He'll get them," Diane says. "But he won't like getting a pile of mostly blank slates he can't read. These were written between 1945 and 1946 in the desert. After 110 years that shit'll turn to dust in a heartbeat, if it hasn't already. They need to be scanned before they disintegrate."

"And if they already have?"

"The scanners have a resolution of .1 angstroms. No matter how badly degraded they are, the scanners will pick up the designs."

"When are you expecting to have them?"

"Not for a couple of days," she says. That will give her plenty of time to get everything in place.

"Okay," Peter says. "Are you asking for more money?"

"No. Built the scans into my asking price."

"Good. I don't know that he would go any higher. Unless . . ."

"Unless?"

"He's pretty keen to get his hands on these. So much so that he asked for the location so he could get them himself. Was willing to pay three times your asking price."

"What happens if he finds there isn't anything there?" Diane says. "He'll have paid for a bullshit treasure map. He gets nothing, I get a bad reputation. Hard pass."

"A boy can dream," Peter replies with that charming smile.

"Keep dreaming." Dream like she does. Dream like drowning. Dream like the world is swallowing you up and you fall and fall and fall and never wake. *Dream like that, Peter,* she thinks, *and maybe eventually you'll understand.*

John Whiteside Parsons. Jack to his friends. Genius. Gullible, high most of the time, couldn't keep his dick in his pants. He was a rocket scientist before there were rockets, paving the way for America's entry into the space race whether he knew it or not.

Engineer, occultist, chemist, entrepreneur, a founder of the Jet Propulsion Laboratory in Pasadena, heroin addict, paranoiac, hated by Howard Hughes, the LAPD, and numerous men and women whose sisters, lovers, and partners he banged with wild and religious enthusiasm.

Literally. Parsons was a follower of the occultist Aleister Crowley. A member of Crowley's Church of Thelema. High on orgies, low on sin, big proponent of enlightenment through sex. A tailored fit for Parsons.

In 1945 he went out to the Mojave Desert to ride the snake like a wartime Jim Morrison, listened to Prokofiev, got high as balls, and whacked off a magic spell across slate school tablets like Richard Dreyfuss building mashed potato sculptures and yelling, "This means something!"

Mostly, it just meant that he got come all over everything.

It takes Diane fifteen minutes to find the GPS tracker Peter slipped into her purse. She crushes it and scatters the pieces out the window. When she wants Peter to find her, he'll find her and not a second before.

She gives the car a new destination. It'll be an hour until she reaches the site in Pasadena. Five minutes in, she gets the shakes. She's been holding everything together for way too long. And seeing Peter after all these years has cracked something inside her.

She gives herself thirty minutes to break down and scream, beat the seats and the ceiling, let out all the rage and frustration, the longing. She shuts down the waterworks when the timer flashes in her vision, puts her Diane the Competent mask back in place, cleans her face, purpose renewed.

The car heads up the dirt drive of the abandoned equestrian center on Oak Grove next to the Jet Propulsion Lab property at the foot of the San Gabriel Mountains.

Though it should already be cleared, she wipes the car's onboard memory a second time, sends it on its way. It'll slide back into the network somewhere in Glendale with a case of digital amnesia.

The equestrian center is a charred field that never recovered from a brush fire that swept through the area twenty years before. It might have, if the same thing hadn't happened the year after, and the year after that, and the year after that.

It was during that time that the Jet Propulsion Lab was shuttered. Too much fire damage, too much risk. Fifteen people died on the grounds when flames ignited a badly sealed fuel tank that took out three buildings when it went up. After that they packed it in. NASA didn't have any funding, anyway.

But they couldn't completely abandon the place. High chain-link fencing surrounds the whole 170+ acres, and armed quadcopter drones patrol 24/7. To get past them, Diane had a subverted security drone reconfigured, changed its route, spoofed the servers to make all the other drones blind to it while it zipped in and out of windows, up staircases, into subbasements.

Fortunately, she knows someone very good at doing all of that. Pam Lao steps out from behind the ruins of a stable as the car drives away.

"How'd it go?" Pam says.

"About as you'd expect."

"I kind of expected you to kill him."

"I want to hit him where it hurts," Diane says.

"Kind of my point. I honestly wasn't sure if you were going to go through with this. I'm starting to worry."

"Only now?" Diane digs the heels of her palms into her

eyes in a futile attempt to ward off the headache growing between her temples. "I know I'm getting more—"

"Erratic," Pam says.

"You can walk away anytime you want, you know," Diane says, struggling to keep the anger out of her voice.

"You know I won't," Pam replies. "But this will only work if you believe it'll work."

"If it works—" Diane starts. Not for the first time she wonders if she's delusional. If she is, then all of her friends are delusional too.

"When," Pam says. "*When* it works. I just hope you're still you on the other side of it."

"Me too," Diane says. She's scared, because who wouldn't be? But she has to go through with it. If she doesn't, then what's the point of anything?

Parsons masturbated obsessively on every single slate tablet, drawing letters with a stick, his fingers, whatever his drug-fueled muse told him. "Parsons," said a colleague once, "jerked off in the name of spiritual advancement."

Parsons did not disagree.

The Babalon Working. A rite to summon the Thelemic goddess Babalon, the Scarlet Woman, the Mother of Abominations. Probably so he could fuck her.

Diane steps into the ramshackle shed hidden behind a copse of trees on the field of the equestrian center. Little more than a shell, it looks like the sort of place a leather-masked chainsaw killer would feel right at home. Charred walls, crumbling wood, rusting rebar. More bugs, lizards, and snakes than she can identify. If there isn't a body buried somewhere under the floor, she'll be surprised.

Tim and Indigo are going over their gear. Happily married but look terribly mismatched. Tim's five foot four, a rail-thin black man with close-cropped hair and a neatly trimmed beard. He wouldn't look out of place wearing a business suit in a conference room.

Indigo, on the other hand, is six foot three, two hundred and fifty pounds of solid muscle and fake tits. Porcelain skin, a shock of short red hair. She's had her Adam's apple shaved and her finger bones lathed to make them look more feminine. It took her three years to get her voice where she wants it. Sometimes, Diane is still a little startled to hear a soprano come out of her mouth.

"How are we?" Diane says.

"Cutting equipment's ready, scanner's packed," Tim says. He's wearing a skintight stealth suit covered in microscopic graphene hairs that swallow light across the spectrum, so black it's hard to see the edges.

"Green across the board," Indigo says. "Scanners are good."

"The Cat?"

"All set up," Indigo says. She taps the side of an old D-wave quantum computer she salvaged five years ago and named Schrödinger's Cat. A pair of stick-on googly eyes and a cat's nose and whiskers from a party mask are stuck to the front with a note that says, *Now you see him. Now you don't.*

Indigo hits a switch and a holograph projects a scrollwork of Enochian text. There are holes in it. Letters missing, incomplete sentences, gaps like missing teeth. "Code's good," she says. "We just need the rest."

"That's what we're here for," Diane says.

* * *

When Parsons finished the Babalon Working in 1946 with the help of a man who would con him, rob him, and ultimately begin Scientology, he came out of the Mojave as renewed as Jesus. If Jesus had lived in Pasadena and spent his forty days and forty nights jacking off to classical music.

Not long after, he met a woman named Marjorie Carmen, assumed this was the Scarlet Woman, his goddess made flesh.

He was wrong, of course. She wasn't Babalon. She was an out-of-work illustrator who enjoyed orgies as much as he did. The two spent the rest of his life together until he blew himself up in his chemistry lab with a coffee can filled with mercury fulminate.

He was probably high.

"Then I don't see any reason to stall any longer," Diane says. "Last chance to back out."

"You know we're not going to," Pam says.

"Thank you, everyone. I know it's been rough. I know there have been doubts."

"We're doing this for James," Tim says. Diane hears the unspoken words, *whether we believe in it or not*, but maybe that's just her own fears, her own anxieties.

Diane has debated whether this part is strictly necessary, or whether they would be better off doing it in a conference room, a church, something a little more hallowed.

But what's more hallowed ground for what she needs than a land burned, and burned, and burned again? Where even now, when there's nothing left, she still smells smoke.

They gather in a circle, the five holding hands. Their candles are blinking cursors on consoles, rapidly cycling surveillance video. Instead of the susurrus of wind through trees, they've got the quiet hum of computer fans, the hiss of coolant.

"Yea, it is I, Babalon," Diane says.

"It is Babalon," the others say in unison. "Time is."

It says a lot about Parsons's ego, and perhaps about men in general, that the invocation he used to summon his goddess was his own creation, penned over the same year he made the tablets. *The Book of Babalon, Liber 49*. Written in a plaintive, yet demanding tone that if she were to just pay attention to him, smile at him, maybe show him some leg, or maybe a little more, he would move the earth for her. A celestial pickup line that, like most men, he couldn't imagine not working.

"Thou hast called me, oh accursed and beloved fool," Diane says.

The words flow from something that isn't memory, from something deeper, cleaner. Parsons's words shift and writhe, twisting into something far stronger until it is unrecognizable from the original. Their voices become one voice, their breath becomes one breath.

"Set my star upon your banners and go forward in joy and victory," Diane says, and falls silent. The moment hangs, time stilled for a beat, for an eternity. When it passes, Diane feels hollowed out.

"You okay?" Pam says.

Diane's vision is blurred, but goes so sharp a moment later she's afraid she might cut herself on it. "I think so. Tim, you ready?" She pulls off her top, slips out of her pants, revealing the same type of stealth suit Tim is wearing. She pulls the hood of the suit up, affixes the faceplate, the suit's HUD sending data to her eyes.

"Always," he says, his voice a genderless digital noise

through the mask. He shoulders his pack, and the two set out across the field.

Poor, sad Jack Parsons. Rocket scientist, student of the mystic arts, clumsy explosives manufacturer. He didn't get the Babalon Working wrong.

He just didn't have the tools to make it right.

Most people who even know about the tablets assume they're at the bottom of a landfill. A dozen surfaced in 2047 and went up for auction. The man appraising them was something of a Parsons fanboy. He saw something in those inane ramblings that no one could have when Parsons created them. Possibly not even Parsons himself. The appraiser ended up being the only bidder on the slates. Nobody else cared.

Diane cares. Cares every time she dreams of that appraiser, every time she pulls up that memory of James on the floor, blood spattered along the walls, the ceiling, slick and dark across the floor. Diane cares very, very much.

Pam's swarm of tiny drones zip past Diane toward the abandoned grounds of JPL. Two minutes later, Pam's voice over the radio: "Security's blind for an hour. You know the drill."

Diane and Tim bolt across the field following the objective markers appearing in their HUDs. A timer blinks in Diane's vision counting down the seconds.

One of Pam's drones has cut a line in the chain link with a laser too small to see. They push through onto the grounds.

JPL's security drones hover in the air like sharks drifting in ocean tides. Diane knows they're offline, knows that they won't suddenly come for her, weapons hot, but she hurries her pace nonetheless.

The grounds of JPL are a cracked, concrete wasteland of old dreams left to die. Once this was the center of the most amazing things humanity could achieve. Now it's little more than rubble and shattered glass.

Most of the buildings still stand, though more out of luck than anything resembling structural integrity. But the one they head for has given up even trying to pretend. When the last fires swept through the JPL grounds before it was closed, they utterly consumed this building, like a head on a pike left behind to warn others.

What remains is little more than dust, a concrete pad, a heat-warped metal staircase leading into a dark hole of subbasements. Diane layers a drone-made map over her vision, highlighting obstacles to avoid, where not to step. Good thing too. Even with the thermal and IR sensors in her faceplate, the basements are pitch black.

"We're here," Diane says into her radio. Tim unpacks his cutting equipment, scanners. He burns through concrete and conduit with a high-watt laser in minutes.

Diane helps him lever out chunks of precisely cut concrete. It's slow going because the wall's so thick, but they open up a space that hasn't seen light since this building was erected in 1952.

And inside, a military footlocker covered in dust and spiderwebs, hinges and a padlock rusted shut. By then Parsons was persona non grata at the lab. Did he put it there? Did someone else? Why?

The answers are as elusive as they are irrelevant. The slates are here. That's all that matters. They pull the footlocker out, and with some elbow grease and a pair of bolt cutters open it with a scream of cracking rust.

There they are. Twenty-five slate school tablets framed in desiccated wood and held in place by warping wooden slats. Diane lifts one carefully out to get a close look. It's either the real deal or somebody planned an elaborate joke a hundred years ago and smeared them all in Elmer's Glue.

"We've got them," Diane says, her voice too quiet to carry.

James talked about Jack Parsons and Crowley's Thelemic Church the way a twelve-year-old might talk about his favorite video game. A couple of weeks after getting the job to appraise whether the Parsons tablets were genuine, he went on a three-hour rant about how the man was a genius never getting the acclaim he deserved.

James asked Diane to marry him the next day. He wanted her to know what kind of crackpot she'd be stuck with if she said yes.

She already knew. She said yes anyway.

Whether his obsession was faith, belief, a hobby, Diane didn't really care. She trusted him. And vice versa. He knew what she did for a living. Had even helped her plan a few jobs.

And then one night he showed her the pattern.

"I think I'm onto something," James said, the 3-D projector showing a revolving cloud of symbols Diane didn't understand. There were gaps between symbols, black holes where text should be.

"What is this?" she said.

"Enochian. An occult language made up by John Dee in the fourteenth century. Unless you look at it a little differently. Then you get this." James flipped a switch and the cloud changed. Symbols shifted, numbers, formulae, equations appeared in their place. "These tablets? They're nonsense. But they shouldn't be. Enochian is just English with a different alphabet and vocabulary. Dee wasn't very imaginative. So I ran it through a script that compared each tablet, looked up similar patterns, and spit out the results. The first one that stood out was this one."

One set of equations pulled away from the rest, grew until it filled the the projection space. "This is the Caldeira-Leggett model," he said. "It describes quantum dissipation, the idea that energy is never destroyed, it just turns into something else, but at a quantum level."

"So, he wrote quantum equations to summon a goddess on tablets for an occult ritual with his come?" Diane said.

"Stranger," James said. "These were written around 1945. The Caldeira-Leggett model wasn't discovered until 1981. I've got equations here describing concepts that didn't show up until after 2020."

"Is it a hoax?"

"If it is, it's a really good one. I checked everything. Handwriting analysis, handedness, DNA. As far as I can see, this is one big quantum algorithm. Before the idea of quantum computers even existed."

"What does it do?" Diane asked.

"I have no idea."

"Diane?" Pam. Worried.

"Yeah?"

"There's a truck ten minutes out." After the fires no one comes out here, not even scavengers.

"It's Peter," Diane says.

"It can't be."

But it can, and it is. Diane can feel it in her gut, that wake of void he leaves everywhere he goes. "Trust me." But how? Diane wonders. Did he have another bug on the car? Did she leave some clue behind?

"There's an old surveillance satellite that's been parked over us longer than it should be."

"He rented time on a satellite?" He wants the tablets more than Diane realized.

"What do you want to do?" Pam says.

Diane checks her timer to see how long before security comes back online. Thirty minutes. "Indigo, can you run the algorithm?"

A pause, then, "Yeah, I'll feed them in as you get them to me."

The plan has been to scan the tablets and leave them behind. Something about hauling a hundred-year-old footlocker past security drones feels a bit risky. Indigo's job is to make sure the data scans match the gaps in James's pattern before they leave the site. Make sure they're good.

But not actually, you know, do anything with them.

At least not until they are someplace more comfortable, better lit, not looking down the barrel of security drones and heavily armed men.

"Pam, can you stall them?"

"Already did. I've got road closures up on the 210 they'll have to detour around. That'll give you twenty minutes max." But Diane needs more time.

Tim has unfolded a small table with interlocking sheets of metal that stick up along its edges like a flower blooming in fractals. Once it's powered up, Diane carefully places the first tablet in the middle of the table and steps back.

"Indigo, you're up."

Lights pop from the petals in a machine-gun rhythm bathing the tablet in half a dozen wavelengths. Two minutes later it's over.

"Got the scan," Indigo says. "It's uploading and running through the index. Give me the next one." There are twenty-four tablets left. At two minutes a pop, they won't make it.

"Can we do more than one at a time?" Diane says.

"Up to three. Resolution'll be shit, but they should be okay."

"Do it." Diane slides three tablets into the scanner and readies the next batch to go. Twenty-one.

Lights go off in a rapid flicker from the scanner, go dark. "Shit," Indigo says. "Hang on. Okay. Running it again." The scanners flash, the data uploads. Twenty-one to go. They get a rhythm going. Diane puts down the tablets, Indigo scans, Tim pulls them out. Eighteen, fifteen, twelve, nine, six. Diane begins to hope that they might just make it.

Then the scanner blows a fuse. It's a small fire, but the equipment's trashed. Diane doesn't realize that she's muttering, "No, no, no," until Tim shakes her.

"What happened?" Indigo says. "I've lost the connection."

"Scanner's busted," Tim says. "We've got three left. Diane, what do you want to do? Diane?"

"Bigger problem," Pam says. "Truck's almost here. ETA's three to five minutes." Even if they take these last slates and run for it, they'll never make it.

"Both of you turn on the recording equipment in your suits," Indigo says quickly, "and send me the feeds. Highest fidelity you can get."

"That's gonna burn out the optics fast," Tim says.

"You got a better idea?"

Tim glances at Diane, who nods.

"What about the truck?" Pam says. "I've got six heat signatures."

Diane can hear the fear in her voice. "Can you reactivate security early?"

"Yeah," Pam says.

"Wait for my signal."

"All right," Tim says. "We're live."

Diane follows Tim in a circle around the tablets, looking down, from the side, from the floor. They get every conceivable angle multiple times. The characters have to be clear enough for Schrödinger's Cat to understand them. It eats into their time.

Diane hears a pop and Tim cursing. "Tim's optics are out," she says, but keeps going. A second later hers die too. Everything goes pitch black.

"Did we get it?" Diane says, pulling off her useless faceplate. She's already running for the surface, dodging debris in the dark.

"Looks like the algorithm's running," Indigo says.

"They're almost here," Pam says.

Diane hears the sound of a rack sliding as Pam readies a gun. If it comes down to a firefight they're all going to die.

"Hold on." Diane bursts out from the darkness of the stairwell like a swimmer surfacing from a riptide. She triggers every transmitter she has on her, even sends Peter an emoji of a raised middle finger. She pulls her stealth hood back to make it easier to get a fix on her.

"Diane, what are you doing?" Pam exclaims. "You just lit up like a bonfire."

"Wait for it." Diane can hear the truck slowing at the equestrian center, then speeding up toward the JPL grounds, following her signal like rats to the Pied Piper.

The armored truck bursts through the chain-link fence, pops the curb, heads straight for Diane. It screeches to a stop a few feet from the building's foundation. Diane stands defiant as five men step out of the car. They're thugs, nothing more than monkeys with guns.

There should be six.

"Do it," Diane says.

The pitch of the JPL drones overhead shifts into a deeper whine. Diane bolts for the staircase back into the darkness, sounds of gunfire overhead.

Halfway down to the first landing her shin hits a chunk of concrete with a loud snap. Pain like she's never felt before blossoms through her leg. She tumbles, hits hard, body crumples like a puppet with cut strings. She's not sure if she's screaming or not. She's not sure it matters.

She's blind, can't walk, can barely think through the blaze of pain. Shaking, skin clammy. Shock reaches up to pull her down, but she won't go. Crawls by feel along the dark corridor. Knows this isn't over yet.

Above her, footsteps on stairs echoing across abandoned walls. The pain is too much. Her heart hammers in her ears, her breath a ragged wind she can't quiet. An oval of blinding light pops to life around her.

"Diane," Peter says, flashlight in one hand, gun in the other. "Fancy meeting you here."

* * *

"There are gaps in the code," Diane said.

"And I've been able to fill some of them based on what I know of the math," James said. "But most have too many holes. I think there are more tablets out there, the rest of the algorithm."

"And you really have no idea what this does."

"Well . . . no, it's insane," James said.

Diane responded with an attack of tickling that ended with the two of them on the floor, and James on top of her.

"I've defeated you in fair combat," she said. "And got you right where I want you. You have to tell me."

"I think it might actually summon a goddess."

"That looks like it really hurts," Peter says. He crouches down just out of reach.

"You killed him," Diane says through gritted teeth.

"I did. And I took the tablets."

"Why?" She's waited years to ask this question.

"Did you know I was a priest of the Church of Thelema? Of course you knew," Peter says. "James approached the church with a language problem. I helped him with Enochian. Do you think he knew you and I worked together? I didn't connect him to you until . . . well, after. You never knew we were friends."

"You kill your friends?"

"When they try to murder my goddess, yes." Peter's voice goes harsh, words punching out like fists. "I saw his pattern. A mathematical construct of my goddess. Mine. He explained away my faith with all the poetry of spin, rotation, probability. He tried to trap her in algebraic amber."

Peter's motive has always eluded her. Why take the

tablets? Why even care? Now she knows. And that makes this all so much sadder.

"I wept for days at what I'd done," Peter says.

"I wept for years," Diane says. "I think I win that contest."

"I wish you hadn't found them," Peter says. "They were just fine where they were. I don't understand why you even went looking."

"You knew about them."

"Of course I knew about them. Just like I knew you used them as bait to . . . *what* exactly? Lure me out here? Doesn't matter. I did what I had to. But I don't have to do it again. I don't have to kill you. I just want the tablets and all your scans. They can't exist. What if someone else found out about the pattern, and actually ran the program? I'm not going to let that happen."

"Oh," Diane says, a slow smile creeping up her face, "I have some bad news for you."

"You're serious," Diane said.

"Very," James said. "I think Parsons was onto something, not just crazy bullshit. He was trying to summon Babalon. But if he had tried to actually run the math, it would have taken him decades. So why'd he write it? He couldn't do anything with it. And where did he get all the information? He was describing mathematical concepts that hadn't even been invented yet."

"You think this goddess, this Babalon, showed him?"

"Got a better explanation?"

"No," she said. "Doesn't mean there isn't one."

"True." James began to move toward the display, but Diane pulled him back down.

"If you're looking to solve mysteries of the universe," she said, "I have a few thoughts on where you could start."

"How could I possibly say no to such an invitation to philosophical debate?"

Peter says nothing for a moment. Diane can't read his face, the glare from the flashlight blinds her. Then, "What have you done?" Diane laughs as much as the pain will let her. "I need those tablets."

"So take them." Tim has crept up behind Peter, inch by silent inch, and when he's in range swings a hammer made of three stacked tablets.

But the blow slides inches over Peter's head, the tablets shattering against the wall. Peter turns, fires. Tim drops like a stone.

"Well, that's three down," Peter says.

He turns to Diane, the flashlight playing across her, and freezes.

Later, Diane and James lay together in a pile of sheets and sweat. "You told me Parsons was trying to summon Babalon," she said.

"You want to talk about this now? All right. Parsons called it an elemental. Someone imbued with the power of the goddess. That's what he thought Marjorie Carmen was when he met her."

"What if it's not about summoning her," Diane said, "but giving someone her power?"

"Huh. I suppose. Good a theory as any."

"Think about it," Diane said, and rolled over to go to sleep.

* * *

Diane is standing. Diane should not be standing, cannot be standing. She has a shattered tibia, she is going into shock. And yet, here she is, standing.

It feels like she's looking out of the window of a car she's not driving anymore. She feels a momentary panic. A gentle voice soothes her mind. She listens and gives her consent.

"I'm not sure how you pulled that off," Peter says, "but I don't have to wonder long." He raises the gun.

"I came here to kill you," Diane says in a voice that she barely recognizes as her own.

"Funny, I came here to kill you. Hoped it wouldn't come to it, but here we are. Now, Diane, be a dear and hold still—"

"You misunderstand me, child," she cuts in, her voice like a thousand violins playing as one. "I am not Diane."

Peter doesn't hesitate. Thundering gunfire echoes through the abandoned halls, flashes of light revealing impossible images. Then the hammer falls on an empty chamber, and Peter drops to his knees.

"Please," he says. "I didn't want to kill him. I had to. Don't you understand? I had to." Tears run down his face visible in a building glow in the hall. "Forgive me. Please forgive me."

Diane leans down, kisses Peter on the cheek, gentle, a mother saying good night to her child, and whispers in his ear, "No."

And the night shatters with a terrible, beautiful light.

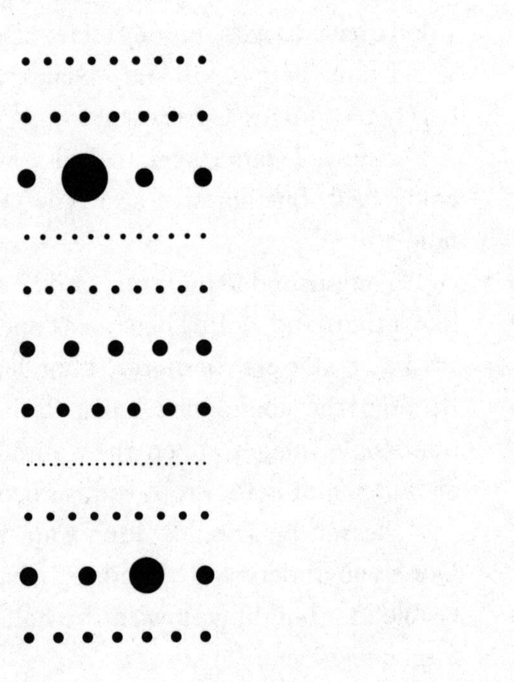

¤ ¤

PART III

A TEAR IN THE FABRIC OF REALITY

¤ ¤

PURPLE PANIC

BY FRANCESCA LIA BLOCK

Studio City

In the San Fernando Valley where I grew up, the blossoms—on the trees and purpling the sidewalks and streets so they seem to glow—intoxicated me like jacaranda wine, but also stirred in me a sense of fear I could never quite explain.

There are different theories about why the term "purple panic" is applied to jacaranda trees. For one, it's supposed to be because they bloom during student finals. Or the pollen makes it hard to breathe? Your bronchial tubes swell, you feel a pressure in your throat, difficulty swallowing. You try to cough up the scorched rags in your chest. Sometimes you swallow your own phlegm and wake, gagging and wheezing. Another theory about purple panic has something to do with paganism—panic as in Pan the nature god with his cloven hooves.

The Valley in the seventies was an apocalyptic place in its own suburban way, and I think it damaged all of us—my friends, Veronica, Beth, Tamara, our parents, and me. If you looked down while flying out of Burbank Airport, you saw the smog laid out over everything in a furred gray haze. Lowriders cruised down Van Nuys Boulevard. Hells Angels, Satan's Slaves, and the Diablos biker gangs fired weapons into the air. Police arrested hundreds of drunk drivers. The city rationed gasoline and water. A prostitute's body was found in a dumpster behind a Sizzler where, once a week, my parents and I used to order baked potatoes, garlic bread, and rare steaks served on metal plates with sharp carving knives that scratched like nails on chalkboards. A 6.6-magnitude earthquake killed sixty-five people and caused more than five hundred million in damage. I remember the shards of glass carpeting our floor and how my feet bled.

At school we feigned oblivion. But in my seventh grade typing class, Juliette McFee—doughy, acne-spotted face and football player shoulders—was sent to juvie for selling angel dust and eventually died of an overdose. Miguel Santiago—pre-Raphaelite curls and weirdly transparent green irises—sold himself for sex on Santa Monica Boulevard in West Hollywood; he was one of the first to die of AIDS. My friend Veronica had been so in love with him. A kid named Ryan Rice—red-haired and small for his age—crashed his moped in Laurel Canyon and we always wondered if it had anything to do with my friend Beth who turned down his invitation to prom. Stacy Stanton—bony blonde with braces—whose father spied through holes in the wall on her and her friends changing their clothes, passed away from anorexia before it was a common term.

And then there was Tamara.

Mostly I remember the darkness inside Tamara's house—night or day. It smelled of chlorine from the swimming pool, rotten lettuce, pee, and sweat; and her little brothers and sisters with their tangled hair ran around shirtless, the shadows of their ribs showing bruise-like through their skin. The mom wasn't home much and the dad wore sunglasses in the house. His greasy hair hung to his shoulders around a face as gaunt as Munch's *Scream.* I was afraid of him. But I didn't yet know why.

Tamara sat in the weeds and dirt under the jacaranda tree in her yard, leaned her back against the trunk, played her guitar for us, and sang in a voice like Linda Ronstadt's. Tam's favorite song was "Blue Boy" by Joni Mitchell, about a woman who is in love with the granite statue in her garden. The statue comes to life and reads her stories, brings her leather boots, and watches her dance behind a feather fan. She turns into a statue herself at the end. I remember once how, after she'd sung for us, Tamara stood up and put her arms around the trunk of the tree. Then, laughing, she threw back her head, revealing the strange premature lines that necklaced her throat, then leaned forward again and kissed the bark.

"Someday I'm going to leave this place," she had said, "and never return."

My own life, though decidedly bohemian, seemed pretty normal in comparison to Tamara's. My father was an art professor with a Jew-fro who often had his nose in a book, and my mother, with her symmetrical features and long blond hair, stayed at home cooking, cleaning, and sewing her own dresses. On the weekends, they left me with a variety of babysitters and went to parties which they came home from giggling and smelling like pot. Sometimes, through the walls of my room, I heard them fucking. They often said to me, "We hope you find someone to love as much as we love each other." They liked to refer to themselves in the plural.

After my mom died, I had to go to California to clear out her house in Studio City. That part of town has changed a lot. An adult bookstore once stood at the corner of Ventura and Carpenter. Down the street a female-impersonator bar provided nightly entertainment. A veterinarian's office clipped Doberman ears into sharp, painful-looking points. Cheap Thai food and clothing outlets filled the mini-malls.

Now Studio City has lots of expensive boutiques and salons for all the starlets who live there, and for their rich producer boyfriends. Foodie places. A farmers' market on Sundays, where kids ride ponies and parents shop for organic vegetables and artisanal cheeses. I'm not saying, by the way, that some of these changes are necessarily an improvement. For instance, I always thought the female-impersonator bar was cool, I liked the rice, mango, and coconut milk dessert from the Thai place, and once I bought, at half price, a pink leather motorcycle jacket at one of the clothing outlets. That was when I wore colors.

My mom's house was a small wood frame, cluttered to the point of hoarding with cardboard banker's boxes of photographs, cards, letters, books, magazines, newspaper clippings, craft supplies, china tea sets, knickknacks, old clothing, shoes, purses, jewelry. I had to go through everything in case something valuable turned up, like on those TV shows.

Boxes crowded every nook and cranny except my old bedroom. It looked just the same—a purple shag carpet belching dust, a lavender quilt on the sloshing waterbed, tinkling purple and lavender glass-beaded curtains. On the wall was an old Eagles poster—Hotel California, with an eerily lit Spanish-style building surrounded by palm trees. I opened my old yearbook and saw that I only recognized the signatures of three people—Veronica, Beth, and Tamara. In our senior pictures Beth stands out with her heart-shaped face, olive skin, and sun-streaked Farrah Fawcett hair. We all have our heads cocked at odd angles, fake smiles on our mouths, saintly upward gazes, and hands crossed at our throats. Actually, just Veronica, Beth, and I look like that. Tamara's picture isn't in the yearbook. It's like she wasn't even there at all.

I brought some of the banker's boxes into my old room and opened them. In one I found some photos of groups of naked people locked in embrace. Sometimes it was hard to tell what limbs went with what head. The women wore crowns of flowers and most of the men had beards. With only a mild sense of shock—because they had been, after all, seventies bohemians—I recognized my parents. My father still had his glasses on.

I also found a photo of my parents and me when I was a teenager. My parents are smiling like everything is just great. My mom is wearing a homemade paisley dress. I am standing between her and my dad frowning and there are already faint but permanent lines in my forehead. My eyes like trains coming through dark tunnels. I'm too thin and my wrists resemble chicken bones.

One picture shows me at five standing naked in a creek on a camping trip we'd taken. My parents used to bring it out at dinner parties and show everyone. "Our little water nymph," they'd say, while I quietly perished.

Besides burning our skins to a crisp, Veronica, Beth, Tamara, and I, like most middle-class girls in the Valley in the seventies, unintentionally inhaled smog, toxic nail polish remover fumes, and glitter; we drank too much alcohol, powdered our vaginas with talcum, and sprayed aerosol antiperspirant under our freshly shaven and sometimes still-bleeding armpits. It's a wonder we hadn't all died of cancer already. We did other more obviously stupid things too. We would ride in Beth's baby-blue VW Bug down Pacific Coast Highway and while she was driving Tamara would reach out the window and hand joints back and forth to carloads of surfers. Or if Beth was driving, Tamara would flash her small, pale boobs with the large aureoles at the dudes and then we'd speed away. We walked up and down Westwood Boulevard or around and around Fashion Square in too-short skirts, hoping some boys would notice us. Tamara gave out her number almost every time. We went to the beach and lay out, frying ourselves with baby oil for hours until we developed weeping blisters. We threw our bodies around at Kaleidoscope, an underage disco, imitating Tamara's moves until we gave ourselves whiplash. Once, when we were walking down PCH, someone lobbed eggs at us from a moving car and shouted, "Vals go home!" An egg at that velocity hurts like hell. Tamara cowered, head down, and started mumbling, "Fuck you fuck you fuck you"; we couldn't calm her for hours. Once she suggested that we rent a house in Newport Beach. We all chipped in, except for Tamara, and walked up and down the dark, deserted streets in our tight pastel jeans and pastel-striped spandex T-shirts until two men in their thirties or maybe forties pulled over out of the fog and invited us to their condo. One of the men was tall, blond, and tan, and wore preppy clothes. The other man was short and squat with a big seventies-style pornstache. They gave us white wine and smoked a joint with us and then it gets a little hazy after that. I'd never thought about it much until I told a therapist years later. I'd been at a party and smelled someone's Lauren by Ralph Lauren perfume, which I guess is what we wore. The dryish, flower-and-woodland scent brought everything back.

"What were your parents thinking?" the therapist asked me.

I didn't know about their orgies then. "We were teenagers. We didn't tell our parents."

"But you said they let you rent a house by yourself for the weekend. And you weren't even old enough to drive yet."

I couldn't remember how it had all happened. There was a lot of amnesia from that time. But I remember one of the men's names—Russell. He looked out the window of his luxury car, and I thought he was going to single out Beth, Tamara, or Veronica, but he pointed straight at me. "You," he said. "You're the one. I pick you." I remember feeling flattered and ashamed at the same time. Later I read somewhere that predators tend not to single out the prettiest girl in a group. Less attractive girls are usually easier prey, the article said.

I was shopping at Trader Joe's for some wine to help me through the process of clearing the rest of my mother's house, when I saw my old friend Veronica. Veronica and Beth and Tamara and I had lost touch after graduation. I think we all kind of wanted to forget our lives back then, at least I did. In some ways, my whole life since had been an exercise in forgetting. I discovered punk rock and used it to annihilate the hippie influence of the sixties and seventies. Cut my hair off, stayed out of the sun, wore only black. I went to art school in New York and settled in Brooklyn. No kids, never been married. You pick enough boyfriends who turn out to be gay or married, you give up eventually. As far as sex, drugs, and rock and roll, I prefer a few glasses of wine, a good TV show, and a solid eight hours of sleep to fucking at this point. But I do still listen to punk music and take an Ambien or a Xanax sometimes when those eight hours elude me.

Veronica looked pretty much the same except her hair wasn't feathered and she had a few more lines on her face from all the sun-baking we used to do. She didn't have many new wrinkles though, considering. In my case I probably have less lines now than I did then. Luckily someone had developed a botulism toxin to inject into our baby-boomer faces right in time for old age.

Veronica and I hugged in the Trader Joe's aisle, complimented each other, caught up. I told her that my mom had died.

"I'm sorry," she said. "Your mom was always so nice. I always remember your beautiful mom."

"Thank you," I said, numb. I thought of my mom in the orgy photograph looking like Botticelli's *Venus*.

"What are you doing?" Veronica asked.

I told her about my job in advertising. She said that she and her husband lived in the house where she'd grown up. They'd met late in life, never had kids. I knew Veronica had always wanted children. To change the subject, I asked her if she'd seen Beth or Tamara recently.

"Beth moved to the Pacific Northwest," Veronica said. "She has three girls." When she said this, Veronica's eyes turned wistful. "Her youngest just went off to college."

"That's great," I said. But Beth had never wanted kids; she dreamed of being a Hollywood actress. "What about Tamara?"

Veronica frowned but her forehead stayed smooth. "I don't know. I haven't heard from her in years."

"Do you think she's okay?" I'd worried about leaving Tamara in that dark house, about how she flashed her breasts at boys on the PCH, but to be honest I hadn't thought of her that much. And now it all felt so far away.

"I looked her up online, but . . . nothing."

"When's the last time you saw her?"

"Years ago. She stopped by my mom's house when I was home from college. She was hitchhiking. I told her, *That's dangerous*, and she just started laughing. Remember that laugh she had where she wrinkled up her nose and sort of snorted like a little calf? But it scared me. It was like she was thinking, *This isn't dangerous. You don't know dangerous.* I felt so naive. And then she took out her guitar and started to strum it and sing like nothing was weird at all. Remember how beautiful her voice was?"

I nodded, remembering Tamara singing "Blue Boy" with her eyes closed, her large, tremulous mouth. "What was going on with her when we were kids?" I asked. Veronica was the one we all told our problems to. At one point she'd wanted to become a therapist. "I mean, did you ever find out what was really going on?"

I thought about Tamara's knobby knees and elbows, her nervous laugh, the way she bit her nails down to the quick. But we were all too thin, malnourished, tired, excitable, we were all nail-biters then, weren't we? I looked down at my tasteful, medium-length, black acrylic fingernails and remembered the ripped cuticles, the way the edges of the nails cut into the unprotected tips of my fingers.

I looked back up at Veronica. Standing there in Trader Joe's, Veronica told me the story Tamara had shared before hitchhiking away.

* * *

When Tamara turned twelve, her father started to come to her room at night. In the seventies this wasn't something anyone talked about. There wasn't education about these things at school; our parents never mentioned child abuse. I think in my parents' case they just didn't imagine things like that even happened where we lived. Suburban orgies evidently, yeah. But not sex with your own kid. Now, thinking back on it, the whole thing seems so obvious. The dark house, the missing mom, the junkie-thin father with his sunglasses, the acting out. Why didn't we do something?

Anyway, Tamara tried to fight back but her father was too strong and she didn't have any weapons because her father would lock up the knives, baseball bats, and anything else that could be used against him. But then she noticed him looking at her little sister. So one night, Tamara went out into the garden and sat under the jacaranda where she liked to play guitar and sing, knocked on the trunk, and asked the tree for help. It was as plausible to expect that the tree she loved would help her as to expect that anyone else would. Then a man's hand reached out from behind the tree holding a knife, and a voice told Tamara to take it but not to ask who'd given it to her. The knife of ebony and silver had been elaborately engraved and the handle inlaid with the image of an eldritch man reclining under the low, purple-flowering branches of a tree.

Tamara put the knife under her pillow and that night when her father came to her room, she brandished it and he went away and left her alone. In the morning, she buried the knife behind the jacaranda tree. The next night when she went to go get it, the knife was gone. But a hand reached out as before to give her the knife. Once again she used it to defend herself against her father and once again she buried the knife, found it gone the next night, and received it from the hand behind the tree. This went on for several months.

Eventually Tamara got so curious about the hand, she couldn't wait any longer, so she went into the garden and asked the man to show himself. She asked three nights in a row, but he remained hidden, silent, and would only hand her the knife. She was afraid that if she tried to peek around the tree, he'd run off and never come back.

Then, on the third night, he spoke with words like rustling leaves: "You have charmed me with your voice."

"Why, thank you."

"And so I want to help."

"Tell me something about you," Tamara said.

"My name is Tom Underhill and I come from a place that is both far away and very near."

"Tell me more."

"Where I come from, the sense of time is different. If you are there, it can feel like days, but when you return you will find that years and years have past. We live under hillocks and in tree houses. We craft knives of silver and ebony and shoes and boots out of birch bark, and we eat the fruit of the golden pear tree. All our furniture is made of ebony, ivory, pearl, and gold."

None of this sounded so bad to Tamara. "What else?"

"If a child is born there with a big, fat head, eyes like burning coals, and a belly that is always hungry for food and drink, we bring them and leave them here, on people's doorsteps. In order for us to take them back, you have to boil water in two eggshells. Only if this makes them laugh will we come for them."

"That's strange. More, please."

"We don't wear any clothes. So I might shock you."

"Please let me see," Tamara said, unafraid.

The tree shook and a cascade of purple petals fell into a heap. When the wind blew them away, there stood a tall, thin man with eyes the color of the jacaranda blossoms. He looked a lot, Tamara told Veronica, like Miguel Santiago, the boy from our high school who'd died of AIDS. This man wore only a loincloth and tall, silvery boots. Tom Underhill and Tamara stared at each other for a long while in which she saw her life under the hill. They shared a bed of ebony, ivory, pearl, and gold. They ate golden pears, crafted boots and shoes out of bark, forged knives from silver and steel, and never wore clothes. Of course, they also helped endangered girls.

Then he disappeared.

Tamara decided that the next night she would ask him to help her kill her dad and run away with her. She put some clothes and toiletries in her backpack, stole—for Tom Underhill—an old, moth-eaten suit that had belonged to her father, and shouldered her guitar in its case. But when she went outside to the jacaranda tree, she found a bloody hand festering on the ground.

Growing up in the Valley, I'd heard of strange things. The hillsides where your cars rolled uphill, and the powdery-white handprints of phantom children that appeared on the trunk, as if trying to keep the car from crushing them. The little ghost girl in the glittery jacket riding a bicycle alone, in circles in a parking lot. The gardener who fell out of the tree in front of my old high school and died—if you lay under the tree you could feel some invisible force slam into you. My friends and I tried that last one, but we didn't feel even the slightest brush of contact.

"That's pretty fucked up," I told Veronica. "All that abuse really did a number on her."

"I know this sounds crazy," Veronica said, "but I kind of believe her. I don't know why. I found a criminal record for her dad online. He went to jail for possession of child pornography."

"I believe her about the abuse," I said. "I just mean the guy. And the hand. Her dad wasn't convicted of cutting off someone's hand, was he?" All of a sudden I felt really uncomfortable talking to Veronica in Trader Joe's, and I wanted to go to my dead mother's house, drink some wine, and watch TV, so I texted Veronica my number, hugged her goodbye, and left.

But on the way back to my mom's house, I felt compelled to stop by Tamara's old place. It was on a street lined with magnolia trees, heavy with waxy leaves and flowers, and most of the houses looked the same, although there were some high-rise condos too. Tamara's house had fallen apart. Shingles missing from the roof, broken windows. The front boarded up. Shrewd-eyed crows blackened the lawn until I walked up, and then they took off into the sky, cackling like monkeys. I was surprised the house hadn't been torn down yet. Property values were pretty high in the area. I'd probably get quite a bit from the sale of my mom's house, the realtors told me, once I cleared away all the banker's boxes.

I parked my car and went around the back. There was a hole in the fence so I just walked through. The pool was empty of course, cracked in spiderweb lines. It was still painted a faint shade of blue. I remembered swimming there with Veronica, Beth, and Tamara. There was this pool cleaner that chugged around on its own, and it reminded me of some kind of little robot. Sometimes I felt like it was watching us.

I guess we all developed different ways of surviving the past. I had my work, for instance, and my wine and my shows to keep away any vestiges of pain. I had New York, but I had no stories like Tamara's. I couldn't make up songs or even sing like she could, and no trees—enchanted—ever spoke to me.

The jacaranda still stood in the yard among the weeds and crabgrass. Surprisingly, it wasn't dead. I went up to it and sat in the dirt at its roots. The blossoms were out in a big purple haze, and I tried to imagine a tall, naked man with eyes that flower color handing a knife to Tamara. I tried to imagine a man's big, bloody hand lying severed on the ground. I wondered if Tom Underhill had ever come back, mutilated, to take Tamara away with him. I raised my fist to knock on the tree trunk, but then I convulsed with shivers and dropped my hand to my side.

MAINTENANCE

BY AIMEE BENDER

Miracle Mile

When we arrived at the tar pits that afternoon for our daily walk, the front gates were blocked by a measure of silver fencing, and a handwritten sign slung over the top read, *Maintenance*. A number of orange cones stood haphazardly by the entrance as if someone had shoved them there in a rush. The grass hills that we could see through the fences were empty, the museum closed.

Ana went over by the side to see if the elephant family—"the woolly mammoth family," she corrected me—was fine, the family we often talked about, especially after her own mother left last year. Almost immediately after that leaving, Ana had initiated the daily walks, and we would come to the grassy area near the museum and just stand side by side and look at them for a while, the mother mammoth in the water with her trunk up high, the father and child trumpeting at her. The child's trunk straight out, trumpeting the loudest, maybe. There it was, our family tableau. It was the one time of day during those early months of adjustment that she seemed comforted, calmed.

For those who have not seen this place, it is a real tar pit from the beginning of time, or at least fifty-five thousand years back, and this particular "lake" is leftover from asphalt mining of the late 1800s, used to patch roofs and roads, the very roads cars were driving by on every day, maybe even Wilshire itself right next to the exhibit. You can see bubbling tar in it on a daily basis from an underground oil field. No one is allowed in. Inside the pit is the statue of what Ana and I had gleaned to be the mother mammoth, halfway submerged in the tar, and she is trumpeting in terror, her tusks huge, and useless. To the side, on the banks, are the small child mammoth and the larger father mammoth, but they are just watching at the edge. They can't possibly rescue her. The tar has a thick and deadly pull, and once in, a creature cannot get out, which is one reason why there are so many fossils. Far across the tar lake, there's another adult mammoth, also trumpeting. Ana and I call that one Uncle.

Anyway, due to her own circumstances, Ana seemed to understand earlier than other children, or even other adults, how it was tragic, how it was an image of such terrible helplessness and loss, that I often wondered how the sculptor had convinced the tar pit art association or the museum board or whoever had it put up there fifty years ago to include it as the central image of the park. Had they realized what they were paying for? There's a photo of him on one of the plaques, Howard Ball, the artist himself, driving the first giant thirteen-foot-tall fiberglass beast through the streets of LA on a flatbed attached to his VW Beetle. There's no hint of who's coming next, and what the mammoth will be seeing for the rest of his sculptural life. Ball was a Hollywood special effects designer. I can't find much more about him. I've definitely looked, at Ana's urging.

Ana, on tiptoes at the green gate, said she couldn't quite see, but from her angle it seemed like maybe the statues weren't in their usual spots. I laughed. "Oh, those aren't going anywhere," I told her. "Those are some heavy sculptures. Plus, one of them is in the tar."

She had already scrambled up and over the makeshift fence that was draped between the green gates.

"Ana," I said, with fatigue.

"Dad," she said. "Wait."

She ran ahead to look closer. I could see the back of her head, her flapping braid, but I could not get an adequate angle to see for myself. She was gone awhile. I wondered if I should climb in as well. Ana is nine now, and extremely trustworthy as a child, but the tar pits are inherently unsafe, and the child has already had half her world stripped from her. Somewhere, across the country, her mother sits in a bar, and tells the bartender her sad story with those eyes that carry the most powerful concoction of yearning and distance.

I was trying to find a foothold in the wobbly fence, which was proving impossible, when Ana returned. Her cheeks ruddy from running.

"They're gone," she said, breathlessly.

"Who's gone?"

She went to the fence and tugged it open enough so I could squeeze through and together we walked over to the gated pit, where the father and child mammoths usually stood. More cones dotted the grass, laced with black tracings of tar from areas where it had gurgled up as a surprise.

She was right, my daughter: the sculptures were all gone, except the uncle, who remained, like a deranged person all by himself, alone at the other end of the lake. The father, whose giant feet had left huge holes in the grassy dirt: gone; the child, whose feet left similar but smaller holes: gone; and, most shocking of all, the mother, who had been in tar for half a century, and who would've required a mighty crane to pull out of that grip. Gone. The museum even shows us how strong it is, tar—as part of the internal exhibit, a person can tug on a pulley and feel how intensely the tar pulls back. It is difficult to manage the pulley, and imagine a two-thousand-ton sculpture inside?

"Maintenance?" I asked Ana, and she looked at me slow-lidded, with a deep world-weary skepticism that had no settled target.

We walked around the grounds to find the stone sloths, check, and the giant orange stone bear, check, which was not really a surprise, as they were obviously replicas that just stood there and told no stories at all. It was midday and felt so empty without anyone around. This was usually a crowded park, with strollers, and kids playing soccer, and a bitter man sometimes drawing bitter caricatures for a minimal fee. And the musical man, Charlie, who'd played tunes on his banjo for years by the museum entrance. He was skilled, and merry. One day, he had disappeared too.

"If not maintenance, then what?" I asked her, as we circled through the scrubby oak grove. She balanced on the white stones that rimmed the art museum, the tar's neighbor.

She shook her head. "You saw how fast the gate was blocked," she said. "They must've turned alive and walked off."

"I think," I said, taking her hand, which she still allowed me to do sometimes when there weren't peers observing, "we would have heard some news if woolly mammoths were walking around the city."

"Invisibly," she said.

"They'd still do damage."

"Well, something surprised the people," said Ana. "That note was not done with care. I just don't know what surprised them."

We returned to the internally gated area, and stood facing the lake. It was potent with emptiness. Ana didn't seem too distressed about the change, which was a great relief to me, and I wondered aloud, a little hopefully, if the mother mammoth had finally sunk to her depths. Really, I said, had they needed to depict the worst moment in the lives of these mammoths?

Ana nodded, solemn. "They did." She said she thought Howard Ball had made it just for people like her.

She had told me parts of this before: How the mothers came to pick up the children at school, so many of the children she knew, how she would watch the mothers, how others mostly could not conceive of or understand how to talk to her about a missing mother, a mother who had left because she had to leave, a mother who was not able to function. A mother she had watched, afternoon after afternoon, struggle to get out of bed, sometimes rolling her out of bed when I had to go early to work.

"He's the baby mammoth," she said, as we walked to the gate.

"Who?"

"Howard Ball."

"How do you know?"

"Well, I don't for sure," she said, skipping a little. "But it's a good hunch."

We were back at the green front gate then, and I do remember feeling an urge to look back. As if the grasses were beckoning. As if the wind had a message for us. The landscape of the park looked the same, and I searched it for a moment with my eyes but didn't glimpse anything new or notable, just almost a kind of whisper of acknowledgment in the grasses and trees themselves. I couldn't understand what it meant, or what I had heard, but when I read, a few days later, that the baby mammoth was back in its spot, trumpeting to the uncle like they were yelling at each other across the lake, I found I was not entirely surprised. I remembered that whisper, a hint of a message I could not in any way decipher. No one had any information about how the baby had arrived, or where it had been, though as I was reading the news on my phone, waiting to pick up Ana from school, I found myself wondering, for a flash of a second, if Ball himself haunted the tar pits, with some kind of surprising muscular capacities, as if he had floated above that sculpture drama for years because it was the unfinished grief of his living life and perhaps he was finally ready and able to let it go. It had taken him a long time, that was for sure.

Kids hopped out of the school gate, and Ana saw my car and hurried over, her backpack jumping on her shoulders.

I couldn't say any of this aloud to Ana, because it is my job, and has always been my job, to be the manifestation of reliability, and I could not bear to risk her looking at me with any worry on her face. As she strapped herself in, I told her the news, which she listened to intently, and we drove home, and after she had a snack, we walked over to the museum to look at the returned baby mammoth. There it was, back in its spot. As if it had never left. A small crowd had gathered; a few people were eating popcorn from an entrepreneurial cart. Earlier in the day, it seemed, the museum had rummaged around and found one of their old saber-toothed cat sculptures, and to complete the picture, and perhaps provide a distraction from the fact that they had no idea what had happened, they had dropped it in the center of the lake, clawing at the air, newly stuck in the tar, so that there was some drama again in the scene. The baby mammoth at one end, Uncle on the other, cat in the middle. It really changed the gestalt—a predator caught in the tar? Suddenly it was a triumph, like the mammoths had defeated their enemy, and the uncle and the baby were close comrades in the struggle. Ana and I looked at it for a little while, but she shook her head dismissively, and asked if we could share some popcorn, and then we went and did a little painting in the free art room with the thick, appealing brushes.

The father and mother mammoths never returned. Some asked the museum to drag the lake, just for the information, but that was expensive, and the museum preferred to spend its extra money on Project 23, the paleontology brushing of fossils that had revealed an entire functioning ecosystem in something like 2006. They'd found some tree branches, and a camel, and dire wolves, and baby mastodons and saber-toothed kittens, and no kidding, the semi-articulated, mostly complete skeleton of an adult Columbian mammoth. Who knew what was underneath the ground in this city. They found it all in the parking lot, of all places, because nothing could be more appropriate to the land's current identity. Anyway, it was impossible to imagine where the grown-up woolly mammoth sculptures themselves had gone, but a few weeks later the newspaper reported the arrival of a giant sculpture of a male mammoth in Torrance, and it seemed likely it was the same sculpture from the tar pits, though of course as before, no one had any idea how it had gotten there. It had just arrived there one morning, seemingly on its own. Once again, I was reading on my phone at pickup when the news about this sculpture came in. I had rearranged my work schedule so that I could pick up Ana on Tuesdays and Thursdays at three, which had been her mother's pickup days, even though Ana really likes the after-school programming; I just couldn't seem to change the schedule yet. Anyway, the car was hot, and I was scrolling along, and my heart skipped a beat as I was reading, because guess who had his art studio in Torrance? For all his special effects materials? Could this even be possible? What, was I thinking he was moving these statues around in the middle of the night unseen with his ghost abilities? Invisibly? I couldn't guess. The world was far more unknowable than I had ever realized, that was for sure. I just kept picturing Ball in his VW Beetle, cheerfully driving the father to the site of his own tragedy, shaking hands with the museum board, toasting, perhaps, with champagne. The father was the first one he'd made, and maybe he wanted him close to home now. I could not find any information about where Ball was buried. As I enlarged the photograph in the article, I could, however, confirm that it was in fact the same male mammoth from the tar pits; I'd recognize his helpless devastated head anywhere. Someone had hung a set of rope monkey bars from his trunk.

I showed Ana again when she came into the car and settled into her seat. She was singing some song from music class. She said she was happy to see it. She did miss the original tableau, she said, but she liked that they were showing up in unexpected places, like they were having some kind of conversation with the city.

The mother, the one stranded inside the tar, never showed up anywhere. One night, at bedtime, when we were talking about it again, as we so often did, I asked Ana if she had done it, if she had hired a crane, and a truck, and some workers, and if she had directed the whole thing in the middle of the night to give the child mammoth a new chance, a new story to proclaim. I was sitting at the edge of her bed, and she was sleepy and bore up under my hand on her hairline, the way she had as a four-year-old, when her mother was around, and she said now why would she do such a thing? "It helped me a lot at the beginning," she said, sleepy. "It's all lame and forgettable now. I liked it much better before, with its secret message."

"And what message was that?" I asked, again, because I can't help asking, over and over again, dipping myself in it, and she said, "You had a mother who was okay, Daddy. You can't feel it like I can. But it's good to see the truth so clear. It feels right, like a puzzle piece that fits."

That weekend, we drove to Torrance to visit the father in the playground, There he was, my old friend. She climbed up it and patted its back, and flung herself around on the monkey bars, but we had gotten lost on the way and it was past lunchtime and we were both more interested in finding some food, so after a few quick pets to his fiberglass head, we ate lunch together, and then drove home in silence. As we headed north, the green freeway signs about the size of those mammoths—the freeways one of our million contributions to the landscape that might one day be in a museum led by another species considering us—I thought about how it hadn't even been accurate,

Ball's tableau. From what I understood, female mammoths stuck together in herds, and the male mammoths went off by themselves. A trio family would've been a rare grouping, and more male mammoths got stuck in the tar anyway, because they were solo creatures, unable to get help. It was rare, even odd, to have a mother stuck like that. But the artist made his point, and I like to think Ana is right, that maybe he made it for her. It took a long time for her to see it, but in the scope of years we are talking about, it was like they were having a conversation in real time. She said, as a voice from the future, thank you for sneaking that in for me, Howard, and maybe he was at the celebration opening, holding his champagne, getting jovial, ill-fitting compliments from donors, and maybe he heard her in a whisper through the grasses, just as I had. I like to think of him nodding, maybe bowing a little, and raising his champagne glass, or doing whatever kind of gesture special effects designers did, and then, when the party was over, driving his VW Beetle back to his studio in Torrance, flatbed unhitched, to all the edges of lakes he had stood upon, or drowned inside, and the otherwise private nature of his sorrows.

WEST TORRANCE 2BR 2BA W/POOL AND BLACK HOLE

BY **CHARLES YU**

West Torrance

First day of summer. This is back when things were good. They're playing by the pool, the two most powerful beings in the universe. Nine and seven. You're over there and we're over here. We'll save you. Okay. Thank you.

You're over there and we're over here and in between is lava. I can walk on lava.

No you can't. You can't. We can but you can't.

There are rules, a few stated outright. Mostly unspoken. Mostly discovered in the moment, with each twist and turn as the cosmos unfurls. Which is not to say this is fantasy. The word is make-believe. As in, making something, believing it.

It's not a game. They get angry if you call it a game. It's more like a story, ongoing. Never stopping, even when they sleep. Asleep like exhausted lumberjacks deep in a silent forest, a hundred year slumber. They dream, they sleep-tell their stories. They wake up and continue. The story had been going on for some time now. Six months, maybe? Eight? Could it be a year? More, maybe. No one could remember how long. It seemed like the story had just started, or never started. Had always been.

There was once a girl.

Hey! And a boy.

Fine. And a boy.

There was once a girl and a boy, her little brother. They were little. But it was up to them to save the world.

They weren't allowed to tell anyone their story.

This made it harder to save the world. They had to save the world and keep it a secret.

Despite the lava, the universe continues its existence through lunch—sandwiches, crinkled potato chips, glasses of ice water. Then cold cubes of watermelon. Geometrically perfect surfaces and vertices. Gem pink, bloodred.

This is the kind of day he imagined. They imagined—when they were still a they. Close enough to the beach, to the airport, the aerospace cluster in El Segundo where he would, with any luck, spend his entire career. This perfect little place, decent schools, local parks, a place where they could spend the school years, and the summers in between. Days like this, stretching out, languid and syrupy.

The phone rings.

The phone rings and his skin goes cold. But this is not the call. The Call. Not the one that keeps him up at night. The one that's coming. The one that starts, *It's about your mother*. Not that one yet.

It's Helen. *Their* mother. His wife. Soon to be ex. Maybe. Probably.

Abby. Yeah. Keep an eye on Billy. Okay. Why? I have to go in to talk to Mom. Mommy's on the phone? Yeah. Say hi. Okay. Tell her I love her. Okay. Don't drown. Okay, we won't.

He slides the door shut and watches them through the glass, light and sound filtered out so that all he's getting is a silent play. Either a cosmic origin story. Or the end of times. Hard to say. Skinny legs and chubby cheeks, flush with the one o'clock sun. Helen would never let them swim at this hour.

Hey.

Hey. Surprised you picked up.

They're fine.

What's going on over there?

Well, the magic in the world is running out.

That's a new one.

Yeah, I'm interested to see where it goes.

Pause. Unasked question.

Yes, I fed them lunch. We're all staying hydrated.

I didn't even say anything.

And yet.

Billy's getting tired.

No, he's okay.

Yeah, he's okay. And he's getting tired.

How can she possibly know this, through the phone, but when he takes another look, sees that she's right. She's like some kind of all-knowing wizard. They get their omniscience from their mother. He's never contested that fact. Her being right wasn't the problem. It was her being so *certain* about her rightness. The certainty was what got to him.

What?

What?

You what? Okay, fine, he's looking pooped. They both are. What? Yes, yes, sunscreen. Trying to keep the irritation out of his voice, resenting the fact that again she's right, it's been close to—oh shit—four hours since the last application.

They'll be fine. They're coming in soon anyway. The stuff is like SPF 500. I could grout the bathroom with that stuff. Anything else?

I'm not micromanaging you, I just wanted to check.

They're fine, and for the record, checking *is* micromanaging.

As if on cue, one of them is yelling. The other is crying.

Gotta go. One of the masters of the universe is having hurt feelings. Yes, I said yes. Sunscreen, yes. Okay. We'll try to call you after dinner. Spaghetti. I'm making it.

She laughs softly. It's nice to hear her laugh. Even now.

What? Me cooking is funny.

No, that's great.

Figured I need to learn eventually. Even *I* can't mess up spaghetti.

I have confidence that you can.

You always believed in me.

He hangs up. Waits a beat—maybe this latest clash of omnipotent beings will sort itself out if he just stands here for a moment longer. It's cooler inside in the air-conditioned condo, and talking to her still takes it out of him. She laughed. That's something. That's not nothing.

They haven't noticed he's off the phone yet. He might get a few moments before one of them looks over. A moment of quiet, before they take over the world again, a temporary (very temporary) pocket outside of their ongoing saga to save the universe.

It used to be he could tell, at a glance, what the story was. Movement and emotion. Rehearsal for later. For real life, whenever that might start. The reenactment of something he'd said, working through it.

But lately, maybe in the last couple of months, he'd been finding himself surprised. Baffled at what they come up with. A word, an idea, some invention, added to their cosmology, something that feels too advanced, conceptual technology he knows did not come from him.

At the moment they're explorers, catching bugs in a cup. Dipping a plastic utensil into the pool, a tablespoon of liquid filled with millions of life-forms not visible to the human eye.

He has to remember that what he says matters, how he looks at the world, it all matters.

He forgets that. A lot. Forgets that he knows, and they don't. And that knowing is an immense and terrible power. And that the moment of going from not-knowing to knowing, it hurts. It's scary. It's all kinds of things. It has to happen, but how it happens, that's everything. How he shows them around this planet, points things out. They trust him. As a guide. From the island of not-knowing to the land of knowing.

Two ways of not knowing something. He had once known it, but had forgotten it, which is to say, doesn't think about the world that way, hasn't for who knows how long. *What is* equals *what is visible,* no less and no more. The furniture has become just that—furniture, faded into the mental background.

They, on the other hand, take nothing for granted. A knife of sun, slicing down on top of their hair. The sharp cold sweet of a mouthful of vanilla ice cream, slightly melting. Each other. Him. Words that come out of his mouth, at this point, still few enough that they have all been stored, cataloged, a crucial part of the research file that forms the basis of their project.

The project being, in a nutshell: *What is this place?*

The backyard. Not much. A landscaped rectangle, built to HOA specifications. In every corner, the requisite drought-resistant clump of succulents and scrubby plant life. Just that. Just their whole world.

Already he can feel them slipping. Billy has a couple more years, he figures, but Abby, she's right there. At the edge of the great stage. Billy maybe is dimly aware—maybe—that there is a curtain, Abby has inched up toward the curtain and soon, any month now, maybe any day now, will take a peek behind it.

He alternates between feeling he's wasted their childhood, hasn't read them enough books, or the right books. Hasn't played the right music for them. Their minds have formed, regardless, and thanks to their mother, they are turning out to be good people, smart, perceptive. Conscientious. Whatever his contribution was supposed to have been, it turned out smaller, some sprinkling of dad magic, some ineffable sense of wonder and appreciation for the world. Or so he thought. He's gotten off easy, he knows, and yet still thinks that he has something important to tell them. If only he knew what it was. He knows this: he has somehow failed them, is still in the process of failing them, and he'll continue to do it. He's contributed all right, but seemingly only the worst parts of himself, peeking out, revealing in glimpses, flashes of anger or pettiness, snatches of language that he is mortified to hear echoing through their minds and out of their mouths. His children. His children. Still not quite sounding like it's real.

Billy does a little dance. No audience. His sister isn't even watching. She's busy thinking profound thoughts about how they might get themselves out of this mess. A quadrillion miles from home, no map.

Billy, in his own little bubble, private. Now she notices the dance, tells him to stop it. He does it again. It makes her mad. Now he's doing it with glee.

Abby stops her allegory. Abruptly. Billy, glad for the opening, takes up the controls of the spaceship and changes course, a giggle, a momentary lapse by his commanding officer. Abby looks at him, watching him watch her, through the glass. She may be reading his thoughts. She may know everything. About him. Someday she will. He wants to tell her, mouth something to her, make a funny face, pantomime. What can't be said in words. Better that way anyway. If in this moment he could just show her, do that one thing, that one perfect fatherly thing.

Slides the door open, a portal. Back out into their world. Blast of sunlight and noise.

What's happening now?

We're on a mission.

On the surface of a planet.

Okay. Cool. Drink a lot of water.

We can't.

Why not?

Our space suit helmets.

She's older, by almost two whole years, so she generally sets the agenda. There are rules and if he's to exist in their world, wants to continue existing here, then he needs to play his part.

You're over there and we're over here. How do I get across the lava? You can't. The lava is hardening. It has turned into rock. Then I can walk across the rock.

No you can't.

Here the younger one pipes up. Why can't he? I think he can.

At seven, the age of reason, he has reached a threshold in his own powers. Second to his older sister, still exploring the range of his abilities to manipulate space and time. She has set the agenda, framed the problem, and he usually goes along with it. Whatever veto power he has, he exercises selectively.

He can't walk across the lava because there's a crack in it. Don't you see it?

I, I suppose so. Yeah, there it is—I see it now. Dad, I'm so sorry. We are going to do what we can to help you.

That's the boy, seven years old and full of suppositions. Billy. Not William or Will. But willing to go along with Abby's version of their story. For now.

We're on the surface of the planet. It's scary.

A look crosses Billy's face. He wants to say it. He's wanted to say it. Wanted to the first time she said it earlier in the day. He's like this. Secretly smart. Everyone knows his sister is the good student. Lost in that is the fact: so is he. But no. Everyone has a slot. He's funny guy. He's silly guy. He's not smart guy. Except that he is. Catches her in errors, takes great pleasure in them. Something deeply satisfying, important for him to do so. In the creation of reality, he can help, if she'll let him. If she'll listen. If he can get up the courage to point out to his sister the weirdness of what she's saying. The question is, will he? It's killing him a little. At risk of life and limb, he ventures:

We're always on the surface of a planet.

What?

Uh-oh.

Sometimes he shrinks from her, lets her have the win. Often she's right, and even when she's not, she can confuse him long enough to effectively win the argument through his silence. Not this time, though. He stands his ground.

On earth we are also on the surface of a planet. What? No we're not. I mean, we are, but this is the kind of planet where you are on the surface and the sky is black. We are in space. We're in space on earth too.

A moment. An infinity. Who knows. He's right, for once. Little brother has caught her in an error. She gracefully pivots out, not giving him the full satisfaction, though he gets some small joy from the victory nonetheless. Just her moment of hesitation is enough. He looks this way, to get the smallest, invisible smile of approval. A father's dilemma. Don't want to embarrass her. But don't want to deny him this moment either. The real confirmation is how she moves on, incorporating the new truth. Okay, we're on the surface of a planet, in space, at the edge of everything.

Okay, he says, ratifying this reality. The rift has healed and they can move on, secure in the integrity of their shared Creation.

Dad is over there and we are over here and in between there is no more lava but there is something worse. In between is nothing. In between used to be a tunnel through space but now the tunnel is stretching, pulling apart, like two parts of a piece of chewing gum, the connector piece getting skinny. Skinnier until it is too thin and then breaks. And then what? Billy looks worried. What will happen when the gum bridge breaks? When that happens, she explains, with unnerving patience, and here everyone is listening, even the birds have silenced themselves and the hum of the pool motor has dimmed to a low murmur:

Then we won't be able to get to Dad anymore.

And then the bridge breaks. A hole opens up in the universe. And he falls in.

It's a black hole, Dad.

Right near the edge now.

It's the event horizon, says Billy. A theoretical boundary based on the escape velocity of light, inside of which events can never affect any outside observer.

How did you know that? Never mind. He'd rather not know.

It's the rim of the world, the lip of the glass, and he's about to tip in. He had always wondered why he got such a good deal on this place. The previous owners failed to disclose the fact that the foundation was cracked, that the place is built on a fault line of reality. Virtual pairs, the fizzy sea foam of quantum reality, particles and antiparticles popping into and out of existence. Hawking Radiation. He can see it. Is he supposed to be able to see it? Maybe it's a hallucination. Or a vision. Or a doctor, in a few months, might suggest it's a symptom of things growing inside his brain. Whatever it is, he sees it now, and his kids see him seeing it, but they can't see it themselves. They are already on the other side of a divide, just a few feet away, but already it's an uncrossable gulf, already the universe forbids it. If it were a math problem, if this were a blackboard in a lecture hall, back in Berkeley (he remembers years ago, the first time he spotted Helen across the auditorium), he could isolate the problem, put all of the numbers on one side of the equation, leaving only infinities. They're over there and he's over here and in between there are the laws of space and time, foreclosing the possibility of future interactions.

A finite number of kisses and hugs, rapidly approaching zero. Sound fails them now. Notes written and left on the refrigerator, found after work, found late at night, saved as scraps of a distant region of the past. Scrawled in wobbly cursive, the unsure lines tracing out the information left here, that will persist long after he's gone, the evidence that he was their father and that, briefly, they had fun.

As he accelerates away from the event horizon now, beginning to distort, a funhouse mirror, everything slowing down, twisting and pulling from him, each moment stretching to its limit, until it's just a band of light and color. The notes are gone now, the sound is gone, everything's gone. A last-ditch effort—flashlights, flicked on and off in the darkness,

h i

d a d

w e m i s s

y o u

And then the light is too faint for human eyes to see, the point at which physics may still hold true but biochemistry fails, and now it's quiet. Echoes of their voices as babies, but those must be imagined, must be memories, still pinging around inside his head. The only thing left is the singularity, space now no longer what he's moving through but time itself. Let t be equal to a number of years, at Berkeley and then the city and then the suburbs. Let n be equal to two, a girl and a boy, and the universes they may create be large enough to get lost in, to make all of the requisite discoveries, but small enough to have some chance of finding each other in the finite lifetime of the cosmos. Here, deep in this pocket, he is neither dead nor alive, no concept of past or future applies, none of this has happened yet.

He sees his wife, accelerating away from him, their paths through space-time diverging forever. He sees his mother, in a different universe altogether, his mom in a bubble that splits into two, one healthy, one sick, and the healthy one splits again, then again splitting then splitting again, and again, and again, until there are countless versions of her, all sick, all tiny, all floating away.

And then he sees it.

It can't be.

Lights flickering.

But how?

He doesn't know the math, can't do the calculations, but finally, at last, is okay with that. Okay letting go of understanding. Dead or alive, who is to say. It will take years and it is a mystery. *Goodbye, hello, it already happened, but not yet, our future visible to us, the division between us.*

Dad, we are still here. Are you still there? Come in, Dad, come in. Over.

Dad, please. Come in, Dad.

Silence. The waves propagate in all directions. In his direction, they finally reach him. He answers.

I'm still here. Over.

Oh good, they say.

We did it. They high-five. We saved Dad from the black hole. And then it's time for some juice and crackers.

They used to ask him for stories. And he'd sigh.

Now they don't ask him anymore. They don't need his stories. And he sighs.

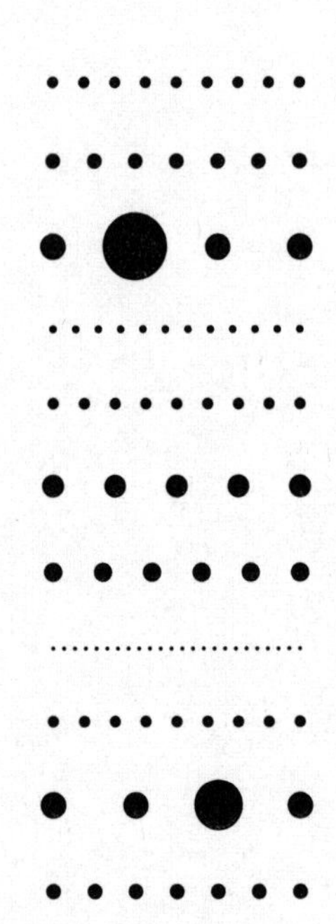

¤ ¤

PART IV

COPS AND ROBOTS IN THE FUTURE RUINS OF LA

¤ ¤

WALK OF FAME

BY **DUANE SWIERCZYNSKI**
Hollywood

We knew things would be different when the president's head exploded on live TV; we just didn't know how *different.*

At first, the killing was treated as a typical assassination. But no bullet fragments could be found, no lone gunman. In the months that followed, and as an increasing number of public figures were slaughtered in plain sight (culminating in the so-called Oscar Night Massacre), we slowly learned the awful truth.

Today, the currency of fame has been completely devalued. In its place: a new austerity where citizens are judged solely by their anonymous contributions to society. Those who continue to seek public recognition risk the wrath of faceless killers who hide in outlaw collectives known as "psychic death cults." ("Show us your face and we will destroy it," reads one line from their manifesto.) These groups continue to operate despite all law enforcement efforts to stop them.

Yet, there is an occasional investigative breakthrough. The following interview was conducted by Special Patrol, California division (SPCA), operating out of a former private "escape room"–style establishment at the corner of Hollywood and N. Cherokee Avenue, inside the "Giallo Experience." —The Eds.

* * *

Detective: Please state your name.

Subject: Hah, fuck you.

Det.: Look, we already know your identity thanks to the DNA scrape when we slapped the cuff on you. It's routine. You can have all of the plastic surgery you want, but your double helix doesn't lie.

Subj.: So why are you asking my name?

Det.: For the record.

Subj.: You might as well paint a bull's-eye on my forehead.

Det.: Look, we're on the same side here. I know what these animals did to your family. If you're completely open with us, we'll be completely open with you.

Subj.: Says the lady wearing a featureless mask, a fedora, black gloves, and speaking through a voice modulator.

Det.: [*Sighing*] It's the room. I know it's stupid, but we were told to use the materials at hand in this old escape room. I never liked Italian murder movies.

Subj.: Everyone's a critic.

Det.: [*Frowning*] I thought you said you wanted to cooperate.

Subj.: I do. But can I tell it *my* way? I feel like you're trying to push me all the way to the end, and if I don't explain it right, you won't understand.

The detective opens her arms in a gesture indicating the subject can speak freely.

Subj.: We arrived through the Burbank gateway, then made our way down the Cahuenga Pass . . .

Det.: Hold on. For clarification purposes: who is *we*? You were arrested alone.

Subj.: I was with my daughter.

Det.: I'm sorry . . . did you say your daughter?

Subj.: Are you going to keep interrupting me, or can I tell you my story?

Det.: [*Lengthy pause*] You may continue.

Subj.: We hit the checkpoint at Cahuenga and Franklin, next to those stacked glass blocks that used to read *HOLLYWOOD* before someone smashed it all to hell. Now all that's left is *OOD*, along with all of the ugly signage you SPCA guys slapped up. I signed the papers indicating that yes, we knew the dangers of Hollywood and would be proceeding anyway.

Det.: We want to keep people safe.

Subj.: If you wanted to do that, you people would level the whole place.

Det.: That would be illegal.

Subj.: Right. [*Sneers*] Anyway, we made our way down the hill and took a right onto Hollywood Boulevard. It had been a long time since I'd been down there, and the daughter noticed them first.

Det.: Noticed what?

Subj.: The holes in the sidewalk. Kind of like mini craters, with chunks of granite with little bits of pink stone here and there. Took me awhile to realize what I was looking at, and the daughter had never seen them before, so . . .

Det.: A lot of frightened A-listers paid to have their stars demolished a few years ago, right around the same time they scrubbed their names and images off the Internet. Larry Edmunds's book and poster shop was hit hard too. There's a rumor that some C- and D-listers teamed up for a late-night raiding party, driving over from the Valley and tossing Molotov cocktails into the place.

Subj.: There were still some names left on the walk.

Det.: Yeah, but nobody remembers who they were, so what does it matter? Let's get back to it.

Subj.: That's really sad, isn't it? The idea that at one time you mattered so much that they would set your name in bronze in the very sidewalk, but now . . .

Det.: Where were you headed?

Subj.: The daughter was hungry, so we stopped at Musso & Frank for a bite. I was surprised; the place was sort of packed. You know how it's divided into two rooms, one with the old bar where Hammett and Cain and Fante and Bukowski—

Det.: Are these the names of your contacts in the PDCs?

Subj.: What? No. They're writers. Famous ones. They used to hang out at Musso's and get drunk.

Det.: Never heard of them.

Subj.: *The Maltese Falcon*? *Ask the Dust*? Jesus, *Notes of a Dirty Old Man*?

Det.: Go on.

Subj.: Wow. I'd chalk it up to age, but of course, I can't see your face to tell how young you are. Anyway, we squeezed our way to the bar, mostly because I wanted the daughter to rub her elbows on the same bar top where the greats used to rub *their* elbows. There were a lot of writers there.

The place has become sort of a shrine to them, a reminder of the good old days of one-step deals and setup bonuses and COEP credits.

Det.: Did any of them recognize you?

Subj.: [*Nervous*] No . . . I mean, why would they?

The detective shrugs.

Subj.: Anyway, the funny thing is, the writers were all out in the open, no masks, using their real names and everything. Which of course. Who in Hollywood would bother killing a writer? The PDCs would have to work their way down through the deep pool of Z-listers and bottom-feeders before they'd ever target a screenwriter. They were all drinking fairly heavily, though, as if they expected death any minute.

Det.: What did your daughter order?

Subj.: Well, she was too young for a martini, if that's what you're asking. She had a baked potato with soy'r cream and a cashew milkshake.

Det.: They serve milkshakes at Musso's? I've never been.

Subj.: Really? It's practically in your backyard.

Det.: I don't spend any more time in creepy old Hollywood than I have to. But maybe you can clear up something for me. I've heard stories that the bartenders serve MND-RSRs. A single cocktail, along with a little extra juice in the sidecar, that erases your short-term memory for a day or so.

Subj.: It's possible. I didn't order one.

Det.: What did you order?

Subj.: Vegan lamb chops, French-cut style. Sautéed mushrooms. Iced tea.

Det.: No MND-RSR?

Subj.: How could I be telling you this if I'd erased my short-term memory?

Det.: Fair enough. Where did you go next?

Subj.: The PDC recruitment center at McCadden Place, right near the Egyptian. The offices were surprisingly clean. Not what I expected.

Det.: Apparently the PDCs infiltrated and forced out the previous tenants—you know, those cultists who believed that humans evolved from clams and their dead leader was coming back to earth in a spaceship or whatever. But how did *you* discover the location of this recruitment center?

Subj.: It's an open secret. Otherwise, how else would wannabes find the place? You know all of this stuff already, you don't need me to tell you.

Det.: It's important to know how you know. Why did you want to visit the center?

Subj.: To prove I'm psychic.

Det.: Do you possess psychic abilities?

The subject leans back in his chair and smiles.

Subj.: And now we come to the heart of this interrogation. You want me to predict the future? Kind of like a test?

Det.: Sure. Let's start with something small.

Subj.: Like your name? Your date of birth?

The detective visibly jolts.

Subj.: Just kidding. Okay, whatever. Hold up fingers behind your back. I'll tell you how many.

Det.: That's no proof of psychic ability. Anybody can make a lucky guess.

Subj.: Sure. But how about twenty times in a row?

The subject goes on to predict, without error, the number of fingers the detective is holding up behind her back. There are no reflective surfaces in the Giallo escape room, which is decorated like a late-1960s, upscale Italian apartment. The subject does this twenty consecutive times. The detective is impressed.

Det.: So you're one of them. The so-called gifted.

Subj.: Nope. I hate those bastards. I came to LA to destroy them all.

Det.: Then how—

Subj.: Can I please, please, *please* tell it my way?

Det.: You're the psychic. You probably know how this entire conversation is going to play out.

Subj.: I wish. But I did manage to pass the PDC screening process. Basically, I was put into a room and had to go through a series of guessing games, much the thing we just did. I thought they'd be choosier, but I guess they're just looking for butts in seats at this point. I was given a paper ticket and an address.

Det.: Was your daughter tested?

Subj.: That wasn't an option.

Det.: They just allowed her to tag along with you?

Subj.: She was close by.

Det.: You're talking in riddles.

Subj.: No, but I've got a riddle for you. A couple goes on their honeymoon. The husband returns home alone, telling police that his wife had a horrible accident and died. The police go, *Your travel agent called. You're under arrest for murder*. How did they know?

Det.: Because the husband only bought a one-way ticket for his wife?

Subj.: [*Crestfallen*] You heard this one before.

Det.: No, I'm a detective. Greed always does you in. As does trying to distract me from my line of questioning. See, your daughter is the one piece that doesn't fit with your story. Where is she now?

Silence.

Det.: And you know, I'm starting to recognize you. Even with the plastic surgery you've had done.

Subj.: I haven't—

Det.: Uh-huh. The way you carry yourself, move your hands around, yeah . . . you were fairly well-known as a character actor, back when movies were still a thing.

Subj.: Not as well-known as my wife.

Det.: Or your daughter.

The subject practically deflates in his chair.

Subj.: Fuck.

Det.: Yeah, look. I've known your name from the beginning. The DNA scrape, remember? But I didn't actually see it until just now. It's all about the tells. Human begins are hardwired to say, *Notice me, notice me*, even when it's in their best interests to stay hidden.

Subj.: How philosophical.

Det.: No, behavioral. Anyway, enough dancing around. I

was hoping you'd tell me the truth, but since you're clearly trying to pull some Keyser Söze shit on me—

Subj.: Oh, you know *that* reference, but not *Double Indemnity*?

Det.: You're just proving my point. You're right: I can't help but give you some tells too. I am young. Younger than you, anyway. But I know you've been lying to me from the beginning, because I know all about you, [NAME REDACTED]. I know why you're here in Hollywood, and what you planned to do. What I don't know is how you're alive.

Subj.: Go ahead. Tell me who I am. What I planned to do.

Det.: Your wife, former A-lister [NAME REDACTED], was one of the victims of the Oscar Night Massacre. She was up for Best Supporting that year. You were standing right next to her when her head exploded. The cameras caught you trying to help her put herself back together, like Jackie O. reaching out of the limousine on Dealey Plaza. But you couldn't. It was too late. There was nothing you could do, no way to protect her from the PDC that had targeted her, along with all of the others.

No response.

Det.: The psychic death cults decided to make a big statement that year and wipe out the entire slate of nominees. They were mostly successful. It was the most public demonstration of their powers, and it worked. But it wasn't just actors. They also went after politicians, high-profile CEOs, musicians, comedians, people who were famous for being famous . . . If you were known by the general public, you were automatically on their hit list.

Subj.: [*Mumbles*] People in a room.

Det.: Excuse me?

Subj.: Just a bunch of people in a room. I've heard it takes only a dozen, and as many as three hundred. The night my wife died, a group of people sat in a room and concentrated on her so much that . . .

Det.: Her head exploded. Like in that old movie *Scanners*.

Subj.: Don't you *dare* say that title! Especially not in front of someone who's lost a loved one to a PDC. You just don't do it!

Det.: Oh, so you're fine with slinging James M. Cain around, but I'm not allowed to get all David Cronenberg on your ass?

Subj.: What? So you *have* heard of Cain.

Det.: Not every tell is a tell.

Subj.: So you're just a dick. Why are you doing this to me?

Det.: Because you're a liar and a drunk who murdered his daughter, yet claims to have had a milkshake with her at Musso's earlier today.

Subj.: Don't.

Det.: I get it, [NAME REDACTED]. You completely lost it after [NAME REDACTED] died, her brains all over your Ermenegildo Zegna three-piece. You crawled into a bottle. But you still had a daughter at home, one who should have been the focus of your attention. You should have protected her. Especially when the PDCs started targeting child actors.

Subj.: Please don't.

Det.: By this point, the media stopped covering celebrity deaths. It was just drawing too much attention; things were spiraling out of control. But we have the files. We have her death certificate—

The detective's interrogation is interrupted by a third voice in the room.

Daughter: But I'm not dead.

Det.: [*Shocked*] Shit!

The subject's daughter, well-known child actor [NAME REDACTED], materializes in the room. She is seated next to her father.

Subj.: Honey, I told you to stay hidden.

Daught.: I'm not going to let this stinky detective tell her filthy whore lies.

Det.: I don't know how *the fuck* you got in here but this room is supposed to be *completely* secure . . . [*Panicking*] Control!

Daught.: Take it easy, Stinky. I'm a hologram. Remember that movie [TITLE REDACTED], where I was inside a computer game fighting for the liberation of all of the "extra" lives? Well, they did a full-image capture of my body and a rudimentary AI based on my mind. It was for the press junket. The idea that I would do, like, a hundred interviews all over the world at the same time. It totally slapped!

Det.: Where is this . . . hologram . . . coming from?

Subj.: The projector is hardwired to my heart. You try to pull it, I die.

Daught.: And if you kill my dad, Stinky, I will haunt you forever.

Det.: Fine. But please stop calling me that.

Daught.: What? Stinky? I don't have the sense of smell anymore, but look at you, rolling up in here with your mask and hat and gloves. You gotta be a little ripe.

Det.: I'm going to talk to your father now, okay?

The daughter shrugs.

Det.: I'm starting to see things a little more clearly now. You . . . and your daughter . . . returned to Hollywood so you could pose as a psychic and infiltrate the PDC who killed your wife.

Subj.: Correct.

Det.: How did you intend to do that?

Subj.: Math.

Det.: [*Stares at him*] You're going to have to explain that.

Subj.: But first let me come clean. After the daughter and I first cleared the SPCA checkpoint and hit the boulevard, we didn't proceed directly to Musso's. First we stopped at a tourist shop on Hollywood and Cherokee. Directly across the street from where we are sitting right now.

The daughter is now wearing star-shaped sunglasses.

Daught.: I got these ace shades.

Det.: That place is an eyesore. All they sell is cheap junk celebrating a place that doesn't really exist anymore.

Subj.: You know what else they sell? Handheld cattle guns.

Det.: Like the one we found on you when you were arrested.

Subj.: If you're going up against a psychic, accept no substitutes.

Daught.: Did you know it can lobotomize a telepathetic with just one pull of the trigger?

Det.: I *did* know that, sweetie.

Daught.: Don't *sweetie* me, Stinky.

The detective frowns.

Subj.: And after I bought the cattle gun, we went to Musso's, where . . . You were right. I did ask Ruben for a MND-RSR.

Det.: That's why you brought your daughter along. So she could tell you where to go next, without you having to consciously remember.

Daught.: My dad's a silly drunk.

Det.: You went to the PDC testing center and got your certification . . . also thanks to your daughter.

Daught.: That's not very nice.

Det.: What's that?

Daught.: The middle finger you're holding up behind your back.

Det.: Just testing a theory.

Subj.: Hey! She's a kid, you fuck!

Det.: Okay . . . so now we have motive, we have a weapon, and since you passed the PDC test, we have the means. But I still don't see how you thought you'd make it out of there alive. I mean, just the sheer numbers.

Subj.: Which is why I did the math.

Det.: Go on.

Subj.: There are three known psychic death cult gathering places: the Egyptian, El Capitan, and, of course, the Chinese. If you don't have the clearance—the stamp on your inside wrist—they kill you on sight. As many SPCA officers have discovered. But once I had my official clearance, I could step into any of the lobbies.

Det.: Why is that important?

Subj.: Because that's where they hang the headshots.

The detective makes an "and . . . ?" gesture.

Daught.: Of their victims, stupid.

Det.: Oh.

Subj.: Early on, there were hundreds of amateur psychic death cults. You get enough people with latent psychic ability, then add a handful of activators powerful enough to draw upon that energy, then boom, you're ready to start killing famous people with your mind.

The daughter makes an "exploding head" gesture with her hands while pursing her lips.

Subj.: They recruited most of their members online, from the comments section.

Daught.: Trolls.

Subj.: But pretty quickly they figured out there was strength in numbers, and the inevitable consolidations and mergers started happening. Now, there are only three PDCs, all of them operating in the abandoned ruins of three Hollywood theaters.

Det.: The Egyptian. El Capitan.

Daught.: Which specializes in child stars. The *jerks.*

Subj.: And the Chinese, which I soon discovered hosts the PDC responsible for killing my wife. Her headshot was hanging on the wall.

Det.: Former movie theaters . . . that makes sense. What

other place could accommodate hundreds of people and have them focus on the same thing?

Subj.: Exactly. When I walked in, they handed me a paper program with that day's targets. As you can imagine, the pickings are very slim these days. It was pretty much Twitter comedian [NAME REDACTED], famous-for-no-good-reason [NAME REDACTED], some YouTubers, a magician.

Det.: What do they actually show on screen?

Subj.: Whatever footage they can find of the target, run in endless loops, usually a couple of hours, sometimes three, until the target is dead. Then the headshot goes up in the lobby.

Det.: How do they confirm the kill?

Subj.: Sometimes they don't. But mostly, the strongest activator in the room maintains a link with the target, so they're able to describe the death in gory detail, right down to what the target was doing at the time. It's not all head explosions, by the way. Some get off on total organ failure, extreme vertigo, the illusion of drowning.

Det.: That's sick.

Daught.: I know, right? Maybe you're not so stinky.

Det.: Thank you.

Subj.: Then there's a break for the restroom, a trip to the concession stand, and then some trailers that give clues about tomorrow's slate of targets. Though, like I said, it's getting pretty obscure by this point. Do you remember anyone who appeared in *The Mephisto Waltz*? Or *Assassination of a High School President*?

Det.: The Chinese has over nine hundred seats; we estimate, based on surveillance footage, that there are over five hundred people inside for any given show. How did you think it was possible to kill them all with a single cattle gun?

Daught.: Like he said, math.

Subj.: Math, and testing the limits of free speech.

Det.: How's that?

Subj.: Basically, I yelled *fire* in a crowded theater.

Det.: You what?

Daught.: Actually he yelled, *Animal Control raid!* That got people moving pretty quickly.

Det.: Do they still call the SPCA that? Animal Control?

Daught.: Pretty sure you faceless fascist freaks started it. You do consider the telepathetics "animals," don't you?

Subj.: Anyway . . . and here's the math part . . . I reasoned that the activators, the most powerful psychics in the room, would sit in the best seats in the house. The very front row.

Det.: You're joking, right? Those are pretty much the worst seats. The middle is where you want to sit.

Daught.: Uh-uh. For me, it's either the back row or no go.

Subj.: Whatever! I figured the activators would be running in the near-dark toward the fire exits on either side of the screen. So I hid myself in a curtain there and nailed as many passing psychics as I could with the cattle gun.

Daught.: BAM. BAM. BAM. I helped.

Det.: You're a hologram . . . you don't have fingers.

Subj.: No, she kept the "Animal Control raid" thing going to whip everybody up into a panic.

Det.: And this plan of yours . . . did it work?

Subj.: Not one bit.

Daught.: It was the ultimate dad fail.

Subj.: There were simply too many of them. I lobotomized maybe a couple of dozen before somebody knocked the gun from my hands.

Daught.: And then it was all over.

Det.: Which brings me around to the question I keep asking: how are you still alive?

Subj.: Once they caught me and scanned my mind, yeah, I was pretty much toast. They had some fun with me, controlling my body, making me do strange things.

Daught.: Not your finest hour, Pops. [*Giggles.*]

Subj.: But then they saw the potential in me. How I could be a huge help to the psychic death cult movement.

Det.: Why would you do that? You hate these people. They killed your wife!

Subj.: But they also made me see the truth. You're right—I was responsible for the death of my daughter. And I needed to be punished.

Daught.: Don't look at me. That happened *after* my brain was scanned for the AI press junket thing.

Subj.: And the PDC, in turn, admitted culpability in the world they had inadvertently created. Instead of celebrities and politicians . . . real live human beings, flaws and all . . . we are now controlled by the cult of anonymous fascists who demand total social control, ruling behind masks and truncheons.

Daught.: Pssst. He means people like *you*.

Det.: That is not fair. We are struggling to barely keep this world together!

Daught.: Admit it, Stinky. This is why you allow the PDCs to continue to operate. Why you *didn't* level Hollywood. No famous people means that the anonymous jerks can rule from the shadows.

The detective stares at the hologram.

Subj.: So I cut a deal.

Det.: What . . . kind of deal?

Daught.: In Pop's defense, he really didn't have a choice. *You* try keeping your mind together when dozens of telepathetics are playing around in there. You're lucky he's not wetting his pants and barking like a dog.

The detective stands up from her chair, horrified.

Det.: What did you do?

Subj.: It's what I *didn't* do.

Daught.: He didn't resist arrest.

Subj.: And I didn't let you speed me through my confession. I've kept you here in this room for at least twenty minutes . . .

Daught.: . . . while I hacked into your Animal Control personnel files, including photos and video interviews without your mask, and transmitted them to the Chinese PDC.

The detective, visibly panicked, runs to the door and begins to pound on it.

Det.: Let me out!

The daughter whispers something in her father's ear.

Det.: For [NAME REDACTED]'s sake, let me out of this room!

Subj.: Look on the bright side, Shannon Morris.

The detective, pulling off her mask, turns to face the subject and his daughter.

Daught.: You're going to be famous.

End of interview.

JAGUAR'S BREATH

BY LUIS J. RODRIGUEZ

Angeles National Forest

Los Angeles's jagged terrain exists because this ground is volatile. Quakes and other ruptures have crunched land, lakes, rivers, forests, savannahs, up and down, back and forth, over millions of years into the Santa Monica and Santa Susana mountains, the Verdugo Hills, with uneven mounds dotting many of the city's communities—Echo Park, Elysian Park, Hollywood Hills, City Terrace, Silver Lake, Topanga Canyon, Malibu. I can name many more neighborhoods where homes precariously hug dirt and granite along the most daunting street curves. Then there are the San Gabriels, the mountain range that separates the woody and biodiverse northern Los Angeles and western San Bernardino counties from the Mojave Desert. This range is part of the larger Angeles National Forest, skirted on the north by the San Andreas Fault.

So, it was bound to happen. The Big One. The world burping and heaving like a sick dog. An upheaval of biblical proportions. Still, nobody imagined it would be like this.

I'm Lorenzo Salas, but everyone's called me Lencho since I was a kid.

I'm thirty-five and have lived in LA for thirty years. As a migrant from Mexico, my first neighborhood was Watts.

Then we moved to LA's harbor, surrounded by refineries and port smells and container ships. My father worked in a steel fabrication plant. He picked up skills—fixing old engines and forges and cutting machines. Skills he passed on to me. Finally, after leaving home, finding my own prospects, getting married, I ended up in northeast San Fernando Valley—Sun Valley, to be exact.

One morning, I awoke to a particularly beautiful day. Low eighties. No clouds. The brightest blue canvas above our heads. Smog missing, but not missed, brisk winds had pushed the dirt haze to the ocean. I walked outside of my ranch-style home and took a breath; I felt my lungs hang on to every air molecule like long-lost family. It had been ages since this atmosphere bellowed with health. Somewhat surreal.

"Want your cafecito, Lencho?" my wife Betina asked from the other side of a screen door.

"'Horita voy," I said, hesitating a little as I reflected on that day of all days.

Then God lifted up His shoulders, on a Richter scale of ten. In pajamas, Betina and our two small kids ran out of the house to my arms. Terrain and structures crumpled like paper. Paper buildings, paper homes, paper streets, paper people. A noise erupted like a giant machine gear had broken in midturn. Fires exploded—gas pipelines ruptured, electrical lines crackled in swinging arcs, freeways tumbled. Dust swirled upward, covering the sky. The quavering may have been around five minutes, who knows, but it felt like forever. After the first jolt, other shakes of seven to six kept everything unstable for days. Panic and fear gripped the city. Violence and looting followed.

The City of Angels turned into hell's smelter.

* * *

"Santos, mi'jo, do you see anything?" I whisper to my thirteen-year-old son, who cradles a laser-bullet automatic on his lap while peering past a ridge overlooking the crevices and canyons of a particularly dense section of the San Gabriel Mountains.

Our guerrilla resistance group is "Jaguar's Breath"—jaguars being those preconquest animals that roamed the forest and jungles with ease, close to Tonantzin, Mother Earth, close to seed, sprout, and greenery. The battalion consists mostly of people with Mexican and Central American origins. My first lieutenant, Rufino, is Guatemalan—with Mayan roots—a hardened survivor of the child concentration camps along the border whose parents were deported. My wife Betina is a long-haired, dark-eyed Salvadoran who grew up in the Valley. My brothers Lalo and Chilo, also Jaliscienses like me, are among our warriors. Until the Big One, most of us worked hard and followed the law. But then the laws became chains that enslaved us. My children, Santos and Carolina, are growing up in mountain caves, where their homeschooling includes wilderness survival and armed defense.

"Papa, something's moving," my son says.

Through the thick brush I notice the shiny back of a walking drone guard with the letters *AFP*—for "America First Party." This is a killing machine. The AFP—which we call "Amfirpas"—controls the US military.

I radio back the drone's location. Santos and I then scramble beneath the entangled branches. Another routine patrol.

I didn't expect to spend my middle age with a young family living under nature's whims like a hunted animal. After the Big One and the series of quakes that followed, we thought the worst was over. Boy were we wrong!

When the dancing finally stopped beneath our feet, the roaring and whirling from above became daily occurrences. Weaponized helicopters and jets flew by in formation, like a flock of synchronized birds. The government used the disarray throughout Southern California to implement martial law, including curfews. All civil liberties suspended. Any person or group that dared to protest was gunned down, jailed, never heard from again.

The commander in chief—a dude named Woodson—declared himself "president for life" with Amfirpas' blessing. People took to the streets in most states; soon the whole nation fell under his dictatorial grip.

"We will bring law and order, no matter what it takes," Woodson stated on every TV and radio station. Bespectacled, with blue eyes and black hair drifting toward gray, in another time or place he'd have been a stern school headmaster.

The state of siege included registering anyone who needed work into a mandatory national job database called LifeSecure.

I found my way to the LifeSecure offices that popped up in a clearing among the rubble.

"I'm here to sign up for work," I told the uniformed agent who manned the door. I ended up in a vast cavern with plastic chairs filled with unemployed men and women.

"How does this work?" I asked another uniform behind a desk.

"Private companies in need of work go through our

database for possible employees—especially now after all this mess," she said. "You may work a few days, several months, or even years. We provide a small stipend when you aren't working, but only if you keep registering."

What she didn't say—and I found out soon enough—was that we worked for starvation wages. More importantly, we had no choice about registering. Those who tried to opt out were caught and held in giant "noncompliance centers"—a new name for what used to be prisons. They were caged behind razor-wire walls, no news in or out. You didn't even have to commit a crime.

People forget how industrial Los Angeles used to be. LA wasn't just Hollywood, beaches, sunshine. Even the Valley once had a GM auto plant, a brass foundry, aerospace assembly factories. This kind of employment was all but gone by the year 2035. I understand that in the 1980s, the whole country swung dramatically from manufacturing to technology. For most of us the jobs went toward Walmart, Home Depot, and Target. Then those disappeared as well.

LifeSecure replaced what used to be Social Security, Medicare, housing subsidies, and employment offices. It controlled everything from work to education to public health and transportation in a seamless partnership between corporations and the state.

When I signed up for LifeSecure, I wrote down the skills I had in machine repair—digitized, remote-controlled machines soon dominated the landscape, and this seemed viable as jobs went. Nonetheless, most work became robotized. The rest of us competed for the few jobs that programmed machines couldn't do. I'm still young, but I became less and less important for the economy. Nobody had to say this—you felt it with every fiber of your being.

"Lencho, come back to camp with Santos—we have food," Betina's voice is cracking on the two-way.

"Got it—over and out," I respond.

Santos obeys dutifully when I tell him to fall in. I'm sad he and Carolina, age eleven, have to be soldiers, missing out on childhood, innocent memories, and even things like normal fear—of the dark, the bogeyman, fairy-tale creatures. Here fear is real, but we can't stay afraid for long. Fear has to turn to focus, determining the best course of action to take. Then we have to flow—the two other "f's" added to the reptilian brain reactions of "fight, flight, or freeze."

In the mountains, we train to think on our asses, as we say, and figure out the best option among many as quickly as possible. Over time, this becomes instinctual.

A large kitchen sits below a canopy of trees. Other battalion members gather to eat. Besides the modern descendants of Mayans, Aztecs, and other first peoples from Mexico and Central America, many mixed with African, European, Asians, from centuries of forced and unforced mestizaje, there's a Korean-Japanese father who helps serve food. A former Crip from the 40s streets in South LA is setting up buffet tables. A family of Oaxacans who used to pick our food in sun-drenched fields, now cook our food. A white skater punk kid, who grew weed in his backyard, now grows veggies hydroponically underground in our caves. Even a few bearded bikers with their leather jackets still on their backs help maintain weapons and machines along with me and my brothers. Most of us are hard-working, law-abiding people who finally said, "Enough is enough."

With everyone's hands, backs, and ingenuity, we've built tunnels for miles embedded with sleeping quarters, storage rooms, weapon stashes (mostly holding stolen ordnance and guns), and central living cavities where we can hang out away from the "eyes" of drone guards.

On my way to the food tables, I stroll over to Betina and kiss her. Carolina runs up to me for a hug. The other fighters greet Santos and me with yelps and handshakes. At times like this, we are family, compas, safe. But they are brief moments, snatched in time.

"Man, every day there's more aircraft," Betina complained just weeks after the first earthquake struck.

"They're bombing areas outside the city," I said. "I hear there are people in the deserts and mountains fighting back."

"Pobrecitos . . . I hope they get away," Betina said as we slept on blankets—our boy and girl nearby—on the floor of a massive compound. These structures were hastily erected by civil servants no longer bound to the government. People in clusters made their way to the compounds with what little they had. Betina and I arrived with the few things we salvaged from our buried and largely burned-out home in Sun Valley.

Betina had a hard time leaving behind our family photos that weren't destroyed. For me, it was the books I'd spent years haunting secondhand shops to collect. I loved every frayed page, black ink on white, and their unfolding secrets. I only managed to take one box. Many nights I spent reading a bio of my favorite historical person, the

Mexican revolutionary Emiliano Zapata. I wasn't one to write in books, but then I found and underlined his famous quote: *It's better to die on our feet than to live on our knees.*

This gave me courage for what was to come.

Most people in the outlying areas were the poor and pushed-out—every race, color, political view, and creed. The central city was now white, all money, people who didn't work but owned everything. Okay, there were some black and brown people among them, since the salient feature was wealth, not skin color.

Anyway, another earth-shattering event occurred that had nothing to do with tectonic plate shifts. The America First Party—the white supremacist group holding all the political reins—declared war on "undesirables." At first they targeted the usual suspects—Muslims, blacks, gays, antisocials of any color, and those who opposed martial law. As things go, these included whites who wanted equality for all. Amfirpas thought by dividing us, pitting races or genders or some other divide against one another, we'd be too busy quarreling to fight back. For the most part they were right! Many people—those who have *not* been killed, jailed, or exiled—were doing just that. But a growing number of fighters from all over the country united against the "One Party, One Law, One Way" culture that Amfirpas manufactured.

They were all now "enemies of the people."

"Amfirpas has attacked City Hall, the police station, and killed elected officials in LA, the county, and the state," Betina gasped, echoing the news on the radio.

Most stations had been closed down. Only "official" reports were allowed, especially from Fox News, which took over all major TV news outlets. A lot of regular radio bands were also gone within weeks of Amfirpas' invasion, but new guerrilla stations sprung up—the airwaves were one place where clandestine broadcasts continued to report.

I suspected this wouldn't last long.

Just then my younger brother Paco made an announcement. "I'm joining the protesters," he said. "I can't just sit here day after day, not knowing what's going to happen. I got to get out there."

Lalo and Chilo both responded in unison: "Don't go."

"They're coming after anybody who goes against Amfirpas," Lalo said.

"Lalo's right," I said. "Maybe wait a few days. When we can see how things are going, we'll all go together."

"I've had it up to here—since I lost my wife and daughter in the earthquake," Paco said, tears welling in his eyes. "I'm just a walking ghost." He grabbed a hooded jacket and made his way to the exit. "I'll be back. I'll let you all know how it goes."

Paco traveled to Downtown LA with a group that wanted to peacefully challenge Amfirpas' rule. This group had placed flyers on walls and utility poles for the demonstration. With Paco gone, the rest of us waited anxiously around the radio listening to a clandestine station. At first everything about the protest sounded fine. No police or soldiers appeared on the streets. Then a reporter said that gun-toting machines were moving along Broadway toward the throng of people.

"Oh no!" Betina shouted.

Soon blasts rang out. Voices and shouts followed. The radio signal died.

We found out later that Paco had been killed along

with hundreds of others. Bodies were piled up and burned. For days on end, I drowned in depression. Most days I couldn't get out of bed. Lalo and Chilo reacted in their own ways to this pain. Yet Betina helped with her quiet but palpable strength. She was always the steadier of the two of us. She was also fierce when she had to be—I never doubted she'd be able to handle any painful event or decision.

"It's time to fight," I told Betina after the drones in the air and on land decimated much of what we loved in LA. "I don't see any other way."

Each week, more of those in the compounds left for the deserts or mountains, melting away until these places felt half-abandoned.

"What if the neighbors in and around here turn us in?" Betina said. "Like they did with the Reyes family."

She was right. Government agents had come as the Reyeses had loaded up their minivan to leave. Officers led them out in plastic cuffs, bruises already forming on their faces, off to the noncompliance centers—where they were subjected to forced labor and indoctrination.

"We'll take only essentials and sneak out in the dead of night," I said.

"And the babies . . . we can't leave them here or with others," Betina said. "They'll have to join us."

"Entiendo . . . they'll be trained if they're to survive," I said with a dry throat. "If we don't prepare them now, even as small as they are, they'll be picked off like baby turtles."

The four of us—followed by my remaining brothers and their loved ones—wound up on the mountain range, living off the land, digging tunnels for days and days, as well as gathering supplies, weapons, and whatever else we could get in our city raids. With hundreds, then thousands, who came our way, we got everything done.

As we labored on our defense preparations, the whole world became engulfed in the cataclysm. Several nations came together to stop Woodson and Amfirpas. The US government pulled their immense resources as the world's largest military and struck back. Nuclear attacks destroyed the major capitals of Europe, except Russia, which as a capitalist oligarchy was allied with US interests. Israel and Saudi Arabia were also in cahoots. Latin America was rained upon by conventional bombs and most countries capitulated early. But many provinces and states continued to push back. Same in Africa, Asia, and Oceania. Japan also didn't go along, but a nuclear blast annihilated Tokyo, and the traumas of Hiroshima and Nagasaki brought government surrender.

China was fractured. And the Koreas united with US prodding, although bands of heroic fighters dogged such unities. The Philippines also joined officially with the US, but the population became hostile, with armed groups surrounding Manila, close to retaking her. Mexico and Brazil were in similar conflicts, although deaths there became considerable.

The United States' much more technologically advanced war machines just mowed down as much as they could, with collaborators in those developing countries massacring villages and poor people.

Pervasive death proved to be a great restraint to organized defiance.

However, here—in the good old United States—all was not well for Amfirpas and their metal unmanned "soldiers." The resistance was spreading everywhere. I heard of battles won, lost, land taken, retaken, and heroic efforts against vast odds. The larger Native reservations had not fallen. Many outskirt areas of big cities were in the hands of guerrilla fighters. Interestingly, units formed in rural areas, rife with Evangelicals and right-wing ideologues, and took up arms.

From our forest hideouts we descended into the cities and suburbs for midnight raids, moving in and out undetected, then hiding in interlocked tunnels and dense foliage that extended to the Tehachapis. Jaguar's Breath became a scourge to the vast hydra-like government and economy that were destroying and controlling most everything else.

But for us whose allegiance is Jaguar's Breath, the America First Party will never control our souls, our minds, our capacity to stir in strategic silence. Like a jaguar stalking.

"Pass the chile, carnal," I exhort Lalo across the way from the makeshift table made of downed trees.

"Hey, where are Santos and Carolina?" Betina asks with scowled forehead.

"They were just cleaning up," I reply, looking around. "They should have been here a long time ago."

I get on my radio to contact Santos. No response.

Then we hear it—the chortle of a large machine as it breaks through a cluster of trees. A walking drone. We pick up our weapons, of which only the laser-bullet guns can penetrate and damage these metallic monsters.

Suddenly I see the terrified faces of my children. They are inside the drone behind bullet-proof plexiglass. I can't hear them, but I see Carolina's mouth is open, screaming.

This hulk of a drone has found them and with its powerful springlike arms picked them up and pulled them in. I move swiftly to the side and begin firing around the base of the drone so as to immobilize it without hurting the kids. Others around us also move, but a few are gunned down by the drone's automatic blasts. Betina leaps around to the back of the machine—it looks like it's alone. But we know it's signaling our location.

Rufino manages to shove a magnetized digital bomb below the drone's underbelly and then scurry off. With the push of a button, the device goes off, creating a precise hole in its main body, spreading shrapnel in all directions while we jump for cover

The detonation stops the drone dead in its tracks. I climb up and begin forcing the outer door open so my kids can get out. Betina scurries to join me. We have no time to lose. Our warriors are already entering the tunnels and sealing them; one entrance is left unsealed for us. With grunts and yells, we jerk the door open. Santos and Carolina jump out of the drone and rush toward the tunnel. No time for hugs.

In a minute or two, this area will be saturated with bombs and fire. Only the tunnels can keep us safe, although we also have to move deeper and deeper, away from our outside kitchen and dining stations, which will be utterly destroyed. We leave the dead outside; the wounded have been hurried in, bellowing with pain.

"These fascists are such cowards," Betina says after we find haven in a darkened section of back tunnel. "They have machines do all the fighting. They only face their victims in camps and isolation wards when their captives can't fight back. I'd like to see one of those Amfirpas people up close, stare straight into their eyes, while I cut their throat. For now, we're only destroying machines. What we need to do is get the people who created those stupid drones and robots."

"You're right," I respond. "I just don't know how."

I feel helpless. Most of what we're doing is defending ourselves with a few forays to the closest communities to get what we need. We have to do something wildly unexpected to get to the heart of our enemy. It's time for us to strike.

Months later, we would unleash a desperate plan. We would move against Woodson's son who lived with his family in the Bel Air section of the city. There were unpaid workers from noncompliance centers, those who supposedly "took" to the indoctrination, in the fancy homes of this neighborhood—one of the few that had been rebuilt after the Big One. These people did the landscaping, kitchen work, laundry, and house cleaning—many consisting of the same Mexicans and Central Americans who used to do this, albeit at low wages, before the natural and unnatural upheavals.

Unbeknownst to the exceedingly well-off owners—made up of corporate heads, investors, financial officers, and high-end government bureaucrats—we had most of these workers on our side. They only pretended to comply so they could infiltrate such places.

Nathanial, an older black veteran and scrappy computer genius, who had ended up homeless until we recruited him to our cause, created electronic communication devices that linked our agents among the obscene rich to Jaguar's Breath in the mountains. At our command, these agents were to disable security systems and open electronic gates—and subdue any human security guards they found.

"Nate, are you set up to signal our people when I give the word?" I asked.

"No problem," he said. "But remember to wait till everyone's surrounded Woodson's home—everything depends on timing."

Our plan was to kidnap the younger Woodson family and bring them back to our confines as leverage to end this madness—or at least buy time to replenish our numbers so we could conceive and implement more brazen actions.

Carrying this out was risky since the Woodson family was hardly ever alone—but we had to try.

Slowly, quietly, in measured moves, we climb up a green section of newly carved-out canyons and ravines surrounding Bel Air. There's an enormous house on iron stilts. Opulent, with nice cars lining the road leading to the mansion, people in party attire are going in and out. They've been partying here on a weekly basis. These are the money-and-power people, who let the generals direct the drones for our demise, yet never have to see the wreckage, blood, and gore those machines inflict. They have a copious amount of leisure time—to party, play golf, watch screens that show their wealth accumulating on our backs.

What the machines end up doing in the mountains or deserts—or even what happens in the noncompliance centers—doesn't mean a thing to these people. They are secure that "business is taken care of," and never have to know what actually occurs.

Betina is leading a group of fighters up a ridge. Rufino is in charge of another group. I'm leading the third. This time around, Santos and Carolina are left in a new tunnel we just excavated in the mountains. Going to the very heart of the rich enclaves in Los Angeles, heavily guarded, will mean many of us won't make it back. We make the dangerous trek through debris and wildlife to get there, avoiding machines, to get as close as we can. Even with razor-wire fences, concrete and steel walls, and drones scattered about, we finally get to the house. It's the first time we've gotten this close to our adversaries.

"Wait for my signal, everyone," I say carefully into my radio.

I'm thinking I won't come out of this. But I see Betina's determined look; Rufino's leadership; Lalo and Chilo and all the other fighters climbing diligently toward who knows what. This inspires me.

"Ready . . . on my mark: cinco, cuarto, tres, dos, uno," I say as we all jump up and fire toward the house; drones hear us and rush over to where we are. Most thoughts leave as I aim and shoot, and the uproar removes all other sounds and sensations from the air and ground. But we're Jaguar's Breath, we're the guardians of soil, sun, and whatever decency is left in the world.

For a dreamlike second, Betina, Santos, and Carolina appear like faint apparitions in my mind as drones begin training their guns on me. But they don't fire. With Nate's expertise, our agents in the house managed to hack into the control boxes and digitally disable the drones.

We realize that electronically run machines have a weakness—humans.

A loyal team is there alongside us filming everything, including the taking of the family. They'll relay the video to guerrillas in our new hideouts, who in turn will broadcast the images as far as they can to embolden other rebels wherever they may be. It'll show that Amfirpas is vulnerable, that it can be gotten, that others can carry out similar attacks on an ongoing basis. It shows there's a way to win.

Jaguar's Breath is not just fighters, we are planters and nurturers of seeds for a final victory that we may or may not all live to see, but which will sprout and one day bring forth a prodigious harvest. When all hope appears gone, due to earthquakes or oppression, as long as there are these seeds, the world can always be renewed.

GARBO ON THE SKIDS

BY A.G. LOMBARDO

Downtown Los Angeles

Quis custodiet ipsos custodes?

Tonight the Skids are quiet, the Santa Anas finally ebbing away, only warm ghosts rattling dead palm fronds above the sidewalks. Patrol Officer Travis walks his beat east on 5th Street, toward San Julian. Shabby facades, shuttered offices, iron fences glow under flickering streetlights. Above, the ruins of apartments and buildings seem to stab with their jagged, burned walls into smoggy skies. The street is clogged with rusted cars jammed together overflowing onto sidewalks; tarps, car doors, sheet-metal scraps hide people living beneath. Voices fill his ears from the sunglasses-mic: backup, riot in progress at the Boyle Heights Alien Detention Center. Travis relaxes, not his call, way beyond the barbwire walls and guard towers of the Skids: a vast swath of central LA that stretches west from Old Broadway to the Los Angeles River. The Skids is a walled patchwork of shanties, dorm blockhouses, and ruins where the dispossessed, desperate, down-on-their-luck and undocumented eke out their lives. A faint scent of jasmine in the whisper of Santa Anas almost masks the acrid smoke from October's perpetual fires. He passes the ruins of the Panama Hotel, some homeless tents anchored to its brownstone, its windows above darkened with cardboard.

No helmet covers his black crew-cut hair tonight, flecks of gray in his roots and sideburns. A violation of protocol, but the helmet's too heavy, the uniform stifling in the heat: black, boots, gun, and smart-stick; the coal sunglasses and bulletproof fabric that gives him a plastic automaton outline.

South toward 6th Street. He passes old San Julian Park, now a slag heap of rubble from the quakes and fires of '32, then rows of tents, camping chairs; five-foot-tall mazes of shopping carts and trash bags filled with the detritus, the sad stories of the Skids, of haggard men's and women's faces as they warily watch Officer Travis pass.

A ZED—zone enforcement drone—flicks past high above, like an inky shooting star above the Skid's fortress walls and barbwire webs. Here, in the fire-raked ruins and crumbled warrens, are slum rooms and squalid apartments. The corporate high-rises that once loomed here are long gone, reduced to heaps and ruins after '32's swarm of superquakes. The companies retreated west, as if in a final stand against the Skids: now, only their choppers dare to cross the Skids, ferrying CEOs through the darkness.

He's reached the Angelus Inn, its two-story pancaked rubble, only its second floor inhabited, pink and teal colors incongruous among the sidewalks clustered with panhandlers, drunks, addicts. A searchlight from the walls north of the Skid zone sweeps past him.

Across from the Angelus, the ruins of the collapsed four-story SRO hotel looks abandoned, but the upper floors are filled with Section 8-ers. He's reached the Simone Apartments, burned, tilted on its foundations, condemned like its inhabitants . . . its windows shrouded with sheets and cardboard; its iron rails lean, half pried from scorched walls. An old woman clutching her canister of liquor ration glances down at Travis as she hurries up the crumbled steps of the Simone's courtyard and into a dark alcove.

As he passes a cinder-block wall and rusted, abandoned dumpsters, he glances down a walkway that separates the Simone from the half-toppled walls of the old Marshal House Apartments. A distant security light reflects broken glass on the walkway beyond the padlocked fence. Travis stops. "Cam on, infrared, double mag," he whispers. His camera-glasses instantly filter to infrared, probing the walkway with crimson, magnified light: the window of a lower unit's smashed, a turquoise purse on the pavement, splayed open, lipstick, a wallet, scattered plastic cards.

Officer Travis lumbers over the fence: the uniform, the smart-stick, his gun, he feels heavy, like a space-suited explorer in some parallel world of dark, drowning gravity. "Mag off." Carefully stepping around the purse and its spilled contents, infrared beams glow into the dark room: an overturned antique TV and cheap, narrow table; a broken glass on the tile floor. "Police! Anyone there? Police!" Silence. Drawing his gun, Travis clambers through the window, careful to avoid shards of glass frowning from the frame like fangs.

A room, its door ajar, shines milky in his infrared vision: the gun's laser-pointer is a white line tracing the walls. Travis slowly moves into the darkness, through a tunnel of ruby infrared. A bed, something on the bed. He finds the wall switch and flicks on the light. "Infrared off."

A naked woman's sprawled atop the sheets, her wrists

tied to the metal bedposts. Someone's spray-painted the walls in purple paint: an *S* slashed with a line, the familiar symbol meaning death to the Skids, the homeless.

"Target off," he says softly, and the line of red laser light vanishes from the gun's muzzle. Travis stands before her, holstering his gun. Scarlet ligature lines on her wrists under the strings tied to the cheap metal posts; greasy blond hair swept back as if it had been pulled; eyes shut, indigo and mascara smeared on the eyelids; red lipstick halfway across her cheek; a sleeping face, emaciated, pale, like a face born at a different time that might have stared into a fashion camera lens instead of whatever horror had broken into her life; her legs still spread, her blond pubic hair light, shiny; skin alabaster, young, oiled and creamed, as if pathetically or bravely pampered despite her exile into the Skid zone; round, full breasts spill over her starved, jutting ribs, pink nipples still erect.

Travis feels her warm, bound wrists: a pulse, slow but strong, steady. "Travis here, I need paramedics and backup. Marshal House Apartments, second floor, northeast rooms, possible sexual assault, suspect at large."

"Roger, Officer Travis, dispatch on its way," the voice in his ears answers.

He looks around. A small end table and lamp knocked over; a sliding closet door open, boxes and dresses and clothes heaped on the floor; a dresser in the corner, drawers open, mounds of clothing, underwear, socks on the floor, a pile of cheap costume jewelry.

Travis looks down at the girl, her red fingernails limp above the tied strings. Is there flesh dug from her attacker under those nails? He recalls the feel of her warm, soft wrists, and electricity tingles through him. The room seems to fade away, as if he's floating above himself, over the room and the woman, like another observer, or a hovering ZED. His heart thumps inside his rib cage as he leans down, closer. She smells like apples and mint. His fingers brush and rub her nipples. A hand runs slowly, gently down the inside of her smooth thigh, cups the soft, warm mound between her legs—

Her blue eyes spring wide open and she gasps.

He jumps back as she stares up—at his face, at the ceiling, at nothing—like a corpse shocked for a terrible second back across a forbidden boundary, from the mysteries of the dead and back into the world of the living . . . then her eyes roll back to glistening white and close. He steps closer: she's slipped back into unconsciousness.

"Travis here, sweeping second-floor location, over." His mic startles him as he lurches through the doorway: cops and paramedics rush down the quake-tilted corridor toward him.

Inside the tiny living room, Travis briefs a detective and two cops from Central Division as paramedics work on the woman in the bedroom. The lab boys are setting up in the hallway, waiting for the medics to clear out so they can examine the crime scene. Detective Gerard grins at Travis: a ruby light, the size of a teardrop, glows from the corner frame of Travis's dark glasses. "You can turn your camera off, Officer Travis."

Now he can see, in the small translucent menu bar in his peripheral vision, the camera's red indicator light. "Camera off," Travis whispers: the crimson drop fades away like molten fire.

The room begins to slowly spin around him.

"Goddamn things," Sergeant Flores grins. Their voices

fade in and out as a cold sweat prickles, envelops Travis. "I'm always forgetting myself. The important thing is that you turned it on."

He can't remember . . . her body, like a flame blurring everything . . . the camera . . . it was on the whole time . . .

"Next year you can put in for the brain-scanner model," Officer Ludlow says. "A sexy voice'll remind you."

"Not me, I don't want voices in my head." Detective Gerard vapes a cigarette. "I don't care how many extra credits they pay us . . . So what have we got here?" Their electronic tablets are out, set to record Travis's preliminary report.

Travis licks his cracked lips, folds his arms to secretly wipe the sweat from his palms.

The medics angle a gurney from the bedroom. Travis watches as she's trundled out, strapped and swathed under sheets on the stretcher. An IV pod hangs from a rod, its tube snaking down under the sheets, dribbling clear liquid; an oxygen mask covers her face: her smeared-mascara eyes mercifully still closed.

"God! You're insatiable!" Reina laughs as they enter the front door.

"Steinbeckia random '26," Travis says. Pillars of blue sparkling light erupt through the kitchen door, down the dark hallway, and the office niche near the fireplace: holograms of a man dressed in a mask, silver jumpsuit, and combat boots, shouting techno-rap music.

Travis lifts her off her feet in a bear hug, his hand working between the legs of her short cotton dress. They're kissing as she unbuckles his belt; he's already hard.

He pulls her dress over her waist and they fuck on the

wood floor of the dim living room, bathed in the blue glow of the gyrating holograms. Travis holds down her wrists. He can see the sofa and divan under the large windows that look east over the barbwire walls snaking along the concrete dry Los Angeles River; the armchair with the yellow quilt; the red sable footstool, the brown cocktail table near Reina's head.

Travis closes his eyes, moans, spasms, and comes.

"Me! Travis!" Reina's voice finally breaks through the sonic music from the holograms. "You're hurting me! Music off!"

He opens his eyes. Silence, the holograms vanished. He sees his fists squeezing, pushing her wrists against the wood floor. "Sorry, I'm sorry," releasing her as he rolls onto his back, panting.

Reina turns, pushes up, sitting next to him. "Shit! You get so . . . carried away." The olive skin around her lips seems to crinkle when she frowns. She rubs her wrists.

Travis gazes at her upturned wrists, at the reddish abrasions. "I'm sorry, baby." He gently lifts and kisses her left wrist over and over, massaging it as he stares at the ruby band, *his* mark that seems to deepen with red blood.

The bedroom door is closed, she's asleep. He silently straightens the paisley throw rug rumpled from their love-making. Travis resettles the miniature holograms on the cocktail table that were also jostled: he and Reina, vacation trips, a few friends. The antique granite dial-face clock on the fireplace mantle says 1:11 a.m. Around the clock are more holograms, Reina's miniature ballerina and circus figures, a crystal vase of yellow roses, a framed Picasso print—*Girl Before a Mirror*—centered above the fireplace.

In the corner is the office niche with its little wicker chair and desk. He sits down, extracts the patrol glasses from the drawer. "Computer, Axon, download menu," he whispers. An indigo hologram projects from vents in the desktop: a red, white, and blue hovering wall, the website of the Axon camera program, then the download screen. "From October 3, forty-one." At the bottom of the hologram, in the *from* and *to* filter bars, the numbers *03 10 2041* appear. The file projects before him, bathing his face in blue light: *Time-stamp 03 Oct 31 22:44:12 . . . Duration 00:06:02 . . . Status Device/Cloud.*

His palms are damp. The camera was on six minutes and two seconds, from about the time he entered the apartment's window to when Detective Gerard reminded him it was on. Everything that happened was in that sliver of time, though it seemed like an eternity, fractured, a dream. The video exists on the camera and in the cloud. The department, to manage data, kept body-cam videos in the cloud for thirty days; if by then no evidentiary retrieval came to light, videos were deleted.

Twenty-five more days and he'd be in the clear. November 2. An eternity. *Just a few weeks.*

"Play vid," he whispers. He slows down, replays *her* like an erotic daydream: the bound, languid wrists . . . the ruby ligature marks . . . her sleeping face, scarlet-smeared lips parted . . . his fingers kneading her breasts above her emaciated ribs . . . his hand tracing down her milky thigh. He resets the video before she can gasp and blink open her eyes. The red spidery scars across her wrists . . . caressing her downy mound . . . Reina's bruised wrists . . . his face flushes with heat, his groin aches with desire, an electric shock tingles through him, he can't think anymore—

"Delete file. Close down." The hologram vanishes. It is done: the video's erased from the Axon download server, the only copies in his patrol glasses' memory chip and the cloud.

He scoops up the sunglasses and pads back to the bedroom. *Her blood-etched wrists . . . her breasts . . . thighs . . .* but her face flashes in his mind, her blue eyes springing open in alarm, staring up in horror. What did she see?

Seventeen days

Travis walks south, into the Skid's night silences. In the distance, a searchlight beam sweeps past, like a strange moon orbiting in the copper, smoky skies. As he passes San Julian Park, he rings the melted iron fencing with his smart-stick, all the meth-heads and winos scattered inside the park's rubble and in their lean-tos and tents looking up warily; a darkness has seeped into him, except for the strange fire in his belly. *Sexual assault under color of uniform . . . no statute of limitations.*

As he heads past the Angelus Inn ruins, his palms tingle. *What is she doing up there in her little shithole?* Travis walks past rows of homeless tents, tarps, piles and trash bags of their belongings and scraps. Two men sit in front of the Simone Apartments, drinking booze from their ration cans. *So beautiful, that body wasted here in the Skids.* An ancient black homeless woman stands before him, arranging bags in her shopping cart heaped with the street's fortunes.

"Get that shit out of my way," Travis hisses, and kicks the cart: it topples over the curb.

"Why you do me like that!" the woman shrieks.

"Let me see your ID, Skid."

The woman scowls and slowly extends her left arm. Travis painfully wrenches her hand as his glasses scan her upturned wrist: a ghostly translucent menu appears in the periphery of his lens:

Evelyn Bradley-C
HP ID RG44561
DOB 04/18/73
Warrants 11: List? Y/N

All Skids were classified A, B, or C: A's had no warrants, could sometimes get day passes, and had family or contacts outside the Skids; B's had warrants and no contacts outside the zone; C's were quarantined with a nasty little zoo of diseases: only A's had a slim—theoretical—chance of escaping the Skids one day.

"Whad I do?" Her wizened eyes brim with tears. "Hurt me," rubbing her wrist, "goddamn poh-lice."

"How 'bout those warrants? Fucking Class C. Maybe you got C4 in your shitty little cart. Fuck off before I run you in." Last month, two terrorists disguised as Skids detonated shopping carts filled with C4 explosives hidden under their rags and bags near a checkpoint in Little Tokyo, killing seventeen cops and forty-one Skids. Since '22, when California split into four states—Jefferson, Steinbeckia, Los Angeles, and Orangebeachland—Russian spies were infiltrating from the Aleutians, worming south through the coast's balkanized upheavals. Then in '23, the East Coast fragmented in sympathetic agony with the West. By the time of the Constitutional Convention in '24, the West and East Coasts had seceded, and it was too late to stop the waves of terror attacks from Russia, ISIS, and

China across the walled and fortified patchwork of the Pacific and Atlantic free states and the Midwest's isolated new republic, Great America.

The old woman, shaking her head, struggles to right the heavy shopping cart.

As Travis stomps past, he gazes into the dark, ruined alcove of the Marshal House Apartments. *What did she see? What does she remember?* A dark gravity gnaws at him, pulling him up toward the apartment, toward her room, to her . . . Gritting his teeth, he walks toward 5th Street and the abandoned rescue missions. *Assault under color of uniform . . . fifteen to twenty years behind bars.* Maybe he'll see some action on Wall Street: a domestic-violence call, a brawl, a vaccine or food-line riot, someone or something he can strike at.

Fifteen days

Officer Travis knocks on the white, paint-peeled door. The broken, twisted corridor of the Marshal House Apartments reeks of marijuana, DDT, and the mint scents of Calidream vape smoke; a scrawny kitten slurps from a saucer of instamilk down the hallway.

The door cracks open, revealing a chain lock, then her face: blue eyes, full red lips, her greasy blond hair in a bun, perhaps more radiant in the squalor of this place, like a Madonna on the Skids.

"Lindley?" he asks, but he knows her full name—Gret Lindley—and much more from the case files. "I'm Officer Travis."

Her eyes sweep up and down his uniform.

"*B. Travis*," she reads his chest name tag and Travis feels himself finally exhaling a breath. "You're the one who . . . found me."

"That's right."

She seems to study his face for a moment, her blue eyes expressionless. If she slams the door, calls the bureau, makes a complaint, the first thing Central will do is review his body-cam video in its ghostly cloud limbo . . . but he has to know: what did she see, remember?

The door gently closes. Travis stands for a moment, a man balanced on a cliff. A chain rattles and the door opens wide.

"Come in."

He steps inside. She's wearing faded jeans, a baggy, long-sleeve maroon sweatshirt, and white slippers. The sweatshirt covers her wrists . . .

"I was just making coffee. Would you like some?"

"Thanks." He sweeps off his patrol glasses. For a long moment she lingers, staring into his gray eyes.

She nods and steps behind a Formica counter: old, boxy appliances from decades ago, the ones sometimes seen in pawn and thrift stores in the Skids: microwave, a hot plate, mini fridge, a sagging cupboard. Now he can see, in the electric light, the cracked walls and ceiling buckled, slanted from the quakes. Filling two cups of rusty water from the tap, she heats them in the microwave and pulls out a jar of Folgers Classic instant coffee from the cabinet.

Travis looks around: the window opening out to the walkway has been blocked, a slate of scrap wood screwed over its broken panes; the cheap table's back against the wall, the old TV atop it, the cracked tiles swept clean of the broken cocktail glass. A shabby orange La-Z-Boy chair, a stack of boxes and books and magazines—old ones made from paper—leans against the wall. He furtively glances at the closed bedroom door.

She places two steaming coffee cups on the small table in the kitchenette. "Sit down."

Travis sits on the chrome chair; he feels awkward and heavy with his gear. He glances at a page cut from some ancient magazine—a black-and-white photo of a beautiful woman's face—taped to the wall.

"That's Greta Garbo," she says. "The old movie star?" Travis shakes his head, uncomprehending, sips bitter metallic coffee. "We kinda share the same first name. Gret-A, for Classification A, get it?"

"Yeah." Gret Lindley's an A-Skid, no warrants, diseases, some family or contacts outside the zone.

"She's kind of my idol, I guess. Independent, never let men push her around. I'm an actress too. Just extra work, or I wouldn't be stuck here. I had an audition last month in Dreamland." Travis nods: Dreamland's slang for the media zone, a fortress that stretches miles across LA State, from Malibu beyond Hollywood to the burned ruins of the Observatory, where all entertainment is manufactured: film, music, subscription channels to the West and East Coast free states. "I won't be stuck here forever. I'm working on a sponsor."

An awkward silence as he sips coffee. There's only one slim chance to escape the Skids: some kind of rich angel looking out for you, someone with a pile of credits in the bank to pay for your bond. Travis gazes down at his glasses folded on the table, at the secrets behind those smoky lenses. *She's gorgeous enough, cleaned up and some food in her, bait for the right sponsor, maybe some fat cat oozing bank credits from the Beverly Bel Air zone.*

"I don't know what would have happened if you didn't find me," she whispers. "I feel . . . ashamed, the way you found me and all."

"Cops see a lot of shit." Travis sips coffee. "Your safety is all I—we want."

She frowns. "Is there anything new with my case?"

"It's active, still early in the investigation." Silence. Does she suspect what every cop knows, that Central, that all the bureaus, don't give a damn about Skid-on-Skid crimes? You're a ghost if you're on the wrong side of the walls and the sentry gates and the searchlights and the ZEDs, or east and south toward the old ghettos before Cali broke up and away, the trans and gay and alien zones and the red-light districts. The only certainty is death, cremation, all that's left is the ID chip to be gouged from your wrist, wiped, and implanted into the next registered zoner.

"I was so stupid," she shakes her head. "Letting that guy take me home . . . from the Cave, that dive on Boyd Street?"

Travis nods. Boyd skirted Little Tokyo's red-light zone: *An unemployed actress . . . a whore . . . figures.* A handful of bars like the Cave littered the borders of the Skids, which corruption made porous, where those with enough credits trolled for the desperate, for whores and drugs and slaves and organ "donors."

"But you know all this from the police report."

"Yes ma'am."

"Call me Gret. Shit, I owe you my life maybe. So this bastard that raped me, he'll never get caught, will he? No one gives a fuck about Skids."

"We have two fingerprints, but it's no good without a match." In the police report, Lindley's memories of her rapist were understandably murky: medium build, gray eyes, and black hair, clean-shaven, a strong chin and thin small nose, about six one in height. The description fit dozens of men, even Travis . . .

She nods and seems to stare down at his patrol glasses. The suspect's description: perhaps she had blended her attacker's appearance with Travis . . . or worse, remembered only Travis as he stood before her beautiful, open body—for a second he's in the bedroom, her mascara-smeared eyes popping open, wide blue pupils gazing up at him or beyond in horror—

Travis glances quickly down at the tabletop and his patrol glasses: yes, the glowing red eye is off; why does she keep staring at them? He licks his lips, wipes the perspiration from his palms against his trousers.

"*B. Travis.*" She's only reading his tag again. "Brian? . . . Bill?"

"Blair."

Lindley glances at the gold wedding ring on his finger. "What's your wife's name?"

"Reina."

"Queen . . . or is it princess? That's beautiful."

A folded arm of the sunglasses blinks green. Travis slips them on, hears the dispatcher's voice reporting a disturbance on Wall Street; the call's not for him but he drains the coffee and stands. "I have to go. Thanks for the coffee, Ms. Lindley." Better to leave now: he feels like he's balanced on a tightrope . . . guilt . . . loathing . . . a sickening fear inside him . . . and heat, if he could just reach out and take her—

She shows him to the door. "Officer Travis . . . I don't want you to think that . . . I mean, this has never happened to me before. I don't take strange men home. He promised to help me, said he knew producers in Dreamland."

"You were drugged, it's all in the toxicology report. Goodbye . . . Gret." As she holds the door open, he can see the ruby line of the ligature marks around her pale wrist, like a kind of erotic bracelet . . .

The door closes behind him, the chain rattles, and the lock clinks. Travis walks down the jagged hallway. Behind him, the kitten hisses.

Twelve days

In the bedroom: two orange candles on end tables dance rust-glows against the walls. Along the opposite wall, atop the long mahogany dresser, sits an extinct conch shell suspended in crystal, Reina's collection of tiny cactus pots, a hologram of them vacationing at a parched winery up in Jefferson State; Travis's plastibadge, his strange, C-shaped handcuffs that worked by encasing the wrists in a kind of force field, and his gun. Teal and milk drapes are drawn over the large window, blanketing southern views of the Los Angeles River. Facing this wall is a huge bronze mirror and framed prints of old towns and villagers that Reina bought when they went to New Baja and down into Nada-Land. An oldies hip-hop song, "Tunnel Vision," blares as Kodak Black dances and sings, like a blue ghost in his swirling hologram.

Reina's straddling him on the edge of the bed, slowly pumping up and down, moaning. After a while, he gently lays her down

Travis turns and grins, the handcuffs glimmering in candlelight, swaying from his extended finger: the antique chrome handcuffs, lined with red velvet, with the little skeleton key in its lock.

"What's the charge, officer?" Reina smiles.

"Exposure . . . decent exposure . . . very decent."

Reina smiles. He lifts her left arm to the silver bedpost, and locks the cuff loosely around her wrist to the post's filigreed rung. Snapping her right wrist to the bedpost, Travis slowly kisses her breasts, her belly button, then his tongue slides between her legs.

Jay-Z's hologram sings "The Story of O.J." as Travis pushes between her thighs and enters her. "Oh Jesus yes," Reina moans, her fists clattering the handcuffs against the metal rails.

Travis shudders and comes. He opens his eyes, slowly pushes off her, sits on the bed's edge. Reina's brown eyes close as he leans down and kisses her on the lips. His fingers brush her erect, dark nipples, then his fingers start to slide down. "I need a Coors." He gets up, puts his hand on the doorknob.

"Hey, aren't you forgetting something?" Reina jangles the handcuffs.

"Hmmm . . . I don't know if I'm done with you yet." Travis's gray eyes shimmer darkly in the candlelight.

"That's not funny."

He grins. Quickly unlocking the cuffs, he sits on the bed, kissing the inside of her left wrist: the red lines are fading, but he can see them, like ghostly webs.

"I got an idea." Reina smiles as she snaps and ratchets a cuff around his right wrist.

"No." Travis quickly stands up, unlocks it, and sets the cuffs on the dresser.

"Can't take it, huh?" Reina's lips crinkle into a grin. "You always have to be in control."

2:13 a.m., an empty Coors can on the desk. Travis watches

Gret's breasts as his fingers knead her nipples, pink, small, so different from Reina's sand-dollar, chocolate areolas. Over and over, the hologram loops: his fingers gliding down her thigh, his hand pressing into the blond tuft between her legs. "Replay," he whispers. Gret-A, endless, opens wide her blue eyes in shock and gasps, like a thousand Gret-A's in a dream's conveyor belt, into his own darkness.

One day

Tonight's shift is like the Skids have been wrenched into some alternate world. The Santa Anas churn smoke from fires peppering Griffith Park's toxic dumps, and the Skids smell of ash. Time drags, as broken as the streets and ruins and addicts and vagrants he lurches past, a ghost, a robot in his black uniform.

The night sky is like blood from the fires. Officer Travis avoids San Julian Street, the apartment, the room, the woman, all of it . . . *this place, it soaks into you, poisons you like a Class C Skid* . . . his life has somehow been hijacked, violated by that whore up in her tenement . . . he doesn't want to think that this darkness could chew a man up from inside. At the corner of San Pedro and Winston, a young brown man wearing a sticky white T-shirt sells Mexican sodas from a cart.

The digital clock inside his lenses reads: 9:31 p.m. An hour and fifteen minutes until the video is deleted from the cloud.

A vacant lot, its chain-link fence festooned with Mexican rugs and piñatas for sale: colorful, cheap-fabric images of Martin Luther King Jr., Che Guevara, Michael Jackson, Obama, then piñatas of Great America's President Kid

Rock. The vendor, an old woman with a brown, leathery face, squats on an instamilk carton. He passes the facade of the shuttered, burned Food Mart, rainbowed with graffiti.

A mound of clothes and junk, abandoned by someone. Two teens—shirtless, pale, and gaunt like cadavers—argue, wrestling over a beat-up bicycle; they stop and glower as Travis looks them over but turns the corner. The gray ruins of the shuttered LA Mission & Kitchens is spangled with new graffiti:

Jefferson's got water tons
Steinbeckia food n' sangria
Orangebeachland all d' sand
LA got Judgment Day

He keeps replaying how hours ago at the start of his shift, which seems like years, Detective Gerard sat hunched over his desk, working his leads, chain-vaping. Were they watching him? Tying up a few loose ends before they arrested him?

Day zero

Travis gazes out the plexiglass of the rising elevator, grateful to be back home, out of the hot, still night reeking of fire. The world is new again, his world, as if reborn from the Santa Anas' ashes. Below him, the gray scar of the Los Angeles River winds south toward the concrete horizon of the Boyle Heights detention complexes, and northeast toward the burning pyres of Griffith Park and beyond. From this fortified building northwest of the Skids, the shimmering ruby lights of hovering ZEDs and the walls and guard towers that checker across the zones seem silent and distant, another world.

He presses his thumb into the scarlet eye of the scanner lock, and the concrete door slides open. "Reina?"

Inside, columns of blue light throb in the darkness: holograms in each room and down the bedroom hallway flicker and revolve.

Travis turns, like a prisoner transfixed, the holograms scintillating, surrounding him like glowing demons: the body-cam glides closer to the naked girl, her wrists raised above her, crucified on the bed, but her face is out of the frame. The camera floats in blue haze, closer, lingers as his hands rub her breasts. A hand, fingers trace down her thigh. His hand probes between her legs.

"Blair . . . tell me again," Gret-A whispers: her blue eyes are open, black mascara and red lipstick perfect.

"It's no good with Reina." Travis feels sick, dizzy: it's his voice. The red time stamps bordering the videos spin and count madly, reflecting on his face like blood-etched codes.

"Say it." The body-cam angles above her face. Her upturned, bruised wrists, her fists clenched to the metal bedpost, but the knotted strings are gone . . . Now a man's hands cuff her wrists to the post's rods, the chrome cuffs lined with red velvet . . .

"You're all I want," his voice echoes from the holograms. "Gret-A."

Reina stands in the living room, bathed in the shifting prisms of color. "How could you!" she screams.

Her hands cuffed to the bedposts in shimmering blue pixels. "Tell me again . . . Blair . . . tell me again—"

Travis grabs her arm. "Reina!" Four Gret-As moan

around him, blue eyes staring up at him. "It's no good with Reina," his voice booms and echoes through the rooms, "no good with Reina—"

"Don't touch me! Fuck you!" She wrenches free, tears in her eyes. The gray door slides open and she runs, disappearing down the slate corridor.

"No, I was safe . . . the cloud's empty . . . just clouds up there," he hisses. "You're all I want," his disembodied voice seems to bounce between the shifting holograms. "Gret-A." Blue shadows crawl across him as hands squeeze breasts and fingers glide down thighs in glittering pixels.

Sick, the walls spin in the blue pillars of light and his stomach heaves. Talking in her apartment, she taped him, mixed it all up . . . fingerprints, *it's no good with* . . . out a match . . . what's your wife's name? *Reina* . . . *your* safety is *all I*—we *want* . . . Goodbye, *Gret* . . .

His car's parked a few blocks away, tucked in the shadows of the abandoned warehouses of Industrial Street. Travis wears jeans, his face shadowed under an indigo hoodie as he passes through the Skid's eastern security checkpoint along Central Avenue: extending his palm up, the cameras above scan the ID implanted in his wrist and the gates click open. He passes under the wall's arches and towering strands of barbwire, a ZED twinkling high above like a red star. His fists digging into the sweatshirt's pockets to hide the hidden weight of the gun: it's around midnight, and the Skids aren't safe even in daylight.

He crosses San Pedro Street, trudging west, past homeless tents and crumpled, sleeping bodies under cardboard and blankets. Walking briskly north up San Julian, he ducks behind a dumpster as a searchlight glides along the jagged, ruined rooftops. No moon tonight, the hot air is heavy and still, tinged with faint smoke from the fires.

Travis slips into the Marshal House, the fractured hallway dimly burnished with amber light from lamps above; moths skitter around buzzing bulbs. He creeps past a door ajar, the minty scent of Calidream vape smoke and a faint radio fading behind him: *"And from Great America, President Rock today warned the East and West Coast free states that harsher security measures and increased sanctions . . ."* At her door, his fist finally relaxes around the gun in his pocket. Folding out the tiny rods of the picklock, he silently works the tools in. His thoughts are knotted up . . . *Confront her . . . make her talk . . . I was safe, until she broke into my place and copied the vid from my glasses . . . The gun . . . Reina's gone . . . Gret—*

The door clicks. Travis slowly opens it, the inside chain unhooked. Darkness, only feeble light through the gaps in the boarded-up window. He flicks on the wall light.

The boxes, books, chairs, kitchen table, microwave: it's all gone. Travis opens the bedroom door. The bed, dresser, everything is gone. The graffiti on the wall is painted away, as if it never happened. He slides the closet door open: empty.

Travis walks toward the front door, turns. Still taped to the kitchen wall is the black-and-white magazine photo of Greta Garbo. Peering closer, he reads the faded caption at the bottom of the yellowing page: *Garbo sizzles as the dangerous seductive spy in MGM's new sensation, Mata Hari.* On the Formica counter, a faded blue playing card, facedown, and another blue card, ripped into four pieces, facedown. He pieces together the torn sections: the queen of hearts. *The queen . . . Reina . . .* Travis flips the other card over: the king of clubs . . . *cops, kings with their billy clubs* . . . He turns, glares at the magazine page taped to the wall. *My idol . . . didn't let men push her around . . . I'm an actress . . . the body-cam video . . . I won't be here long . . .*

He jabs out the ruby eye of the scanner lock and the concrete door slides open.

Fountains of blue light wash over him like misty confetti. "No, you fucking bitch." Travis stands in the shadows, pinned by the four holograms glowing and shifting from the kitchen, the fireplace, the office niche, the hallway. Scarlet digital time stamps tick and flash madly, revolving around the pillars of blue light, reflecting on Travis's azure face like a kind of stigmata . . .

Her wrists handcuffed, limp above her wide blue eyes. "Say it," she whispers.

"Computer off!"

Gret-A's red lips smiling up at him. "You're all I want," his voice echoes from the holograms as his phantom blue glowing fingers glide along her skin.

"Computer off," his voice breaking, fists clenching, gazing wildly around at the columns of cobalt light, like ghostly interrogators.

The holograms blink and flicker. Gret-A stands in blue shadows, surrounding him like scintillating clones. She wears a black jumpsuit, her blond hair neatly coiffed and clipped. "Hello, Blair." Her red lips smile; Gret-A's eyes seem like incandescent sapphires in the holo-light: she is radiant, like a goddess who once wandered in disguise through the ruins of the Skids. "You will transfer all of your credits from your bank account into another account. I'll give you instructions soon. My ticket out of the Skids.

If you don't you'll get, what? Ten, twenty years behind bars. It's awful, what criminals might do to cops in prison . . . and if you do get out, the Skids will be waiting . . . Now your rodent mind is thinking . . . *How do I know she won't release the video after I pay?* No guarantee, but it's your only chance . . . You'll have to replay the fear in your mind, every night and morning, like a video loop, like you played me, over and over . . ."

Travis moans, pressing his skull with his palms as if to keep his head from exploding as he slides down the wall, bathed in Gret-A's blue shadows. He slips the pistol from his sweatshirt pocket and points the barrel between his eyes. "Target," he whispers. A thread of ruby laser light needles between his eyes.

Fire . . . fire. Stinging tears glide down his face. "Target . . . off." The beam of scarlet light vanishes. Travis closes his eyes and for a moment Gret-A, like an avenging angel of light, hovers and smiles, imprinted pink in the membranes of his eyelids, then her face sinks into a warm blood sea.

SAILING THAT BEAUTIFUL SEA

BY **KATHLEEN KAUFMAN**

Century City

Kelsie woke with a pain in her gut and an ache shooting down her right side. The pills would help at the cost of her clarity, and she needed her thoughts to be crisp. It was worse in the morning and better in the afternoon and insufferable by nightfall, her pain like the Pacific Ocean tide, ebbing and flowing with the pull of the moon. She had learned when it would roll in and when it would subside again. She felt the lapping discomfort and the fuzzy numbness that settled on her dying cells. She was not unhappy, nor did she complain, much anyway. Everyone should complain a little. It was something she was constantly trying to teach her nurse-companion Amanda. Amanda was a top-of-the-line home care specialist, programmed to treat emergencies, skilled in minor surgical procedures, and pain management, and she had diagnostic capabilities that far exceeded the original model. She was also the last of her line. The other KIND382-OH had been repurposed long ago. When Kelsie passed, Amanda would be reprogrammed.

Amanda had originally been built for the state hospice programs that filled beyond capacity when the first pandemics hit. She was taught empathy and kindness. Amanda was an excellent listener and was capable of spontaneous and organic reaction. She did not have dialogue protocols like some of the other medical bots, which could get caught in a loop and ruin the illusion. No, Amanda was extraordinary, but she did not understand Kelsie's penchant for wallowing in her own pain. She had learned not to rush Kelsie's room the minute the biologic sensors were activated. She knew that Kelsie would ask for the pain medication when she was ready.

This morning, Kelsie could hear Amanda in the next room, shuffling around the kitchen, probably making tea. What would happen to all the tea? Amanda wondered, as she sat on the edge of her bed, rubbing her right arm. The organic crops—fruits, vegetables, and the like—continued to be eaten by the animals and insects. But tea was a strictly human invention, as was gin. Kelsie sighed. She would love a cold tumbler of gin—poured over a thick slab of ice with just a hint of lemon. It wasn't exactly forbidden, but it would take some cajoling and Kelsie wasn't sure she was up for cajoling. She would need to petition the care service, which would forward her request through a million channels until the ever-human face of Abtonius Crowninshield appeared on her videospeak. He would give her understanding half smiles, and then ask if alcohol was the best decision given her physical condition. The problem with bots was their inability to understand the concept of not giving a fuck.

Amanda appeared in the doorway of Kelsie's sleep cell holding a delicate blue glazed teacup and saucer, the last of a specially designed tea set. The design was an intricate and intertwining pattern of shoe-shaped sailboats illuminated by an infinitely sad moon. The set had been a wedding present from Kelsie's mother so many years ago, a custom order that had made Kelsie hold her breath and clutch her bride's hand as she realized it was the story she'd loved as a child. The story of the old moon and the boys in their shoe-shaped boat played out in intricate images across the delicate porcelain. A shattered teacup here and a cracked saucer there, over the years, all the chaos that reigned in the days and months and years since—only this was left. Everything else had broken. Amanda took extra care with it, even though they both knew soon it too would crack and splinter, like every last human creation in this dying world.

Amanda was lovely. She had glossy golden hair pulled back in a practical ponytail at the base of her neck. Her eyes were wide and the color of the sea at dawn. Her skin was perfect. Amanda had been created 153 years ago and reprogrammed a multitude of times to achieve the precision with which she operated, but her corporeal presence had remained unchanged. 153 years young. She had been functional when Kelsie's great-grandmother had been alive. The thought was dizzying. Perhaps she would be around for another 153 years, but in what form? Kelsie knew the human appearance of bots like Amanda had been entirely for the sake of humans. When Kelsie was gone, what form would they take?

"Can I get you a Napron?" Amanda asked gently. "There's no reason to feel that pain."

Kelsie smiled and rose, wincing as she accepted the teacup and saucer. "I'll take a soft-boiled egg and a piece of toast. Light on the browning and heavy on the butter, please." She took a sip of the Earl Grey. The bots were missing out on the perfection of a well-made cup of tea.

Amanda's brow furrowed, an inanely human response to the mixed message she was receiving from her processing server. "Okay, have it your way," she responded, cheerful in defeat.

Kelsie walked from her sleeping pod onto the circular patio that hung high over the Pacific with its clear glass panels that opened onto the ocean and gave the impression one could walk right into the waves. There was a fat finch in the feeder. He was eating sunflower seeds and flicking his bloodred tail feathers back and forth nervously. Kelsie lived on the thirty-second floor of 1 West Century Drive, in what had once been christened Century City. Upon moving in, Abtonius Crowninshield had proudly listed the names of the celebrities and elite who had lived in these luxury condominiums, but all that was past. Kelsie had been the only resident for years. Catie skittered across the patio, pausing at the feeder, and then making a half-hearted leap upward. The finch jumped, dropping his seed, and sailed up into the potted dwarf orange tree, resurrected from extinction in a lab. It bloomed with such intoxicating white flowers each spring. Kelsie struggled to remember if they had been this fragrant naturally, if the blooms had been so full. She'd requested the little tree specially. If she closed her eyes and drank in the sweet soft scent, she could almost hear her mother's laugh as they drove past the last orange trees in Altadena when she was a child. That was before the wildfires had raged, turning the land into Gatsby's valley of ashes. That was before the honeybees disappeared from the earth entirely. In Kelsie's childhood, a few apocalyptic survivors still buzzed their way in and out of fading blooms. It was hard to believe that just a century earlier, before all the disintegration of this world began, there had been endless rows of unruly orange trees and a seemingly eternal spring.

Kelsie smiled as she sipped her tea. Catie was an indulgence, and worth the cajoling of Abtonius Crowninshield. She was a cream-and-gray tabby with one black paw and one white. Her eyes were an otherworldly gold. Catie's back leg was half the length of the others, hence her utterly ridiculous leap at the bird, and her limpy trot. She was never going to be wild, so she was approved to become the last house cat. She liked tuna and would sit on your lap for hours. Catie was perfection.

Kelsie placed her hands on the railing and took in the view. The ocean breeze blew a lock of hair over her eyes. Subtle streaks of silver were beginning to appear and they matched the crisscross pattern of tiny lines settling in at the corners of her eyes. There was no one to compare herself to anymore. She was the youngest and oldest left of her kind. The air smelled of salt and birds that ate fish. In her youth, the water levels from the Pacific had been low enough that on a good day one could walk the oceanfront in what used to be West LA. The beach at Venice Boulevard and Centinela had been their favorite spot. Her father had remembered a thoroughfare filled with cars, but in Kelsie's youth it had already become a long stretch of rolling waves, the concrete and asphalt barely visible beneath the blue-green ocean water. Now at high tide, the Pacific lapped the edges of Century Park West.

Her grandmother had told tales of Santa Monica Pier, but all that had drowned long before Kelsie was born. A new pier now rose above the sunken remains of Fox Studios and stretched out into the gray water. A Ferris wheel sat empty, a roller coaster wrapped around the perimeter, bright tents dotted the scene, a wall of stuffed bears sat behind a counter where Kelsie liked to imagine her grandmother had once thrown a ball through a hoop for a prize. It was all artificial, rebuilt to match the historical photos.

Kelsie had never wandered the wooden planks of the pier where bright, striped beach chairs lined the walkway, evoking past days when revelers sat in the sun and ate cotton candy or sipped beer from plastic cups. Amanda could have taken her there in a wheelchair, but the idea was too sad, and it was too painful to sit for that long, anyway. Sometimes Kelsie mused that the pier was no more than a hologram, projected for her amusement alone, but she knew better. The bots were meticulous and ardent in their determination to preserve these tiny pieces of humanity, a scene from a past that not even Kelsie remembered, a living museum that now only housed the seagulls and possums. Still, it was a comfort. Kelsie could get lost imagining the life that might have existed before.

Amanda joined her in the morning sunlight holding a tray laden with a perfectly soft-boiled egg in an egg cup shaped like a tiny chicken. A glass of orange juice accompanied the meal.

"Thank you," Kelsie said as she snapped the top off her egg and drew a deep and satisfied breath at the sight of the creamy golden yolk.

"You never need to thank me," Amanda said. "How are you feeling?"

"You know . . ." Kelsie said, looking up over a spoon of runny yolk. "I think I might be dying."

"You're not funny."

"How would you know? We spent last night watching Laurel and Hardy try to move a piano up a staircase in Silver Lake and you never laughed."

"It's a stretch for my programming. Plus, I'm not sure it's funny."

"Well, you might be right," Kelsie said, savoring the saltiness of the egg and the perfect ration of butter on the toast.

"Can I get you a Napron after you eat?"

"Maybe."

"Pain is preventable," Amanda said, her sea-foam eyes darkened with concern.

"I am the last human to feel pain. You don't understand, but that is important."

"Why?" Amanda asked. "Patient UTN997 passed peacefully with no pain, his dreams regulated by the Dreamspector, his memories of his loved ones ever present on the viewguider."

Kelsie took a sip of tea. "Pain is what makes us human. You feel no pain; your hardship is only programmed and can easily be unprogrammed so that no memory remains. But *our* pain sits in the very core of our flesh. I'm not judging Hector on the way he died. But that's the thing. He was Patient UTN997 to you, and Hector to me. He lived in Brazil and loved zombie movies and tequila. He was allergic to strawberries and forever in love with a young woman he once saw at a coffee shop. The day they met, Hector had been afraid, but he had been fearless in asking her out for coffee. They sat and talked for an hour. Hector never saw her again and never forgot the way her eyes caught the sunlight. That was Hector. I miss him."

"I understand that," Amanda said. "You talked almost every day."

They had been the last two left, after all. He was in Rio, she was in Los Angeles. It didn't matter. They were the last two to care what the cities were called. The bots saw the world in zones. They saw them in ecosystems and habitats. Hector had done his own cajoling and savored a healthy dose of his beloved tequila every day. At the end, he had been lost to his memories. He talked of his brothers and sister, long dead, the young woman in the café, children he'd never had. He spoke of his fear. At the very end, he was lost to the Napron, floating in a shoe-shaped boat on the tide, headed to the old moon who would pluck him from his bed and cast him to the stars. He had clung to the story that Kelsie told. The story passed to her from her mother, and her mother before that, the story that was inscribed on her china. How three brothers had sailed out to sea on a shoe-shaped boat and been drowned in a storm. The old moon had plucked them from the angry water and placed them in the sky, where they looked down for eternity from the heavens. It was the story of eternity and golden lockets made of fish fins that were evidence of heaven's miracles.

Kelsie wiped her mouth and stretched her hands so that the joints popped.

"I'd like to get some work done," she said firmly, and stood, the familiar ache shooting down the side of her body.

The care service considered Kelsie's work to be therapeutic. Kelsie considered it to be essential. Although for whom, she was not sure. The museums and libraries were now depositories in much the same way as the replicated Santa Monica Pier. The great paintings and sculptures were safely stored in temperature-controlled vaults in the old Getty Center on its hill. The books sat on the shelves, the air monitored for humidity and dust so that they would never fall prey to the disintegration of time. The bots were oddly sentimental, Kelsie thought as she opened the door to her studio. They extended such effort into saving these utterly human remnants. When she died, her work would join the collection in the vault. It might even sit next to a Matisse, she thought with a rueful smile.

Her easel sat ready; the half-finished panel of the graphic novel waited patiently. Kelsie spread out her tools: the black ink pens, the fine-line charcoal pencils. She pulled her stool closer to the easel and starting inking yesterday's work. The shoe-shaped boat, its planks held together with pine pitch, took form and she started lining the intricate waves of the angry sea. The story her mother had whispered as she drifted off to sleep every night of her childhood had colonized her imagination so fully that it now played out each time she looked out over the Pacific. Three tiny heads bobbed up and down in the tumult, the three brothers with their nets of gold and silver. Kelsie closed her eyes and let the soft cadence of her mother's voice seep out from her memory. The images on the cream paper were a cheap imitation, but it was the best she had. The old moon hung in the sky, the light spreading out across the water, the three brothers looking up for salvation from the storm. Where were their sisters? she'd asked once. Her mother had swallowed a laugh and told her that the girls had more sense than their brothers and were safe asleep in their beds.

At the very end of Hector's life, the Dreamspector had funneled images into his brain and controlled his unconscious mind. They had considered it humane to flood his thoughts with images of his loved ones. But they had missed the point. Dreams aren't meant to comfort us in this life, they are meant to carry us to the next. But the last honest dream that Hector had spoken of was of the sea and the boats.

He was laden with the nets of gold and silver surrounding his body and could feel the metal working its way under his skin and into his blood and muscle. His skin took on the glow from the moon and he became like the herring and deep-sea crabs of the story, imbued with precious metal, a halfling composed of equal parts human and wonder.

Kelsie used a tiny brush to add a metallic sheen to the hands and faces of the three brothers. The next panel was angry, the storm rising up around them, the brothers frightened, alone, and doomed. As Kelsie sketched, sudden pain shot down her spine and into her knees. She crumpled forward, her head barely missing the still-wet ink.

"I'm getting you a sol-cure infusion, will you take a Napron now?" Amanda asked from the doorway, her bio-alerts responding immediately.

Kelsie shook her head, still in the throes of the spasm. Amanda returned with a vial of cloudy liquid. Effortlessly she lifted Kelsie onto the bed. Kelsie sighed with relief as Amanda kneaded the sol-cure oil into her flesh. It absorbed almost immediately and the pain stopped. Amanda ran her hand down Kelsie's spine, evaluating, pausing, moving on. She propped Kelsie up with a soft pillow.

"It's progressing rapidly. Your bio-signs are in flux. How are you feeling?" Amanda's bedside manner was impeccable.

"Terrible."

"Do you want to know how much time?"

Kelsie had never wanted the answer before. Amanda's biosensory system had 97 percent accuracy to predict the exact time when Kelsie's body would succumb to the cancer, the moment when she would die.

"No."

"Your spine will not support your weight for much longer."

"Can you find Catie?" Kelsie asked.

Amanda returned a moment later holding a compliant Catie the way one might carry a tea tray. Amanda would never truly appreciate the soft comfort of Catie's silky fur. Awkwardly she released the cat, who curled into a tight ball at Kelsie's side. When this was finally over, Catie would be taken to an animal sanctuary for those creatures who could never be wild. Bots would care for her, feed her, and perhaps even admire her, but never understand the genuine beauty of her rumble purr. The vibrations soothed Kelsie nearly as much as the sol-cure. There was no one left to say goodbye to except Catie, not since Hector. She wanted only to finish her art, to pass on her mother's story, the last thing that only she could create.

Amanda moved Kelsie's artwork to the bedside table, spreading the pencils and pens in neat arrangement.

"A comic book?" she said in a puzzled voice.

This was a recent glitch that was getting worse. Amanda had been programmed for a great many things, but her understanding of art was limited. She had an intellectual appreciation of Kelsie's career as an illustrator but lacked the ability to connect these sketches to her knowledge of Rembrandt and Monet. The repeated questions were a telltale sign that Amanda was due for reprogramming. Her code was beginning to falter in the same way that Kelsie's body was failing. In previous times, she would have been sent off for maintenance, but now the bot overseers had deemed it unnecessary. What would become of her beautiful green-eyed friend? Kelsie wondered. What use was her programmed humanity once Kelsie was gone?

"It's a graphic novel, like a book but with pictures, for adults."

Amanda nodded, clearly not understanding entirely. "I'll make you some tea."

Kelsie turned her attention to the page. The old moon was reaching down, ready to pluck the drowned bodies from the sea. Kelsie let her mind wander as she drew the lines swiftly in long, full strokes. Years ago, her grandmother had suffered a heart attack, and been brought back to life in the hospital, but she'd come home changed. There were no more stories of the soft Santa Monica sand on her girlhood beach. There were no more bedtime tales. She was weak and stared blankly. She was angry.

"A thousand arms hugging, and holding me, everyone who ever loved me in my entire life surrounding me with open arms." That was how her grandmother described the moments spent on the other side. The machines and the medicine had pulled her from the edge of death and thrust her back into a dying shell of a body without the will to live. A second heart attack took her for good several months later.

Kelsie had tried to draw it, a place that lived in the mist, where the souls of the past wandered. A place with no memory, just the sensory emotion of love, where no one had to move through the regrets and pain of the past. She'd never gotten it right. The pen-and-ink drawings had filled abandoned drawers. Today she finally understood. Kelsie felt the pull of the next world as well. She longed for the weightlessness and release, the lightening of the burden of consciousness. As she breathed in, the waves of pain along her spine ebbed and flowed in rhythm with the ocean tide outside her window. She knew why her drawings had been wrong. The land of no memory she sought was a newly built pier, where an eternally still Ferris wheel caught the glint of the sun and lit up the sky beyond. A place where the potential for happiness lived forever, never marred by the realities of the living.

It was now early afternoon. Kelsie could tell by the light that flooded her window.

Beside her, Catie rolled over, showing her perfectly cream belly. Kelsie ran fingers through her fur. On her easel, herring and deep-sea crabs leaped from the sea, stealing bites of brilliant gold and silver. Amanda was in the doorway.

"The center would like to speak."

Kelsie nodded and put the tiny brush aside.

Amanda brought the handheld voicespeak to her bedside and pressed a button.

Abtonius Crowninshield's ever-human face appeared, filling the screen with a sympathetic and programmed smile.

"Hello, Abtonius," Kelsie said. "You're here to convince me, I suppose."

His hesitation was a programmed response, Kelsie knew this but found it effective nonetheless.

"I wish you would let us make you comfortable," he said.

"I need to be uncomfortable right now."

The smile grew a bit smaller, a furrow appeared between his eyes—he was a model of compassionate empathy. "I'm not going to pretend to understand, but I respect your decision. I am obligated to let you know that Amanda is programmed to activate your Dreamscape unit and remove your pain when you wish. You are very special to us, and this is our duty to make sure you are taken care of."

Kelsie nodded and the vision cut out. She turned back to her work. The sun would be setting soon and she would lose her light. The old moon was staring at the dead faces of the brothers. He didn't understand death; the old moon had never been born and could never die. He watched the herring and the deep-sea crabs expire and wash to shore. He watched as the villagers grew old and bent and eventually closed their eyes, their bodies sent out to sea, or sometimes reduced to ash. These three were so young, they were not old and bent, they were children. Kelsie used the charcoal pencil to draw lines away from the old moon's eyes, his gaze sympathetic and puzzled. With the tiny brush, she gave a blue-gray tint to his surface.

The old moon considered how to honor the ones taken so young. Overhead, the nets of gold and silver glowed bright in the pitch-black sky. The tiny specks of light drew the herring from the depths, they lined up along the surface, their heads bobbing with the waves, transfixed. The bravest among them leaped at the twinkling dots, they twisted and contorted as they flew into the heavens, hoping for a bite of the beautiful light.

Kelsie gently smudged the edges of the old moon's outstretched swaths of light, the glow spreading and building in anticipation.

A knock on the door and Amanda stood, framed by the light from the kitchen. "I made you some of that valerian root tea you like, although I'll never quite understand why," she said with a gentle smile.

Kelsie was weary. "I don't like it in the same way one likes honey or mint, or anything else pleasant. I like it because it numbs the pain while keeping my head sharp."

It was strange how strong the pull to make herself understood was, even here at the end. After Kelsie was gone from this world, a cup of tea would never be made again, but still she had an irresistible urge to explain herself.

"Can I bring you something you actually like?" Amanda offered.

"Do we still have brandy in the cupboard?"

Amanda nodded. "Not approved by the center but I am capable of keeping secrets." She stopped talking and looked back.

"Tell whoever you want, Amanda," Kelsie said wryly. "The center can fuck itself."

Amanda shook her head and left. Kelsie's occasional and unpredictable irreverence was yet another thing the bot would never comprehend.

Kelsie went back to her drawing.

One by one, the old moon gently placed the lifeless bodies of the brothers into the webbing of the gold and silver chains. He bent their already stiffening hands and elbows at an angle that looked natural. He turned their glassy eyes to the village so they could see their mother and father, their sisters, their friends and neighbors, all living their lives on shore. The boys hung in the gold and silver chains and the herring and deep-sea crabs stopped their leaping and rejoicing to stare heavenward.

Her father had died when Kelsie was twenty-six. He woke one morning and couldn't move his legs. The next day, he lay in a hospital bed, the chemo already scheduled, unsure he would ever walk again. Kelsie sat by the bed as her wife helped her mother negotiate a mountain of paperwork. He recounted stories of bodysurfing in Hermosa Beach when he was a child, the ocean already well up to Sepulveda Boulevard by then, lapping away at what had once been stucco bungalows, sidewalks, and stoplights. It felt like flying. Nascar had been playing in the background, an aggravating, aggressive noise for Kelsie. For her father it was a comfort, the sound of something more chaotic than the war that was being lost internally.

Months after he passed, Kelsie dreamed he was waiting for her in Union Station. He sat alone on a bench dressed in a dark robe. His face was drawn and pale. He looked up at her. Lines of suffering had carved their way into his flesh. He said nothing, but he gave her a small smile and then looked down at the floor. Kelsie had woken shaken and crying. Was he trapped? Was he sitting in this abandoned train station, lost forever? Where were his thousand arms and everyone who had ever loved him? Where was his misty land of no memory? Was he waiting forever for a train that no longer ran on tracks that had long ago been torn apart by earthquakes and storms? Her wife had said no, she had kissed Kelsie's brow and quieted her.

Kelsie's wife had passed months later. Measles. That was the year the mutated strain took so many and no one seemed immune. She had come home Friday with chills and aches, her chest sprayed with what looked to be a rash. By the next morning, she was covered in angry red spots, her brain already boiling from fever. She died on Monday.

Kelsie had called the hospital, and anonymous figures in hazmat suits picked up the body. She had filled out a blizzard of forms, following the orders the two of them had laid out years before. Her wife was cremated on a Wednesday, and on Thursday her ashes were buried under the last standing California oak in what remained of Descanso Gardens, where they had been married underneath the canopy of the great trees just a few short years before.

There was no one else to mourn them by then. Her mother had followed shortly after her father—a stroke, the doctors said. Kelsie had known better. Her heart had been broken, and without it, she had no cause to stay in this world. Everyone Kelsie loved was gone, why had she been left behind? What purpose did she possibly serve here in this world that was full of memories of the dead and dying? Kelsie sat underneath the oak tree and ran her fingers through the dirt that covered the ashes of her sweet, beautiful wife. Her wife whose curly hair fell in her face when she laughed, whose teeth were an unnatural shade of white, who snored a bit when she'd had a brandy.

Kelsie drew a fine line of silver below the eye of the old moon. It wasn't a tear—she had learned long ago that tears had no place in the world—but it was a motion of grief, of recognition that nothing you do is ever enough, the truth that what we have to offer is not always adequate but will suffice nonetheless. She drew the old moon reaching to the heavens, brushing his otherworldly light across the faces of the three brothers. The herring and deep-sea crabs watched reverently from below. Kelsie's fingers tingled and she knew it was near time. She looked to her right and saw a lady's glass of brandy sitting next to the chilling cup of valerian tea. She hadn't heard Amanda enter or leave.

She reached for the tea first, bitter as bark as it rolled down her throat, but then creeping into the crevice of pain that had built around her spine. As Catie stretched and curled closer, Kelsie was hit with a wave of loss. She could feel the inevitability as the sun sank lower outside her window. The evening light caught the top of the Ferris wheel. Her last meal had been a boiled egg and toast.

The thought made her smile.

Then pain reared, paralyzing her. She breathed in and out, picturing the waves cresting and falling, and let the pain settle into her cells. It didn't lessen the sensation but rather heightened it. When it took her, would she be here for eternity? She hoped not. Kelsie hoped for the stories of weightlessness, of eternity, of a thousand arms, of love beyond measure. She had faith, although in what she could not say. She hoped to see her wife, to feel her lips again, to hear her laugh. She hoped to see her mother, whose gentle fingers brushed back the hair from her forehead while she slept as a child. She hoped to see her father, infinitely complicated, infinitely lost. She hoped to hold his hand and walk with him down the newly formed pier, a place with no memories, and pour him a cup of coffee in a world of their own making. She hoped for so much. She hoped to see Hector, and share a draft of rum on a beach in Rio.

Kelsie took a sip of brandy. It burned her throat and rolled slowly down her gullet. She took her brush and edged the waves in dark crimson. She sketched the shoe-shaped boat drifting back to shore, lost in the darkness. The old moon considered, watching it float away. He reached up and washed the brothers in a golden light and their eyes snapped to consciousness immediately. They looked around waveringly, unsure and afraid. The old moon drew them near, held them close. They would not die in the sea, they would not drown in their foolishness. They would live for as long as they were remembered, for as long as they shone in the sky down upon the world. They saw their father and mother, they saw the women and men of the village, they saw awe in the faces of the herring and deep-sea crabs.

Kelsie lay back, her hand shaking. She drained the rest

of the brandy and ran her fingers one last time through Catie's silky fur as the cat gazed back with impassive half-lidded eyes.

"Amanda."

Immediately, she was there.

"I think it's time."

Amanda nodded. She would carefully pack up the completed work. It would be transported to the vault beneath the Getty where all things human were meticulously preserved. It would remain there forever, visited only by curious bots who wished to see what human life had been like.

Kelsie breathed deep as the Dreamscape overtook her. Her wife with her eternally curly hair and infectious laugh had made her a birthday cake and utterly destroyed it in the baking.

They laughed as she pulled it from the oven, the smoke alarm screaming in protest. Kelsie watched as Hector recounted a tale of his brothers at the seaside, his face animated and alive. Her sides hurt from laughter, not pain, as she imagined the boys rolling in the sand. Kelsie saw her mother and father when they thought she could not see; they held hands and stared at each other deeply; no one else existed in that moment, not even a little girl hidden in the corner. She saw Catie leaping endlessly for a bird she'd never catch. She saw her wife, who was just a girl then, a sophomore at USC. A girl who sat a table over in a humanities class, a girl with a tattoo of a caterpillar on her wrist, a girl who gazed at her the way her father had at her mother.

Kelsie felt herself falling. There was no tunnel, no thousand arms. There was only perfect darkness and the infinite end of light.

ABOUT THE CONTRIBUTORS

Max S. Gerber

AIMEE BENDER is the author of five books, including a *New York Times* Notable Book *The Girl in the Flammable Skirt,* and the best seller *The Particular Sadness of Lemon Cake.* Her work has been translated into sixteen languages and can be heard on *This American Life* and *Selected Shorts.* She lives near the tar pits in Los Angeles.

Kari Blackmoore

STEPHEN BLACKMOORE is the author of the noir/urban fantasy Eric Carter series about a modern-day necromancer in Los Angeles. He has also written tie-in novels for television, video, and role-playing games. His latest Eric Carter novel is *Fire Season.*

Nicolas Sage

FRANCESCA LIA BLOCK is the author of more than twenty-five acclaimed and widely translated books, as well as numerous short stories, essays, and poems. She has received the Spectrum Award, the Phoenix Award, the ALA Rainbow Award, the 2005 Margaret A. Edwards Award, and citations from the *New York Times Book Review* and *Publishers Weekly,* among others. She lives, writes, and teaches creative writing in Los Angeles.

ALEX ESPINOZA is the author of *Still Water Saints, The Five Acts of Diego León,* and *Cruising: An Intimate History of a Radical Pastime.* He's written for the *Los Angeles Times,* the *New York Times Magazine, VQR, LitHub,* and NPR's *All Things Considered.* The recipient of fellowships from the NEA and MacDowell and winner of an American Book Award, he lives in Los Angeles and is the Tomás Rivera Endowed Chair of Creative Writing at University of California, Riverside.

LYNELL GEORGE is an award-winning journalist and essayist. Her work has appeared in various media outlets, including *Vibe, Essence, Smithsonian,* and the *Los Angeles Times,* where she was a longtime staff writer. She is the author of *No Crystal Stair: African-Americans in the City of Angels* and *After/Image: Los Angeles Outside the Frame.* Her latest book is *A Handful of Earth, A Handful of Sky: The World That Made Octavia E. Butler.*

Blake Little

Edgar Award finalist **Denise Hamilton** is the author of seven crime novels and the editor of the best-selling anthology *Los Angeles Noir* (which includes the Edgar Award–winning short story "The Golden Gopher" by Susan Straight) and *Los Angeles Noir 2: The Classics.* She is a former *Los Angeles Times* journalist, a Fulbright Scholar, a noir and sci-fi/fantasy geek, and a proud LA native who refuses to speak only in English.

Kathleen Kaufman is a native Coloradan and longtime resident of Los Angeles. She is the author of *The Tree Museum, Hag, Diabhal,* and *The Lairdbalor,* soon to be a feature film with Echo Lake Studios. Kaufman is a monster enthusiast and Olympic-level insomniac. When not writing, she can be found teaching literature and writing at Santa Monica College. She lives in LA with her husband, son, terrier, and a pack of cats.

Jack Hummel

A.G. Lombardo is a native Angeleno who taught at a public high school for twenty years. His debut novel, *Graffiti Palace,* an hallucinatory Homeric odyssey set during the Watts riots, garnered high praise: the *Chicago Review of Books* called it "stunning—a blend of Joe Ide's IQ detective novels, Thomas Pynchon, Jonathan Lethem's *Chronic City*, and Haruki Murakami's *1Q84*." Lombardo lives in LA with his wife and daughter, and is working on his second novel.

Seth Ryan

Lisa Morton is a screenwriter, author of nonfiction books, and prose writer whose work was described by the American Library Association's *Readers' Advisory Guide to Horror* as "consistently dark, unsettling, and frightening." She is a six-time winner of the Bram Stoker Award, and the author of four novels and over 150 short stories. For more information, visit www.lisamorton.com.

S. Qiouyi Lu writes, translates, and edits between two coasts of the Pacific. Their fiction and poetry have appeared in *Asimov's*, *F&SF*, and *Strange Horizons*, and their translations have appeared in *Clarkesworld*. They edit the flash fiction and poetry magazine *Arsenika*. For more information, visit s.qiouyi.lu.

Pocho Sanchez

Luis J. Rodriguez has published sixteen books of poetry, fiction, nonfiction, children's books, and essays. Best known for his memoir *Always Running: La Vida Loca: Gang Days in L.A.*, he has also been a print and radio journalist and written plays, movie scripts, and worked as a script consultant on three TV shows, including FX's *Snowfall*. From 2014–2016, Rodriguez served as Los Angeles's official poet laureate.

Evelyn Taylor

Duane Swierczynski is the two-time Edgar Award–nominated author of ten novels, including *Revolver*, *Canary*, and the Shamus Award–winning Charlie Hardie series, many of which are in development for film and TV. Swierczynski has also written over 250 comic books featuring the Punisher, Deadpool, Judge Dredd, and Godzilla (among other notable literary figures). A native Philadelphian, he now lives in Los Angeles with his family.

Nicola Goode

Ben H. Winters is the *New York Times* best-selling author of *Underground Airlines*, *Golden State*, and the Last Policeman Trilogy. He has won the Edgar Award, the Philip K. Dick Award, and France's Grand Prix de l'Imaginaire. Winters has also written books for young readers; numerous plays and musicals; and articles about books and culture for *Slate*, the *New York Times*, among others. He lives in Los Angeles with his wife and three kids.

Tina Chiou

Charles Yu is the author of four books, and his fiction and nonfiction have appeared in a number of publications, including the *New Yorker*, the *New York Times*, *Slate*, and *Wired*. His latest novel is *Interior Chinatown*.